W9-BVS-526

MAGNOLIA SUMMER

MELANIE DICKERSON

GRACEFAITH PRESS

Copyright © 2018 Melanie Dickerson

All rights reserved. No part of this publication may be reproduced, stored in a retrieval system, or transmitted in any form or by any means—electronic, photocopy, recording, mechanical, scanning, or other—without written permission of the author. The only exception is for brief quotations in printed or electronic reviews.

This is a work of fiction set in a fictionalized town in Alabama. Any resemblance to real events or to actual person, living or dead, is coincidental, unless otherwise stated in the Author's Note. Any reference to historical figures, places, or events, whether fictional or actual, is a fictional representation.

Scripture taken from the Holy Bible, King James Version.

Cover: Copyright:

First edition, GraceFaith Press, 2018

❀ Created with Vellum

Deliver the poor and needy;
Free them from the hand of the wicked.
Psalm 82:4

CHAPTER 1

JUNE, 1880, BETHEL SPRINGS, ALABAMA

Truett Beverly aimed his rifle at the noose above James's head. He would only get one shot to sever the rope, but that wasn't what bothered him. How to get away from the half dozen men, all armed and standing near their able-bodied horses after he fired the shot—that was what bothered him.

Even as the sun sank low, the summer heat sent sweat trickling down his neck and over his collarbone. The dark hood concealed Truett's face. Strands of hair clung to his sweaty temples. The long cape hid everything except his boots, but his black gelding was more likely to be recognized than his boots. He could only hope the descending darkness would prevent that.

Sheriff Suggs took the noose from a low, thick branch of the white oak tree and placed it around James's neck. The pale rope stood out against his friend's dark brown skin. In the light of the torches the small lynch mob was holding, Truett imagined he could see James swallow, his throat bobbing against the stiff noose.

Heat boiled up from Truett's gut.

The sheriff's beefy jowls shook at his own words, something about protection of women. He was lynching James for trying to rape his daughter. But it was a lie. James would never do such a thing, not to Almira Suggs nor anyone else. Sheriff Suggs would jump at any excuse, rumor, or made-up story to lynch a black man—especially the one his daughter was in love with.

Truett forced himself not to blink or even breathe as he curled his finger around the trigger. He must do it now, before Sheriff Suggs ended his rant, turned, and sent James's horse charging out from under him.

Truett squeezed the trigger.

The cracking boom of the gun echoed through the woods. The sheriff and his men pivoted, searching the semi-darkness of the woods for the source of the gunshot. After a moment of stunned silence, they called out to each other, struggling to catch their skittish horses' reins and mount them.

Truett had already shoved his gun into the holster on his saddle. He urged his horse into a gallop.

He kept his eyes on James, who leaned forward over his horse's neck. He clutched the pommel of the saddle with his bound hands and hung on, pressing his heels into the horse's sides to move her into the trees, away from the sheriff and his men.

"There he is!"

A glance over his shoulder showed the six men kicking their horses in pursuit. They pointed, cursing and shouting, "Get him!"

Truett hunkered low over Colonel's neck, anticipating the shots that would be fired at him. His heart thundered against his ribs, and he stifled the whoop of triumph that rose into his throat.

As the men closed in on them, Truett caught up with James and the brown mare, and they crashed through the brush.

The whites showed all around the mare's eyes. If only she would keep running, following the lead of Truett's black gelding.

The shouting continued behind them. James turned his head toward Truett.

"We'll never outrun them." James said.

Truett sent his horse tearing down the side of a tree-covered embankment. At the bottom, in the dark and dense foliage, the trail was barely discernable. Truett followed it until he saw a half-fallen tree and turned Colonel sharply to the right.

James's horse followed him. Truett drew to a stop and slid from the saddle. He grabbed both horses' reins and led them into the mouth of the cave. James dismounted as well.

Truett cocked his head toward the cave entrance, listening. His heart beat so hard it vibrated his chest.

The seconds dragged on. Where was Sheriff Suggs and the other men? Had they gone another way? Or were they waiting outside to pounce on them when they ventured out? Truett laid his hand on his gun, straining his eyes toward the entrance of the cave.

Hoof beats approached. The sound grew louder and louder until they were right outside. He pulled his gun out of its holster and braced his feet apart.

The sound gradually grew softer, until Truett once again heard only silence.

The cave was so dark, he could barely make out James's form and couldn't see his face at all. They both just stood there, not moving or making a sound. The quiet was almost a palpable presence in his ears. After almost a full minute, Truett finally took a deep breath.

"Is that you, Truett?" James whispered.

"Who else?" Truett stepped into the half-light at the entrance of the cave and flipped the hood off his head. He grinned at his best friend.

James shook his head. He whispered, his words barely audible, "Truett Beverly, you're the beatinest sight I ever did see. You saved my life." His voice hitched at the last word.

Truett swallowed past the lump in his throat. Sheriff Suggs would've taken James's life and never felt a moment's remorse. He took a step toward James and enveloped him in a bear hug. James didn't hug him back. Then Truett remembered—his hands were still tied.

Truett stepped back. He lifted his hunting knife from its sheath on his belt and sawed the ropes that bound his wrists in two.

"I thought I was dreaming when I heard that rifle crack and the rope fell." James rubbed the back of his hand across his eyes. "But Tru, you could have been killed. If Sheriff Suggs finds out it was you, he'll kill you yet."

Truett placed his hand on his friend's shoulder. "I had to do it, James. Besides, I couldn't let Suggs lynch another innocent man. And you know saving lives is my calling." He grinned.

"Always the hero. You always want to be King Arthur or Sir Gawain, going around saving people, and it's gonna get you killed."

Truett's chest grew tight and he shifted his feet. "Nah, James. Anybody with any conscience woulda' done the same."

"No. Most people wouldn't."

"You're the one you should be thinking about, James, not me. You gotta light a shuck out of here or Suggs'll finish what he started." Truett kept his voice low just in case Suggs or one of his men had circled back around.

"I'll have to leave, now, tonight."

"Where will you go?"

"Ohio, I guess."

It was where he had gone to school. "I'll go with you, make sure you get safely north."

"Listen, Tru."

The urgency in James's voice stopped Truett's hand as he reached for his horse's bridle.

"There is something I need from you, but you gotta be careful." He scrubbed his hand over his short hair and sighed. "I need you to keep an eye on Almira."

"Almira?" *Uh-oh.*

James bowed his head. "We— I— She may be . . ." He shook his head. "I knew better, but I was weak, Tru. I hope God will forgive me." James rubbed his face, then the back of his neck. "No one should blame her. It was my fault. I should have been strong, for her sake. Maybe I deserve to be lynched." He pressed a hand to his forehead. "I'll come back for her. You have to tell her that. I'm coming back as soon as I can to take her back with me."

Truett's heart dropped to his gut. "Does her father know?"

"I don't think so, but he knows enough to justify killing me—at least in his mind. Just promise me, if you find out that she's with child, you'll write and tell me. Suggs will want to kill her if he finds out." He pointed a finger at Truett. "But don't do anything to let him know you're helping me. He'll kill *you*. And this town needs its doctor."

There was something else this town needed much worse, and that was a sheriff who didn't think he was above the law, a lawman who didn't judge innocence and guilt by the color of a man's skin.

But James was right. If Suggs ever discovered who had saved James from being lynched, he would be glad to lynch Truett in his place.

~

SITTING ALONE IN HER ROOM, CELIA WILCOX REREAD THE LETTER her sister had sent her.

DEAR CELIA,

Please come and help us. Mama just sits and mumbles. I'm scared. We have no money, and Daddy's horses broke down the fence last night and ran away. Will has been searching for them since before daylight. Without those horses, I don't know what we'll do. Daddy spent the last of our savings buying them. But the scariest thing is Mama. She doesn't

5

even remember that Daddy's dead sometimes, and when she does remember, she cries for hours. She hardly knows the rest of us exist. I've been taking care of Harley and Tempie, trying to cook on this awful stove—I need you, Celia. I don't want you to give up your dream of your own seamstress shop, but surely Mama will get better. Please come and help, just until things get a little easier around here.

Your affectionate sister,

Lizzie

Celia cried when she read the letter earlier that afternoon, a fist of guilt squeezing her chest. She immediately started packing her trunk, barely able to see through the blur of tears.

Her father had died in February, and it was nearly summer now. She'd spent two weeks grieving with her family, the only time she'd visited since they'd moved to the farm in north Alabama.

Nashville was her home. Her father had agreed to her staying at Mrs. Beasley's boarding house while the rest of the family moved. She loved her father, but . . . a tinge of anger mixed with her sadness now as she contemplated the events of the past year. How could her father have chosen to throw away his money and good sense to buy a farm, leaving his position as a mathematics professor at Vanderbilt University to be a horse breeder?

The decision never made any sense to Celia, and she'd told her father so, as tactfully and respectfully as she could. But he didn't listen. Her poor siblings and mother. They'd happily gone along with Father's scheme, never knowing what heartbreak would come of it.

Ruminating over it wouldn't help. Her next course of action was clear. She had to go and help her little sister take care of her family.

Celia's stomach twisted. She looked around at her drawings,

the dresses she had designed, the patterns she had made. Her sewing materials couldn't be contained in one basket. They were all over. What if Mother was never able to come out of her fog? Never able to deal with the younger children and the household chores? Celia might have to give up her dream of her own seamstress shop.

But she couldn't think about that now. Her family needed her.

CHAPTER 2

Truett's first patient was waiting for him when he arrived an hour late to his office after riding all night. Mrs. Lowry began talking as he unlocked the door.

"Dr. Beverly, I came by to discuss these sour risings I keep having, and to ask your opinion of the benefits of taking Dr. Pierce's Golden Medical Discovery."

"I think you're safe with that particular remedy, Mrs. Lowry." Truett motioned for her to have a seat, but she remained standing.

"Dr. Beverly—I do love calling you that." She smirked, and the wrinkles around her eyes and mouth deepened. "You've grown up so handsome and tall, and such a gentleman. But you always were a good boy. If only I had a daughter instead of four ornery sons." She sighed, her calico bonnet shaking as the fold of skin under her chin rolled over the tightly tied bow.

"But Dr. Beverly, about this medicine. My sister Lavinia says there are some tonics that are just pure alcohol. I surely don't want to take anything like that."

"No, ma'am. Dr. Pierce's remedies contain no alcohol. You can read the ingredient list right on the label on the side of the bottle."

Once he'd convinced her that that particular patented medicine was perfectly safe, she smiled and patted him on the arm.

"Tell your mother I'll come to visit and bring her some of my plum jelly."

"Yes, ma'am." Truett watched her through the window as she walked down the street. Then he sat down, tipped his chair back, and closed his eyes. He said a prayer that James had had an uneventful trip north last night. Truett had ridden with him across the state line and watched him get on the train.

He felt himself drifting off to sleep.

The squeak and hiss of the train's brakes woke him. His eyes sprang open and the chair wobbled beneath him. He leaned forward, setting all four legs back on the floor.

The scent of coal smoke wafted under the door as the train screeched to a stop. As Truett sat up and stretched, muffled shouts preceded the dull thumps of wooden crates being dropped onto the train platform as men unloaded freight that had reached its destination.

He wandered over to the window and peered between the letters painted on the glass: *DR. TRUETT BEVERLY, M. D.* The railroad tracks divided Main Street, and he had a good view of nearly the entire row of buildings, few as they were. The depot was just off to the right. He watched as the train cars gave up a small portion of their load.

A dainty black boot appeared on the top step of the passenger car, and a lady emerged, wearing a lilac-colored traveling suit and an enormous hat, complete with matching feathers and large flowers.

Whew-ee. He hadn't seen the like of that hat since leaving medical school in New York City. And under it . . .

Celia Wilcox.

The breath went right out of him. She had only been to Bethel Springs once, six months ago in December. He'd never forget that day, both of them standing in front of his medical office after she got off the train. He'd been the one to tell her that her father had died. His gut twisted at the memory. She'd covered her mouth with a gloved hand, and that beautiful, well-put-together lady fell apart right in front of his eyes.

Her face crumpled and tears poured down as she gasped and sobbed.

It must have been because she was so young and pretty, tall and fashionable, but he hadn't expected her to break down in front of him. Her tears intensified the sharp stab of guilt through his chest. He'd been called on to save her father's life and he'd failed. Hadn't even been able to extend the man's life long enough for his oldest daughter to get there and say good-bye.

He'd been warned in medical school and by other doctors that such guilt feelings were out of place and unfounded. He couldn't let them into his mind or they would interfere with his endeavors to practice his profession.

Easier said than done. And it was his first death, after all.

Truett moved to the open doorway of his office to better study her flawless features as she stood on the wooden platform beside the train, clutching her little silk purse.

Striking. That was the word that came to mind.

She was not crying today, but she bit her lip, and her dark eyebrows drew together in a crease. She glanced around. Had her brother forgotten to come fetch her? Her eyes sparkled, the sunlight making them flash. Her dark hair was pulled back and mostly hidden under that eye-catching hat. She stood alone until two men walked up and dropped a large trunk beside her.

She spoke briefly to the men—thanking them, most likely— and then gazed down the deserted street. She rubbed her temple. Might she have a headache? He wouldn't be surprised. The train ride from Nashville was a tedious seven hours.

One of the little Posey girls wandered over. She smiled down at the child, spoke, and then glanced up the street again.

Truett couldn't let her stand there feeling stranded. He would offer to take her home.

Just as he stepped out, Curtis Suggs started across the street toward the train depot.

Truett clenched his teeth. Of course the sheriff's varmint of a son would go nosing after Celia, just like the hound dog he was. Truett hurried at a fast walk down the wooden sidewalk.

⁓

WHERE WAS WILL? CELIA GLANCED AROUND. EVERYTHING ALONG the street, the bushes and trees as well as the store fronts—a barber shop, blacksmith's shop, general store, and doctor's office —were covered with the red-orange dust of the red clay streets, giving everything a rusty look.

The locket watch on the chain around her neck told her it was 2:15, which meant the train had arrived on time. Perhaps her family hadn't received her telegram.

One woman strolled the sidewalk, walking toward the general store or the post office. Four men leaned against a hitching post across the street and stared in her direction. She pretended not to notice them, but her stomach did a little flip. Having grown up in Nashville, it unnerved her to feel nearly alone, standing next to the town's main thoroughfare. There was the one woman, but she had just disappeared into the general store. Did the four men mean her any harm? She clutched her small bag against her stomach.

The afternoon sun sent a jolt of pain through her temples. She rubbed her forehead.

How would she ever get her things to her family's home without Will and the wagon? She could walk, but she couldn't leave her trunk and all her possessions sitting there in plain view. Her family had moved here just nine months ago and she had only visited them once since. Who could she ask for help?

"Ma'am?"

Someone tugged on Celia's skirt hem. She looked down at a blond-haired, blue-eyed girl with a smudge of dirt across her cheek. The child's bare feet poked out from under the hem of her feed-sack dress, and her toes were covered with the rusty red dust. Her wide eyes took Celia in from toe to head, including her newest hat, which must seem quite different from the cloth bonnets that the women of Bethel Springs wore.

"Yes?" Celia smiled at the child's broad face and awed expression.

"Are you a Yankee?" The little girl spoke the last word in a whisper.

Celia didn't know whether to laugh or feel offended. Finally, she said, "No, I'm from Tennessee."

"Good. I wouldn't want you to get shot. You're pretty."

"Thank you."

"My pappy shoots Yankees."

"Oh." A nervous laugh bubbled up, but she cleared her throat instead.

"Sadie!"

The little girl's head jerked toward a woman whose dress was almost as stained and worn as her own, and she motioned with a quick jerk of her hand. "Git away from that fancy lady."

The little girl scurried off, glancing back at Celia as she ran.

The four men who had been staring at her ambled across the street, toward Celia. The young man in the lead wore a butter-yellow, side-button shirt. As he stepped onto the train platform and approached her, he removed his hat. The three others shuffled behind him, their mouths agape, eyes fastened on her. She noted the train depot just behind her. If necessary, she should be able to find safety there.

"How do, miss?" The yellow-shirted one said. "My name's Curtis Suggs. I couldn't help noticing, you look as if you might need some assistance."

He appeared pleasant enough, with an accommodating smile, and she liked that he'd stopped a polite distance away. *Thank you, God, for gentlemanly manners.* His dark hair looked clean, as did his shirt and trousers, with no rips or obvious mends—which was an improvement over the unkempt loafers gawking at her from behind him. Wrinkled and ill-fitting, their clothing hung on them like a scarecrow's, their lips and scraggly beards stained brown with tobacco juice.

"Good afternoon, Mr. Suggs. My brother, William Wilcox, was supposed to meet me when I arrived today, but he isn't here. I wouldn't want to put anyone out, but I am in need of a conveyance. If one of you gentlemen happen to be going toward my family's farm . . ." She waved her hand toward the large trunk just behind her.

Curtis Suggs raised his shoulders a notch. "Miss Wilcox, I have a buggy over behind the town hall—my father's the sheriff of this town—and I'd be happy to run yonder for it," he nodded toward a building down the street, "and fetch you home."

Celia studied his face, trying to get an idea of his character, but his features were smooth and expressionless, except for the smile curving his lips.

"I don't want to trouble you—"

"Miss Celia Wilcox." A new voice sounded from over her shoulder. Celia turned to see the town doctor.

An unpleasant, sinking feeling assailed her stomach. The last time she had seen him, he'd informed her of her father's death. "Dr. Beverly."

Besides the fact that Dr. Beverly was dressed so handsomely—even in shirtsleeves and without a coat he far outshone the other men in sophistication—there was something comforting about seeing him again, though she couldn't fathom why. She couldn't look at him without remembering that awful day when he told her Daddy was dead. *I did everything I could,* he'd said.

Perhaps it was the compassion she had seen in his eyes, along with his sincere regret at having not been able to save her father, that made her spirits lift. No, it was probably only because he was familiar to her, he was the town doctor, and her family trusted him.

Their first meeting was embarrassing, to say the least. Though she'd been in too much pain to feel embarrassed at the time, now her cheeks heated at the memory. Never had she broken down so in front of a stranger. But she'd spent the entire train ride praying, *Oh, God, don't let Daddy die.* So when Dr. Beverly told her he was gone, she'd burst out sobbing.

Doctor Beverly's blue eyes gazed directly into hers. "I see you've just arrived. May I escort you home? My horse and buggy are lodged at the livery stable."

He seemed even more handsome than she remembered, and younger, seeming only four or five years older than her own nineteen years, with his lean frame and light brown hair neatly combed. He wore a white shirt with a stand up collar, a charcoal vest, and neatly creased gray trousers.

"Will was supposed to meet me. I sent a telegram, but something must have happened."

Mr. Suggs took a step toward Dr. Beverly. His expression hardened and she couldn't help noticing the way Curtis Suggs glared at the doctor, his chest heaving slightly.

"There's no need for you to leave your office." Mr. Suggs said. "I can take the lady home. Besides, I offered first." He squared his shoulders and sent Dr. Beverly a challenging look, but the doctor appeared not to notice.

"I don't mind leaving my office for a while," Dr. Beverly drawled, looking at Celia as if he didn't notice Mr. Suggs's hostility, then winked at her. "Haven't had an emergency all day."

Her heart fluttered a bit at the warmth of his smile and his flirtatious wink, then frowned at her silly reaction. But on a serious note, she couldn't let them fight over her. She needed to defuse the situation. What should she do?

Taking a ride alone with a stranger like Curtis Suggs could be dangerous, at least to her reputation. She was safer with the doctor, who was their nearest neighbor. He had already endeared himself to her family. And to make it more socially acceptable, she could turn it into a house call by asking him to look in on Mama. She would have to let Mr. Suggs down gently.

She smiled, hoping to soften the blow. "Mr. Suggs, I do thank you for your kind offer to escort me and my belongings to my family's home, but I believe I shall have to accept Dr. Beverly's offer. I'd very much like to get his medical opinion on one of my family members."

"Oh, well, I—"

"Do excuse me. Perhaps I will see you on Sunday, in church . . .?" She nodded as though he had said "yes," and then turned to Dr. Beverly. "When we get there, would you examine my mother and give me your professional opinion about her condition? In her letters, my sister has written some things that concern me." She bent and picked up her carpetbag, then let the doctor take it from her.

She refrained from smiling at Dr. Beverly. She didn't want him to get the mistaken impression that she was being flirtatious. Lord willing, she was only here to help her family for the summer, until her mother was back to normal, and then she would hie herself back to Nashville. After all, she could help them more by sending them money from her seamstress business, especially now that Daddy was gone.

～

TRUETT HAD TROUBLE SUPPRESSING HIS GRIN AT THE WAY MISS Wilcox handled Curtis. Though she may have been safe enough with the man, Truett wasn't about to let Curtis think he could wile his way into her good graces without some competition.

Besides, he couldn't imagine that Suggs would be the kind of man who would interest Miss Celia Wilcox.

Curtis glared at him, and then tipped his hat to Celia and stomped away.

The other boys continued to stand and stare at the handsomely dressed Miss Celia Wilcox, and he couldn't blame them. She was much more sophisticated, no doubt, than anyone they'd seen before, and much too pretty to be standing on Main Street in Bethel Springs without any way to get home.

The train hissed, groaned, and whistled as the iron giant readied for departure, having unloaded all the goods and mail intended for Bethel Springs.

Thankfully, Curtis and his three fellow oglers were making their way across the street.

"Will you be all right while I go get my horse and buggy?"

She gazed up into his eyes. It was only a moment, but looking into her chestnut brown eyes sent a bolt of lightning through him. Did she feel it too? Or was he only being daft?

She glanced away, and he could have sworn she was blushing.

"Yes, thank you. I shall wait here."

He brought his buggy around, and before he could even ask, the same three men who'd been staring at Celia loped back across the street and offered to help Truett load her trunk. She thanked each one, causing them to turn red to the tips of their ears.

She sure had a powerful effect on Bethel Springs's men. How long would it take them—and him—to get used to her and stop gawking? Probably longer than she was prepared to stay.

Truett grasped her elbow and helped her onto the buggy seat. He sat beside her and clicked his tongue at his horse.

She thanked him, pulled a letter from her bag, and started reading.

Normally he would come up with a joke to chide the lady for not engaging in conversation, but he refrained. Celia Wilcox was entitled to her unsociable mood. Exchanging Nashville for Bethel

Springs would be a rude jolt to anyone. From what Celia's family had told him, she couldn't be happy about leaving Nashville. Her father's death and her family's troubles had changed her situation in life, as she had been working and saving her money to start her own seamstress shop.

As they were nearing the town hall, the back of Truett's neck prickled. Was the sheriff inside? After what happened the night before, he would no doubt be furious.

Just then, Sheriff Suggs stepped out of the town hall, placed his hands on his hips, and narrowed his eyes at Truett.

Oh, Lord, here's trouble. Truett's heart jumped into his throat, nearly choking him. *Let him not stop me to ask where I was last night.* He forced himself not to make eye contact with the sheriff. *Just let me drive on past.*

The sheriff stepped into the dusty street and held up a hand, an unmistakable command.

He hauled back on the reins and smiled. "What can I do for you, Sheriff? Your gout paining you again?"

The sheriff didn't answer. He studied Truett's face, then looked at Celia, who had folded her letter and covered it with her hand in her lap. He tipped his hat. "How do, Miss Wilcox—that right?"

"Yes, sir. A pleasure seeing you again."

His small, pale eyes flicked back to Truett. "Where were you yesterday evening?"

CHAPTER 3

Truett's heart pounded against his breast bone. His mind flitted, unbidden, to the image of a noose around his friend's neck.

"Where were you last evening?"

"Why, Sheriff?" He hoped his fear did not show on his face or in his tone. "Did something happen?"

Suggs rolled a wad of tobacco from one side of his mouth to the other and then leaned forward. A stream of brown spit exploded from his mouth, raising a puff of dirt beside the horse's hoof. "Have you seen James Burwell?"

"Not since yesterday." *Lord, forgive me for the lie.* "Is something the matter?"

"Yeah, something's the matter." Suggs's voice boomed. "James Burwell assaulted a white woman and then lit a shuck out of town. Forgive me, Miss Wilcox, for speaking of such matters before you." He nodded and tipped his hat again at her. "But molesting a lady is no small matter in my county." He pierced Truett with his dagger gaze.

"I fully agree, Sheriff." Truett raised his eyebrows and let his facial muscles go slack. "I can hardly believe James would do such a thing, but if he did, he should be punished just as the law dictates. As the great poets say, 'To molest a fair maiden 'tis of the baseness of beasts.'"

"Yeah, well, let me know if you see him." Suggs backed away, as though Truett's poetry was a disease that might rub off on him.

"My good sheriff, I shall." Truett performed a kind of bow from his driver's seat. He flicked the reins and left the sheriff behind. Then he blew out a long breath . . . and turned to find the fair Celia with her delicate brows drawn down in the middle.

"What great poet wrote that? Truett Shakespeare?" Celia let out a surprising and unladylike snort.

"Actually, I prefer Tennyson." He grinned at her, but she only stared, pursing her down-turned lips.

Having grown up in Nashville, she probably thought all the people of Bethel Springs, including him, were ignorant country folk. He couldn't let her think that. So he would make a wager with himself: Not only would he cheer her up and make her smile, he would get her to acknowledge that he was a gentleman of education and culture.

"You think I don't know any poetry?"

Her brows shot up. "Do you?"

The bemused look on her face was just the challenge to get his blood pumping. Staring straight between his horse's ears, he began,

"Strike for the king and die! And if thou diest,
The King is king, and ever wills the highest.
Clang battle-axe and clash brand! Let the King reign!"

He peeked at her to see if she was impressed yet. Her mouth hung open and her eyes had widened. When she saw him looking at her, she closed her mouth.

He went on:

"Blow, for our Sun is mighty in his May!
  Blow, for our Sun is mightier day by day!
  Clang battle-axe and clash brand! Let the King reign!
  The King will follow Christ, and we the King,
  In whom high God hath breathed a secret thing.
  Fall battle-axe and clash brand! Let the King reign!"

He turned toward her. "Are you not now convinced of my culture and refinement?"

She simply smiled, as if he'd just told her a mildly amusing story. "I'm not sure I've read that one. Is it Tennyson?"

"It is."

She nodded, then she picked up her letter from her lap and began to read again.

She was unmoved by his charm. Incredible. But perhaps she was only pretending. At least he had made her smile. But as he drove along, and even when she'd had time to read the letter several times over, silence reigned.

Why did he have such a desire to get a reaction from her and make her talk? James would say he was playing the knight in shining armor again. James was always looking at things scientifically. But Truett was simply a Southern gentleman, with a bit too much emotion.

But it was more than that. Celia Wilcox was beautiful.

His challenge for himself would be to make Celia Wilcox smile again by the time he got her home, and before two weeks were over, to get her to verbally repent of her low opinion of him. If he couldn't, he'd give up and accept that she was beyond even his considerable charm.

~

CELIA PRETENDED TO READ HER LETTER, BUT HER THOUGHTS WENT back to the interchange between the sheriff and Dr. Beverly, whose aim seemed to be making the sheriff think he was a poetry-sotted swain. But why? Did he know where this James Burwell was hiding? If he did, why would the town doctor, ordinarily one of the town's most respectable citizens, try to fool the sheriff?

And the assault of a woman? This town seemed worse by the minute.

Then Dr. Beverly had surprised her by quoting Tennyson, though she wouldn't for the world let him know she was impressed. No, she had no interest in the backwoods doctor. Although he was uncommonly handsome, with hair the color of well-sanded wood that curled perfectly against his forehead and temples, and the darkest blue eyes, which had looked so sad when he told her how sorry he was about her father's death.

She wasn't sure what to make of him. But her hope, her future, was in Nashville. She would not marry anyone who would keep her in Bethel Springs.

Celia focused her attention on her sister's letter, the catalyst for her departure from Nashville. Lizzie's pleading words were uncharacteristic of her calm and patient sister.

She pressed her lips together to stop the tears that sprang to her eyes and stuffed the letter into her fringed silk purse, an item that seemed frivolous now that her family was practically destitute.

Perhaps it was ungracious to criticize, even secretly, her father's decision, but she still couldn't understand him leaving all their friends, not to mention his livelihood at the university. She'd been helpless to talk him out of it. She just tried to be happy for him, happy that he was doing what he'd always dreamed of doing.

Mama went along with whatever Father said, and Celia half believed her father didn't care about her mother's feelings. She'd never in her life heard him ask his wife her opinion of anything, never seen him listen to her as if he was interested in what she had to say. He treated Celia with more respect than he did his own wife. It had always irked Celia and made her wish her mother, just once, would stand up to him.

There was no use thinking about that now. As soon as Mama was herself again—*Lord, please let it be before the end of summer*—Celia would catch the first train back to Nashville. And she hoped by then she would have convinced her family to go back with her.

Just the thought that the dress shop might permanently replace her with someone else, that she would lose her job when she had calculated it would only take her nine more months to save up enough money to open her own shop, sent her heart racing in panic. Was she being selfish to want it so badly? But after all, with the income, she could help her family. They would naturally want to move back to Nashville, and her money could make that happen.

Celia held on to the buggy's seat as it jounced her around over the bumpy road. She gazed into dark woods crowding the edge of the road—pecan trees, magnolias, and oaks mingled their leaves of varying shades of green. Cedars stood like thick, tall brushes in a straight line along the edge of the fields. Mimosa trees, with their tropical foliage and fuzzy pink pom-pom flowers, dangled over the edge of the dirt road. Farther along, honeysuckle vines draped the fences and permeated the hot afternoon with heady perfume.

The countryside had a natural, exuberant beauty one couldn't find in the city. But nature's charm could be dark and dangerous, as it had been for Father.

With God's help, they could find the runaway horses and sell them and the farm and buy a small house near where Celia would open her shop. Then she would no longer have to board with old Mrs. Beasley and endure her snide remarks about a young woman, alone and unmarried, opening her own business as if she were a man.

A thousand *humph*s on old Mrs. Beasley and everyone like her.

"So what do you think of our beautiful countryside, Miss Wilcox? Or may I call you Miss Celia?"

"Either is fine." She smiled, then hoped he didn't think she was flirting with him. "It is beautiful, in a wild sort of way."

"Your family will be overjoyed to see you. They speak of you quite often, about what a talented seamstress you are and how you plan to open your own shop."

"My family is very kind. I shall be happy to see them." Tears pricked the back of her eyelids in response to the sharp longing in her heart. It would be so good to feel her mother's and sister's arms around her.

Down the road and beyond some trees, a column of dark smoke danced lazily toward the sky. It seemed too big to be simply a cooking fire.

She glanced at Dr. Beverly. His face was set in grim lines. He even looked a bit ashen.

"What is it? Is someone's house on fire?"

"I think so." His voice was hollow.

The acrid smell of smoke burned her nose as they drew closer. The doctor grew stiffer and taller in the seat, the reins clenched tightly in his fists, as he urged the horse to move a little faster. Finally, a burned-out house came into view. Its charred stone chimney rose in the clearing from amidst blackened, smoking logs. Flickers of fire licked the remains of the small house.

Celia bit her lip. "Do you suppose whoever lived here was able to get out in time?"

"I reckon they did." His teeth clenched so tight a muscle twitched in his jaw. His eyes narrowed and color returned to his face. He must know something he wasn't telling her.

"Did someone deliberately set this fire?"

"I don't know." He spoke softly and looked away from her.

"Then why do you look angry?"

His chest expanded as he switched the reins lightly over the horse's back to hurry him past the house. The heat from the fire made her dress cling to her back.

"What makes you think I look angry?" His eyebrows lifted in nonchalance.

"Your eyes are still shooting sparks." She wouldn't mention that his jaw looked set in stone. Like a Grecian statue. "Whose house was it?"

"James Burwell's."

Celia stared over her shoulder at what was left of the house. Her chest tightened for a moment in sympathy for James Burwell. Although, if he had truly molested a woman as the sheriff had said . . .

"Do you know James Burwell?"

"We've been friends since we were children. James has the mind of a scientist, continually making discoveries, figuring things out." He turned and looked her in the eye. "Someday he'll find a new way to double corn production, or invent a machine to do the work of a hundred men, or find a thousand new uses for cotton or sorghum molasses. He is a capable, gifted man, and he would never . . . ever hurt a woman."

Something about his expression and his clear blue eyes as he gazed at her made her heart flutter, just as it had when he'd smiled at her at the train depot.

She quickly looked away from him. Heat rose into her own cheeks and an unsettled feeling came over her. How foolish to have such a reaction to a man she hardly knew. But as she thought about what he had said, she was even more certain that he had been trying to deceive the sheriff.

They rode on in silence for a while. She glanced at him out of the corner of her eye. Why wasn't he married? His features were appealing, and he was tall, educated, his only physical flaw being crooked bottom teeth. She marveled that one of Bethel Springs's girls hadn't roped the local doctor like a prize bull. He was the pick of the county, she imagined.

The wagon bumped over the uneven road, which consisted only of two dirt ruts with grass growing down the middle. The scenery alternated from fields of cotton or corn, to thick forests, and back to cotton again. Out of boredom and an effort to make conversation, she asked, "So, Dr. Beverly, where did you attend medical school?"

"Bellevue Medical Seminary, New York City."

"Oh. Why did you move to Bethel Springs? Did you miss the South?"

He shrugged. "I grew up here and my parents asked me to come back. There was a need for a doctor."

"Is your father a farmer?"

"He owned a plantation before the war. Now he works near Columbia, Tennessee, helping my uncle with his brick manufacturing business. But my mother, brother, and I are your family's nearest neighbor to the east. We'll pass the house in a minute."

Before the words were out of his mouth, a thundering of hooves grew closer. The rider rounded the curve a hundred feet ahead of them and Celia immediately recognized her brother.

"Will!"

Celia's twelve-year-old brother reined the horse to a halt beside Dr. Beverly. "It's Griff. Mrs. Beverly can't control him, and she sent me to fetch you."

Dr. Beverly leaped to the ground. "May I borrow your horse?"

Will slipped from the saddle.

"Take Miss Celia home in my buggy." He swung onto Will's horse and was off at a gallop before she could ask a single question.

"Hey there, Celia. I didn't know you was coming." Will grinned as though he hadn't just ridden up like a banshee, and as though his news hadn't just sent the doctor tearing away in like manner.

"What's going on? And why didn't you know I was coming? And don't say, 'I didn't know you *was* coming.' It's '*were* coming.'"

He climbed onto the seat beside her, kissed her on the cheek, and took up the reins. The gelding started forward at an easy pace.

"Us country folk don't set much store by correct grammar."

She could tell he was teasing her by the way his eyebrows lifted and the corners of his mouth twitched. If she weren't so irritated with him, she would throw her arms around her little brother and plant a kiss on his cheek.

"Not funny," she said. But she had never been good at holding grudges, so she hugged and kissed him, and then tousled his beautiful blond head anyway. "Now will you please tell me what's going on? Who's Griff?"

"Griff is Dr. Beverly's brother. Folks say he hit his head when he was a child, and ever since then, well . . . he ain't been right. Most of the time he acts like a child, but when he gets agitated, he's liable to hurt somebody. And I've never seen him as riled as he was a few minutes ago when I left to go fetch Truett."

An animal-like growling came from behind a row of trees, growing louder and fiercer by the moment. She couldn't see anything past the bend in the road. Her heart thumped against her chest as an uneasy feeling crept over her. "What is that sound?"

"That's Griff."

CHAPTER 4

The back of Celia's neck prickled. She wished Will would make the horse go faster. Dr. Beverly could be in danger!

But perhaps it was best they didn't reach them too soon. What if Will was hurt? She shuddered at the thought. After what happened to Daddy, she couldn't bear anything happening to Will.

Just around the bend, another growl sounded, this one more fierce than before. If only the horse would go faster. A few more steps and they'd be able to—

A woman's scream split the air.

Celia's blood turned cold. She glanced at Will's tense face and then followed his gaze toward the bushes just ahead as the buggy crept around the curve.

Beside the road, a man stood holding a huge rock over his head. *Griff.* He was Truett Beverly's brother, all right. Though his hair was darker and he was a bit taller, his features were too similar to Dr. Beverly's to not be his close kin.

His eyes were wild, like a wolf about to pounce on its prey. He aimed his weapon—the gray boulder—at a small, gray-haired woman several feet in front of him.

Celia gasped, her hand flying to her throat. Griff was going to kill that poor woman!

Out of the saddle now, Dr. Beverly crept toward his brother. Suddenly, he shouted, "Run!" and leaped toward his brother.

Griff let out a roar and heaved the rock at the woman, but Dr. Beverly's shoulder struck his brother in the ribs, throwing off his aim and sending the three of them—Griff, Dr. Beverly, and the boulder—to the ground. The heavy rock landed a safe distance away from its target.

The woman had run away when Dr. Beverly had commanded. Now, she took a few steps toward the house, which was nestled among some trees away from the road, and then turned back to watch.

Truett Beverly grappled with his snarling brother. Griff wrapped his hands around the doctor's throat.

Celia grasped the wagon seat, her heart thumping. She wanted to jump down and help him, but she couldn't tear her eyes off the scene below her.

Dr. Beverly used his hands to cover Griff's eyes. Griff let go. With amazing speed, he grasped Griff's wrists and pinned them to the ground. Then he pressed his knee against his brother's heaving chest. The doctor looked almost nonchalant, holding the thrashing man captive.

Will simply drove on past.

"Shouldn't we do something to help him? Maybe go and fetch the sheriff?" Celia turned on the seat to look back, but the trees and the next bend hid them from view.

"Nah." Will frowned from one side of his mouth. "Truett can take care of it. He told me to get you home."

Celia just stared at her brother. Was this a regular occurrence? Were these the neighbors with whom her family was blessed?

What a strange place her father had stranded her family in.

Celia faced forward on the seat. It wasn't far now. In a few minutes, she would see her family. She wanted to ask Will about Mama, but would he even know anything was amiss? Will wasn't the most observant person in the family.

They turned into the small dirt path leading to the white clapboard farmhouse. Celia clutched the strings of her small purse in her fist. When the wagon slowed to a stop, she gathered her skirt in her hand and jumped down from the seat.

Lizzie burst onto the front porch. "Celia! You're here!" Her sleeves were rolled up to her elbows and water dripped from her hands. She smiled wider than the Tennessee River, and Celia rushed to hug her.

She met her on the porch and they flung their arms around each other.

After tearfully saying how much they'd missed each other, Celia pulled away slightly. "Did you get my telegram?"

"No. When did you send it?"

"Two days ago."

"Tuesday. That's the day the pigs found a hole under the fence and ran away." Lizzie smiled ruefully and hugged her sister again. "We were all out hunting for them, but Mama would have been home. She didn't say anything about a telegram."

"It doesn't matter."

Celia squeezed her sister's wet hand. "Washing dishes?"

She shrugged. "I don't mind."

Had all the housework fallen on Lizzie's fourteen-year-old shoulders? "How's Mama?"

Lizzie frowned and shook her head. She clasped Celia's hand and led her into the house.

The small, one-story farmhouse was draped in her mother's touch—a lace tablecloth here, an oil lamp with a frilly fringed shade there. The simple house had a cared-for look, in spite of the twins' toys strewn over the floor.

Lizzie led her through the parlor, or sitting room, down the hallway, which led past bedrooms on both sides, to the kitchen at the back of the house, and there her mother sat in a straight-back chair, staring out the window. The sun was casting bright orange rays into the room.

"Mama, I'm home." Celia crossed the room, intending to give her a hug, but when Mama finally turned to gaze at her, it was with a guarded, slightly puzzled expression.

Celia stopped in the middle of the room. "Mama. It's me, Celia."

"Celia?" Mama stared at her face without a trace of recognition.

What kind of sad joke was this? Her mother didn't recognize her? It had only been six months since she'd been there for the funeral. Was Mama so bad off?

She couldn't speak as she waited for Mama to recognize her.

Her mother's usually plump cheeks were slightly sunken and her lips were red and chapped. Accustomed to seeing her mother's hands busy peeling potatoes, rolling out pie crust, sewing, mending, or embroidering, it was odd to see them lying idly in her lap. Could Mama not accept that Daddy was gone? Did she have to give up, to forget that she had a family of five children who needed her?

"Don't you know me, Mama? Your own daughter?"

"Oh . . . Celia. Of course. Where have you been?" Mama's eyes still looked dull, as if she only half understood what was happening around her.

Celia swallowed, fighting the nausea that threatened to sweep over her. She stepped forward and took her mother's hands in hers. "Mama, I've been in Nashville, working at the dress shop. But I'm here for the summer. Are you all right?"

She stared at Celia with that disinterested glaze over her eyes. "Yes, I am well. How are you?"

Celia felt like crying. This woman wasn't her mother! What made her sit there in a strange stupor as if she had no mind at all?

She took a deep breath. She shouldn't have such thoughts about her mother. Surely this was only temporary. Her mother was suffering deep grief over Daddy's death. She needed Celia's sympathy and understanding. Celia patted her hand. "Everything's going to be all right, Mama. Don't you worry."

Lizzie stepped forward. "Mama, did a telegram come two days ago, on Tuesday?"

Confusion and annoyance creased her forehead and deepened the wrinkles at the corners of her eyes. "A telegram? I don't know. Look over there." She waved her hand at a small basket on the sideboard.

Lizzie stepped to the corner of the room and peered into the basket. "Here it is." She snatched up the piece of paper, then her shoulders slumped. "Mama, why didn't you tell us?" A look of dismay scrunched her face. She met Celia's gaze and frowned, then let out a long slow breath. Celia wanted to say something reassuring, but words failed her.

Tempie and Harley ran into the house and threw their arms around Celia's knees, nearly knocking her over. They squealed and pelted her with questions, then ran off before she could answer them. Tempie went to fetch her corn shuck doll someone had made for her, and Harley showed her his slingshot.

"I killed my first bird!" Dirt smudged his face and neck, but his smile was wide and full of joy.

"That's very good," Celia said, making sure to look impressed. But inwardly she marveled at how Lizzie had managed to care for them, as rambunctious as they were.

If Mama didn't improve, Celia would not be able to leave them again.

CELIA LET THE SECOND BUCKET FALL TO THE BOTTOM OF THE WELL. Night descended around her, and with it came the shrill chirping of crickets and the mournful calling of the whippoorwill. She turned the squeaky windlass to bring the full bucket to the top. As she reached for it, a horse's hooves thudded on the road nearby. Celia turned from the well and strained to see who it was in the shadowy light of the moon and stars.

The rider turned onto their path and made his way toward where she stood beside the well several feet from the front porch. He took off his hat with a flourish and bowed slightly from atop his horse. "Miss Celia."

Truett Beverly. He must have come to get his buggy and return Will's horse.

"Dr. Beverly." She had just seen him a few hours before, but somehow he looked different. Older.

"I apologize for running off and leaving you."

"That's all right. You were occupied with a more pressing matter, as I recall."

He dismounted and walked closer. "I regret you had to see Griff that way . . . for your first impression to have been . . . *that*. He isn't usually in such a state. His brain injury causes his behavior to be erratic."

Could her mother's state be the same as a brain injury? Could Dr. Beverly help her?

"I've come to see your mother as I promised." Dark crescents ringed Truett's eyes. His hair and clothes were slightly disheveled, and he looked as if he needed a shave.

A pang of pity squeezed her stomach, and a sudden urge came over her to put her arms around him.

Oh, dear. Celia took a step backward, almost spilling the bucket of water that teetered on the edge of the well. What was wrong with her?

She was tired, that was all.

"Let me get that for you."

Before she could protest, he stepped forward, took the bucket from her hand, and grabbed the other one from the lip of the well.

"Thank you."

He was standing very close. The light that showed through the kitchen window showed the shadow of stubble on his cheeks and the slight cleft in the center of his chin. His masculine leather-and-horses smell made her heart thump.

"I-I— Would you like to come inside?" What a stupid thing to say! He'd have to come inside. He was carrying her buckets of water. Was she so affected by the man that she would act like an enamored schoolgirl?

"I will check up on your mother if it's a convenient time."

"Yes, thank you." She turned away.

Celia marched quickly up the steps and held the door open for him. The house was quiet, as Lizzie had just gone outside to find the twins. Dr. Beverly put the buckets down by the sink. He straightened and their eyes met again.

"Thank you, Dr. Beverly."

He nodded. "You're most welcome, Miss Celia."

He turned to Mama, who sat staring at the kerosene lamp on the kitchen table in front of her.

"Mrs. Wilcox, it's Dr. Beverly. How are you tonight, ma'am?"

Mama glanced up, as if startled. "Who?"

"Dr. Beverly, ma'am, your neighbor. Do you mind if I ask you a few questions?"

"No, no, go ahead."

Celia watched as Dr. Beverly spoke softly to Mama, convincing her to stretch out her arm to him so he could check her pulse. He asked her how she had been feeling, if she'd had any shortness of breath or fainting spells. She told him no, but her manner and tone reminded Celia of a child who resented being questioned.

Finally, the doctor stood and walked toward Celia, but he did not meet her gaze.

She led him down the hall, through the parlor toward the front door. Outside, Lizzie rounded up the four-year-old twins to get ready for bed. At the door, she turned toward him, impatient to hear what he thought about her mother. But still he said nothing. Finally, he sighed and rubbed the back of his neck.

She winced. "Is it as bad as that?"

He looked up, a half smile on his face, and shook his head. "She seems perfectly healthy. But she's grieving. Your father's death was a terrible shock to her, and it would seem she's dealing with it by withdrawing from people and from life."

"But it's already been six months since Daddy died. How long will this last?"

"Can't say. Could be a few weeks, could be a lot longer. With these kinds of nervous disorders, it's impossible to know for sure."

"Is there anything I can do to help her recover?"

He rubbed his stubbly chin before answering. "Let me write some letters. I have a friend who teaches at the Nashville Medical Seminary, and I know a few professors at Bellevue in New York. I'll see if they can dig up some case studies on this sort of thing. In the meanwhile, we just have to pray for her."

Celia nodded. "Of course. Thank you, doctor. I suppose I should pay you—"

"No, there's no charge for tonight's visit. Good night, Miss Celia." He placed his hat back on his head as he stepped out the door.

∽

LATER THAT NIGHT, AFTER THE TWINS WERE FAST ASLEEP, CELIA LAY in bed beside Lizzie, whispering so as not to wake Will and Harley in the next room. Tempie was apparently now sleeping with Mother in her bed.

"What do you reckon has happened to Mama?"

Lizzie sighed. "I don't know, but I hope she gets over it soon. And I'm sorry for writing you that letter that made you come here. I'd just had a bad day. The twins were running me ragged, fighting and getting lost. A skinned knee, a bump on the head, they were crying and screaming, and all the while Mama sat there like she didn't know she was in the world."

"Oh, Lizzie, I'm so sorry. It was good you wrote to me. You shouldn't have to take care of everything by yourself. I'm here now, and I hope, by the end of the summer, Mama will be her old self again."

"Surely she'll be back to normal by then. Surely in three months she'll be helping me with the housekeeping and the twins." After a short silence, Lizzie whispered, "What do you think about Dr. Beverly?"

Celia tried to make out the expression on Lizzie's face but the room was too dark. "He seems nice enough."

"Oh, Celia, he is nice. He's been such a help to us. I don't know what we would have done without him. He takes Will hunting, fishing, and he brings toys to the twins. I know he feels sorry for us. Will adores him."

She felt her shoulders stiffen. "Feels sorry for us? We don't need his pity."

"Don't be like that. What I wanted to tell you is that I think he'd be the perfect man for you."

"What do you mean? You know I don't intend to marry."

"But Celia—"

"I might marry someday, but not a country doctor from Bethel Springs, Alabama." Celia hoped to put an end to her little sister's matchmaking with her firm tone. But the truth was, she *did* want to marry someday. Just not until after she'd gotten her dress shop open and business was going well. In fact, she'd had an infatuation since she was fifteen, only a year older than Lizzie was now, for one of her father's colleagues at Vanderbilt, a Professor Dent. Of course, the man was much older and she hadn't seen him since her father resigned his position as head of the mathematics department. Perhaps she would run into another Professor Dent later, when she was too old to have children. Then she could hire someone else to take over her dress shop and only work when and as much as wanted to.

"He isn't attached, you know."

"Who?"

"Dr. Beverly!"

"Shh! Do you want Will to wake up and hear you?"

"Listen to me, Celia. He's a good man. He's handsome, and he doesn't seem to be interested in any of the Bethel Springs girls."

"Aren't I the lucky one?" Celia didn't try to hide her sarcasm. "Should I be like Mama and marry now, when I'm nineteen? Make this man my whole life—since no self-respecting husband could let his wife start her own business. And then, when something happens to him, I lose my mind like Mama, my purpose in life gone? No thank you."

Lizzie was quiet and, in truth, Celia had surprised herself with her vehemence.

"I'm sorry." She took a deep breath and lowered her voice back to a whisper. "It's just . . . I hate to destroy your matchmaking, but I'm not the least bit interested in Dr. Beverly."

"Are you sure you don't think he's handsome?" Lizzie's voice still rang with excitement, her enthusiasm unfazed by Celia's outburst. "There are at least three girls every Sunday who fight over who's going to talk to him after church."

"That's hardly tempting." *As if I'd join in the fray!*

"He's like an older brother to us. And if you marry him, he can stay in the family."

"Oh, Lizzie." Celia moaned.

"You don't know what it's been like to move here. Daddy had never lived on a farm. I think he had this romantic idea about it, that we would be like the Swiss Family Robinson, figuring every-thing out by ourselves. But we were lost, Celia. We didn't know how to do anything. Daddy had to get Truett's advice—"

"Truett?"

"Dr. Beverly. That's his name."

"I know that."

Lizzie clutched her arm. Her sister's grip told her she was determined to make her listen. "Daddy sought his advice for everything—plowing, planting, the horses, everything. And you know we always had a cook back in Nashville. We didn't even know how to operate the stove."

"I'm sorry, Lizzie. I didn't know it was as bad as that. But I hardly think I should have to marry the man to show him our gratitude."

"Oh, Celia, you're impossible!"

"Besides, he might not want to marry me, even if I throw myself at him like those other girls." The picture she was forming of him surrounded by silly, smiling women made her ashamed of her fellow females.

Celia went on. "I tried to talk Daddy out of coming here. I still can't believe he gave up his position at Vanderbilt."

"I know, but it's done, and we're here."

"But that's another thing, Lizzie. Don't you see? We don't have to stay here."

"What do you mean?"

"We could sell the farm and move Mama back home. Perhaps if she was around her old friends again, and in a familiar setting, she would make her way out of this fog she's in."

"I don't know, Celia. I kind of like it here. It's peaceful, it's beautiful, and I've made friends."

"Friends? With whom? The squirrels?"

"We have other neighbors besides the Beverlys. Olean Prichard lives on the other side of us. She's exactly my age. And every Sunday I see the other girls, Henrietta, Tollie, and Mae. Sometimes we go on picnics and hayrides and—"

"Elizabeth Wilcox, are you telling me you'd rather live here than in Nashville?"

"I like it here, Celia. While you've been in Nashville all year, we've been here, settling in. Will likes it, and Harley too. Boys need to explore, Daddy always said—"

"But a lady should always prefer town." Celia took her sister's hand and squeezed it gently. "Lizzie, wouldn't you be just as happy in Nashville? You had friends there, too. And we could hire someone again to help us with the cooking and taking care of Harley and Tempie."

"That's part of the problem. I don't believe we could hire anyone to help us. We have no money. And I overheard some men talking at church. They said Daddy paid too much for this place and we wouldn't be able to sell it for anything near what he paid— if we could sell it at all. The place sat empty for years before we came."

Her heart jumped into her throat.

"We have no money, Celia. Daddy spent most of the money we had left buying the horses, and two of them are still missing after the storm."

"Surely we have some money left."

Lizzie shook her head. "Only seven dollars and fifty-three cents. Mama spent a fortune on Daddy's gravestone. It's solid marble, and she had to send away to Nashville to get it."

All the air seemed to get sucked out of the room. She couldn't breathe. She sat up to keep from smothering and fanned herself with her hand.

"Celia, are you all right?"

Panic tightened her chest, making it painful to breathe. She had to go back to Nashville. She couldn't stay here. But . . . her family was destitute?

"Celia? What's wrong?"

She drew in a shallow breath. "I have to go." She realized how crazy her words sounded. Of course, she didn't have to go, but . . . "I have to get back to Nashville. There has to be a way. There has to be some money somewhere, something we could sell . . ."

"We could sell Daddy's horses, but the most valuable ones are still missing."

Surely God wouldn't let her be stuck in Bethel Springs. Would he?

CHAPTER 5

The eastern sky turned pink as Celia dressed for the day. In the kitchen, Lizzie built the fire in the stove for breakfast. Will had gone out to milk the cow. Tempie wandered into Harley and Will's room, clutching her doll to her chest. Celia went in as Tempie was shaking Harley awake.

"All right, little ones, it's time to get dressed." Celia went in search of some clothes for them and found them laid out on the dresser.

Lizzie. Celia sighed. So much responsibility had fallen on her younger sister's shoulders, and she had borne it wonderfully well.

"Let's get you dressed, Tempie."

The little girl snatched her dress out of Celia's hand. "I can do it myself!"

Celia was doubtful, but she decided not to argue. She turned to her little brother. Unlike his twin, Harley sat still while she removed his nightshirt and dressed him in a shirt and pants. The clothing was quite frayed around the hems, with a hole here and there. No matter. They weren't going anywhere today.

She went into the kitchen and tried to help Lizzie with breakfast, but it was soon clear she had no idea how to help. The newest styles and patterns for women's dresses and hats were mysteries meant to be explored, but cooking? An inscrutable business best left to those who understood it.

"Here." Lizzie handed her a lump of white dough. "Drop balls of this onto the pan."

"Biscuits?"

Lizzie smiled and nodded.

When breakfast was ready, Celia went outside and rang the bell by the corner of the front porch. Will came from the barn and Harley emerged from the trees, holding a slingshot and running as fast as his four-year-old legs would carry him.

She went back inside and found Tempie having a pretend tea party on the floor with her two dolls. "Tempie, sweetie, it's time to eat breakfast." But the little girl didn't even look up from her play.

Celia sighed and went to see what else she could help Lizzie do. "Where's Mama?"

"She's not up yet." Lizzie flipped her blond braid over her shoulder as she set a bowl of hominy grits on the table. "She usually sleeps for another couple of hours."

Celia had never known Mama to sleep past sunrise.

As Lizzie had predicted, Mama didn't emerge from her bedroom until two hours later wearing her housecoat, her hair still braided but messy from her night's sleep. Celia waited until Lizzie had poured Mama a cup of coffee and set her breakfast before her. While her mother ate, Celia picked up the mending in her lap and tried to concentrate on her stitches, going over in her head what she would say.

Finally, Mama pushed the plate away, having barely eaten half her food, and stared listlessly out the window. Celia put the mending aside in her sewing basket, sat in the chair beside her, and took her hand in hers.

"Mama, it's me, Celia."

"How are you, dear?"

She felt cheered by her mother's words, although her eyes still looked far away and her voice was a monotone. "Mama, I want us to talk about what we should do now. I think we should move back to Nashville." Celia leaned closer, trying to get her mother to look her in the eye. "Wouldn't you be happy to be back with your friends? We could sell this place and find a small house in town."

Her mother's eyebrows lowered. A scowl deepened the crease between her brown eyes as she focused on Celia. "You are forgetting your place. Your father wants us to live here, and that's where we will live. Your father makes the decisions, not you."

Tears stung Celia's eyes. She loosened her hold on her mother's hand. "But Mama, Daddy's gone. We need to do what is best for the family—"

Mother snatched her hand away. "So you know what's best? Do you question your father's authority?"

Her voice rose with each word, until it was shrill and unfamiliar, like a stranger's. Mama's face had lacked animation ever since Celia had come home, but her expression came alive now. Her jaw clenched, her lips pursed, and her eyes flashed.

"Your Daddy wanted us to live here, and that's where we shall live."

A boulder seemed to press against Celia's chest. She had only seen her mild-mannered mother angry once or twice, and it was nothing compared to the anger she now displayed. Still, desperation forced her to speak.

"Mama, I know you miss him, but staying here isn't going to make him come back. He would want us to move on, to—"

"That's enough!" Her mother rose to her feet and lifted her right hand, as if to strike her. "I don't want to hear any more about it from you! You always did think you were too smart to listen to anyone. You don't know what you're talking about. I will not listen to another word from you."

Tears stung her eyes and she lifted her hand to her cheek, feeling as if her mother really had struck her. Celia stared at her, not knowing what to say, only wishing she could blot out the accusing look in her mother's eyes.

"We're not leaving, and I will not discuss it."

Celia turned away and stumbled out the kitchen door and down the steps.

She ran, her skirt heavy against her legs, across the clearing behind the house, hardly knowing where she was going. Finally, her gaze caught on a few familiar oak trees shading the top of a hill. Beneath them, her father's grave.

She headed for the ostentatious, seven-foot marble obelisk for which her mother had sent away to Nashville. Tears dripped down her cheeks. She wiped them away with the back of her hand and knelt on the grass in front of the mound of dirt.

The grave marker seemed to mock her, too expensive for anyone but a rich man. The white marble gleamed in the dappled sunlight shining through the leaves of the oak tree. *William Ernest Wilcox*, was carved deeply into the stone. The too-true words, *Gone but not forgotten*, written underneath it almost made her laugh.

"Oh, Daddy. How could you leave us this way?" Fresh tears edged the corners of her eyes and spilled out. "We need you." She leaned forward and sobbed into her hands.

A bird trilled and sang from a tree branch above her. From not far away, another bird answered. The song was mournful, as if the two birds were crying to each other, while the sun winked at her through the leaves.

"God, help me. Please." A tear slid to her chin and dripped off. Having left home without a handkerchief, she wiped her face again with her hands. "I didn't want Daddy to die. . . I didn't want him to die. And now, what are we to do? We have no money. But I have to get back to Nashville so I can work and make money for the family. Please, God, please show me the way." She sniffled. "Don't make me stay"—her voice broke on a sob— "here."

A huge old magnolia tree stood nearby, slightly apart from the oak trees, and it spread its gnarled branches over the ground. A white blossom stretched toward Celia, so close she was able to reach over and pluck it. The flower was as big as her two open palms. She raised it to her face, letting her tears drip onto the perfect petals, closing her eyes and inhaling its heady fragrance. The smell conjured up memories of playing in her friend's back yard in Nashville.

She brushed the petals against her cheeks and chin, oddly comforted by the cool, waxy texture. She fingered a broad magnolia leaf. Smooth and green on the surface, it was tough and strong, yet brown and fuzzy and soft underneath.

She could make it through this.

She would make it through this summer, helping Lizzie and Will and taking care of the twins. And somehow, some way, when the summer was over, she had to get back to her real work. How else would they—would she—survive?

～

SUNDAY DAWNED BRIGHT AND HOT. CELIA GOT READY FOR CHURCH. She'd only been out of mourning for a couple of weeks and could now wear her more colorful dresses, which fit in perfectly at her church in Nashville. But here in Bethel Springs she feared she would stand out like a gypsy among Quakers.

"Lizzie, do you think this dress looks all right?"

Lizzie glanced up from the small looking glass on the wall as she pinned her hair up. "You look very pretty. Truett will be impressed."

Celia glared back at her grinning sister. "Lizzie, I'm warning you—"

"Aw, I'm only teasing." She smiled. "You look elegant."

She blew out a breath, already feeling the weight of the humid morning air. She reached for her favorite hat. As she began pinning it in place, Lizzie wrinkled her nose.

"Not that hat, Celia. Wear something . . . smaller."

Celia examined the long, puffy hat with its wide burgundy ribbon trailing down the back. The multiple dyed feathers and silk flowers increased its height by half a foot. She carefully placed it back into its box.

Smaller. It wasn't as if she even owned one of the floppy cotton bonnets everyone around here was so fond of. She searched through her trunk until she found an old hat, now slightly out of fashion, no larger than her two fists. One side of the brim pushed up and it had only a small bow and a cluster of wax grapes at the back. At least it was the right colors, cream and mauve, to match her dress.

Harley and Tempie bickered in the back of the wagon all the way to church. Mother had refused to come, without giving any reason. Celia had never been very close to her mother, had always been closer to Daddy, who treated her more like an adult than a child. She was the oldest and loved spending time with her father, though she suspected he'd wished she was a boy.

Celia sat beside Will, who drove the horses while Lizzie sat with the twins in the back and tried to keep them from fighting.

A lump of dread formed in her chest as they drew closer to the little white church. What kind of people would she meet here? Would the other young women dislike her?

When they arrived, Will stopped the horses in the shade of a group of cottonwoods, which shed the white bits of cotton-like substance that floated through the air all around the church yard. The air was thick with it, like snow that drifted sideways instead of falling to the ground.

Will jumped down and came around the wagon to help her. His small twelve-year-old hand held hers firmly, and she noticed the calluses for the first time. It was no longer the hand of a child, white and dimpled with baby fat. Will was still small for his age, but his hands were scratched and sun-browned, his nails broken and stained. He also displayed an easy confidence she'd never seen in him before.

As soon as her feet were on solid ground, he sauntered off toward some boys who were calling him. Lizzie and the twins also scrambled out of the wagon and scattered.

Celia searched the small knots of people milling around the church yard until she spotted Harley talking to an older woman. The woman bent over him with an indulgent expression.

Where was Tempie?

Celia glanced around until her eye caught the little girl's bright yellow dress. She also stood chattering away to someone who squatted beside her, bringing his face even with hers. Celia blinked once, twice, then gasped. The man talking to Tempie was Dr. Beverly's brother, Griff.

Her face tingled as the blood drained away.

Pursing her lips, Celia strode the ten steps it took her to reach Lizzie, who was talking to two other girls her age. She grabbed her sister's arm and pulled her aside.

"Celia! What in the world—"

"Lizzie, do you see who Tempie's talking to?" Her voice was a half-hysterical hiss, but this was a desperate situation. They had to act—before it was too late. "Help me save her!"

"What do you mean?" Lizzie's gaze darted from Tempie to stare at Celia with lowered eyebrows and round eyes. "She's just talking to Griff."

"He's dangerous!"

"Oh, Celia, he's harmless—most of the time. He'd never hurt Tempie."

"Never hurt Tempie? He tried to bash his own mother's head in with a boulder!"

"You're overreacting."

It was Celia's turn to stare at her sister. Had she lost her mind?

She turned back to see if Tempie was still safe. Griff was tying her bonnet strings under her chin. He didn't look as if he would hurt her. Perhaps she was overreacting, but she remembered how he'd looked when he'd grappled with Truett, making those horrible snarling sounds.

The man's fingers grazed her little sister's cheek. Celia clenched her teeth and marched over to them. She bent down and swept Tempie up in her arms, forcing Griff to let go and leave the strings hanging loose. She ignored the man and walked away with her sister pressed against her chest.

Out of Griff's hearing, she whispered, "Tempie, if you need your bonnet tied, come to me or Lizzie."

Tempie pushed hard against her sister's upper arms. "Let me down!" she screamed. "I want down. I want to go!"

Tempie was struggling so to get down, Celia put her down. The child took off at a run back toward Griff. She immediately started tugging on his trouser leg.

Celia held her breath, waiting to see what Griff would do. Would he become annoyed with the child? She couldn't allow the man to hurt her little sister. She would claw his eyes out before she would allow him to harm one hair on her head. Celia's heart was in her throat as she watched, paralyzed.

Griff stood conversing with two men. He was exclaiming something about a "hooded horseman," his voice animated and his arms flailing. Tempie stared up at him a moment, then wandered off toward a circle of children and began drawing in the dirt with a stick.

Celia let out a breath of relief. But this was not over. Something had to be done. How could this dangerous person be allowed to wander unhindered amongst women and children?

When she turned to look for Lizzie she was still talking and smiling with a group of girls her own age.

She shouldn't bother Lizzie with this concern. Lizzie needed time to enjoy herself with her friends. Celia bit her lip and vowed to keep her eye on Griff. The man was dangerous. Maybe no one else was aware of what he was capable of, but she'd seen it with her own eyes.

She searched the grounds for Dr. Beverly. He also knew how dangerous Griff was. When she caught sight of him, he was talking with a young lady with upswept blond hair and a tiny hat perched on top.

Celia started to march up to him and tell him demand to know how much danger Tempie had been in a few minutes before. But no, that wouldn't be very polite. Besides, seeing him with the pretty young woman and remembering Lizzie's words to her about him, she thought better of it. If she simply approached them and demanded to speak with Dr. Beverly, the woman would no doubt think she had designs on the handsome young doctor. But as soon as that girl moved away from him, she would take up her concerns with Dr. Beverly.

She tried to appear inconspicuous, standing at the perimeter of the church yard and not making eye contact with anyone. Her watchful gaze went from Griff Beverly to his brother and back again.

The woman speaking with Truett smiled and even laughed as she talked. She leaned toward him, tapping him lightly on the arm with her fingertips. In reaction, he leaned away from her, moving his arms slightly farther away from her. Why couldn't the woman take a hint and leave the doctor alone?

As more people arrived in the churchyard, it became increasingly difficult to keep her eye on Griff and Truett and avoid speaking to the people passing by her. A woman and her husband introduced themselves and shook her hand. Another girl, Ruby Prichard, whom she vaguely remembered from the funeral, came up to introduce her brother, Casey, who blushed when she shook his hand.

They moved away, thank the Lord, and she flashed a look at Griff, who was still in the same place, then at Truett Beverly. The flirtatious young lady conversing with him was finally walking away, and he was staring straight at Celia. And walking toward her.

Had he caught her looking at him? Even if he had, he couldn't know she'd been watching him for the last five or ten minutes. She'd better be more careful, though, or she just might have him—and the rest of these people—thinking she had set matrimonial sights on him.

CHAPTER 6

Truett finally broke away from Beulah Pettibone. He'd wanted to go over and talk to Celia ever since he saw them drive up, but Beulah had cornered him, wanting to talk about the cotillion her mama was giving for her eighteenth birthday. He hoped he hadn't hurt her feelings, but she could probably tell he was not interested in the details of the upcoming gathering.

He strode toward Celia Wilcox. She looked perturbed, maybe even angry.

He took her hand. "Miss Celia." He bowed and kissed it lightly before letting go.

She frowned. He grinned. It amused him that she seemed so wholly unimpressed with him. But he'd promised himself he would make her repent of her low opinion of him, so he'd better make some progress today. After all, he didn't know when he'd see her again. And it kept his mind off worrying about James and Almira—and the sheriff.

"Dr. Beverly, I'd like to speak with you."

At that moment the people in the yard began moving toward

the open door of the church. It was time for the church service to start.

"Of course, Miss Celia. If you don't mind being late for church, I don't mind either."

"I don't think this will take long. I couldn't help but notice your, ah, encounter with your brother two days ago. Then this morning he was touching my little sister, Tempie."

"Touching her?"

"He was tying the strings of her bonnet. I don't mean to be impolite, but I was alarmed. After I saw what your brother is capable of, I don't believe it's safe . . ."

"Don't believe what's safe?" He probably shouldn't goad her. Of course he knew exactly what she was getting at. She was afraid for Tempie's safety around Griff. It was a legitimate concern, after what she'd witnessed.

Her eyes were so pretty. Framed by thick black lashes, they were a dark brown, almost black, that matched her thick hair, which fairly glowed in the morning sunlight. Too bad she kept it pulled back so tightly. No feminine tendrils to hang down by each cheek like the other girls.

"Dr. Beverly, are you listening?"

"Of course. You were talking about Griff being a danger to Tempie."

She stared. "Well?"

"It is true, Griff is dangerous when provoked or when he thinks he's being treated unfairly. He has the mind of a five-year-old, but the body and instincts of a man. Not a very good combination, I admit. But the community has adjusted to him. I am able to recognize when he's becoming agitated, and so are many others. I don't believe Griff would ever feel threatened by Tempie, and I assure you, none of the men here would allow anything to happen to your sister."

During his discourse, she folded her arms across her chest, tilting her head to one side.

She finally smiled—a serious smile, but pleasant. "Thank you for explaining the situation, Dr. Beverly. I can't help but wonder, though, if you've considered the other options for him."

"You mean Bryce Hospital in Tuscaloosa?" The hospital for the insane was actually a very progressive and humane program. Truett had toured the facility once years before. The hospital was headed by Peter Bryce, the leader in the field of medicine for the mentally insane, and it had attracted doctors from all over the country—and even the world—who wished to study his revolutionary ideas, much gentler and kinder ways of treating them than were used anywhere else.

But no matter how progressive the hospital was, Truett didn't like being told he should send his brother there. How would she feel if he suggested she do the same thing with her mother?

"I apologize, Dr. Beverly. I wouldn't bring it up at all except that I'm concerned about my younger siblings."

He tried not to be angry with her. After all, he might feel the same way if he were in her shoes. But she didn't know Griff like he did. Griff had a big heart. He loved people with the intensity and trust of a child. But because of his brain injury, he sometimes got agitated and confused. He sometimes lost control.

Truett took a deep breath before he spoke. "We've actually considered it—at least, my father and I have. My mother won't hear of it. She intends to take care of him as long as she lives. But as I said, your young siblings are safe. The other men of the community would intervene well before he could hurt anyone."

"Thank you, Doctor, for explaining." She pursed her lips as though she still wasn't completely satisfied.

She'd only just arrived, but obviously she wasn't afraid to share her opinion. Not only had she not been impressed by his poetry recitation, but she'd insinuated that he couldn't keep his brother from being a danger to little children.

He was in danger of losing his wager with himself. Perhaps

more than ever, he wanted to change her opinion of him. He would win her over yet.

Everyone else had already entered the church. Truett held out his arm to Celia, knowing she would bristle at having to walk into the church on his arm. Sure enough, the slight scowl on her face showed that she didn't want to allow him the liberty.

Still, she accepted his arm, placing her small gloved hand inside the crook of his elbow. And he liked the gentle warmth of it.

～

CELIA WALKED INTO THE CHURCH ON TRUETT BEVERLY'S ARM JUST as the song leader was clearing his throat. The whole church stood, holding hymnals. Several people turned to see who was walking in late. Their eyes grew big as they watched Celia enter on Truett's arm. The blond woman who had been talking with Truett narrowed her eyes and her cheeks turned red.

She searched for Lizzie and finally saw her standing with Will and the twins—in the same pew with Truett's mother and Griff. Lizzie scooted over and left enough room for two people by the inside aisle. Truett led her straight there, and Celia stood beside her sister. Truett picked up the hymnal in the back of the pew in front of them and held it between him and Celia.

Dozens of eyes burned into the back of her head. As well as a few in front that were rudely turned in her direction.

Since there weren't any other hymnals, Celia had no choice but to share with Truett.

She could certainly see where everyone's thoughts had gone. But Truett Beverly was safe from her. If it were proper to do so, she'd announce it to all the unmarried women of the county.

After singing one song, they all sat down and sang two more. Celia was careful to keep her left arm close to her side so as not to come in contact with Truett Beverly's arm, or even his sleeve.

When the preacher stood up to speak, she held her black leather Bible on her lap and got ready to turn to whatever chapter and verse he dictated.

The man spoke slowly and precisely. He called out a Scripture verse, then rattled it off from memory before Celia was able to turn to it in her Bible. His message was good, full of admonitions to live a life worthy of the gospel, though his grammar was somewhat wanting. He called out several other verses, but again, he quoted them before she could even find the correct book.

Truett Beverly sat perfectly still, the small Bible he'd pulled from his pocket cradled in his hands, but when she glanced at his face, he appeared to be reading the Bible instead of listening to the preacher. Why? At the end of the sermon, they sang one more song and someone spoke a collective prayer.

When the service was over, Celia engaged Lizzie in a conversation about the final preparations for dinner, making sure Truett Beverly couldn't talk to her without interrupting.

Finally, when most of the people sitting in front of them had made their way toward the back of the building, Celia stood. Dr. Beverly was nowhere in sight. She set her jaw and lifted her chin. *Good, he's gone.*

She wasn't sure why her eyes kept darting around the churchyard looking for him.

"You must be Lizzie Wilcox's sister."

Celia turned to see a pretty girl with a pale complexion, brown hair, and a shy smile. "I am. Call me Celia."

The girl held out a slim, fragile-looking hand. "I wanted to welcome you to Bethel Springs. I'm Almira Suggs."

❀

TRUETT STOOD OUTSIDE WITH THE REST OF MEN, PRETENDING TO listen to their conversation about fishing in the creek. Instead, he was thinking how Celia had turned her back on him. Apparently she wasn't interested in him, and that was for the best. Even though he still wanted to make her admit he was much more refined and intelligent than she had believed him to be, he needed to remember that he had little to offer Celia, or any woman. He would be quite ungallant if he caused her to think well of him, only to hurt her when she discovered he had no intention of marrying. Because if Sheriff Suggs ever found out he was the hooded horseman who had rescued James Burwell from his noose, Truett wouldn't live long enough to make a woman a widow, much less a wife.

And women generally liked their husbands living.

Truett shoved his hands in his pockets, wandering over to wait in the shade of the trees until his mother and Griff were ready to go, but Sheriff Suggs's wide shoulders caught his eye. Four other men were crowded around him. His head and eyes were lowered, as well as his voice, as he spoke to the men.

Truett started walking in their direction but kept his eyes focused away from them, pretending not to notice the gathering.

He drew closer and was able to make out the mumble of the Sheriff's deep voice. He picked a leaf from the pecan tree he was passing and pretended to study it.

"We'll go over tonight, after dark, and scare him good," went Sheriff Suggs's voice. "He knows where his boy went to, and we'll force it out of him."

Out of the corner of his eye, Truett saw a couple of nods. But he kept his face directed down at his leaf. How many times had he seen James studying a leaf or a flower in exactly the same way? Always curious about everything, the quintessential scientist.

"I won't need more than one or two men. Shouldn't have any trouble with old Cato Burwell."

The men chuckled, a cruel sound.

Slowly Truett moved away from the huddle of men and let the leaf drop from his hand. He knew where and when the sheriff planned to strike next, and he would be waiting.

His blood boiled at what they intended to do to James's father, who had been blinded in an accident when James was a little boy.

Well, Truett had a plan of his own.

~

CELIA SMILED AT ALMIRA. SHE MUST BE AROUND CELIA'S AGE OR A bit younger, and she spoke in a soft, intelligent voice.

"I'm pleased to meet you, Almira."

"I'm the teacher for the school here in Bethel Springs. Your sister Lizzie is bright and a fast learner. Will is too, though not as eager as Lizzie. Boys generally aren't. Most boys, that is." She got a faraway look in her eyes, as if she was thinking of someone else, even though she was still looking at Celia.

"Thank you. Yes, they're both good readers, and Will is especially good at math."

"I sure was sorry about your father's accident, and sorry Lizzie and Will had to quit school. Of course, I understood about them having to take care of your mama and the little ones."

"Thank you. That's very kind of you."

"I hear from Lizzie that you're a dressmaker and hope to open your own shop." Almira smiled, and it was as though the sun had popped out from behind a cloud.

"I do hope." The words argued against her rising fear. Would she ever achieve her dream? After all, their family's tragedy had already prevented Lizzie and Will from attending school. But if Celia could earn the family's living, they could go back.

. "Good morning, Miss Suggs." Lizzie said as she joined them, offering her teacher a smile just before she squeezed Celia's arm. "You won't believe what everybody is talking about! Some men tried to lynch a man—I'm not sure who he was—but then another man, wearing a hood to cover his face, saved him right as they were about to put his head through the noose!"

Celia's free hand fluttered to her neck. "My goodness." One

rarely thought of such things occurring in one's own town. They always seemed to happen in some far off, backward place.

Almira's eyelids flickered and her face went white.

Lizzie took a step forward. "Are you well, Miss Suggs?"

"Oh, of course. I just hate to hear of such goings on, that's all." She lifted a paper fan and started swishing it so vigorously that stray strands of hair blew wildly around her face.

"I think I'm the last person to hear of it," Lizzie went on. "You've heard about it, haven't you Miss Suggs?"

"Well, yes, I did hear something." Almira's face had gone from white to showing a bright spot of red in the middle of each pale cheek.

"Who was the man getting lynched, Miss Suggs? Do you know?"

Celia was alarmed at the obvious discomfort Almira was suffering. The schoolteacher swallowed hard and fluttered her fan even faster, but she couldn't seem to focus on either of them.

"I—I—someone else here could probably tell you." Her voice trailed off.

"Do you know who was doing the lynching?"

"Lizzie, that's enough." Celia rested her hand on her sister's arm. "Well-bred ladies shouldn't speak of such things."

Lizzie glanced at Miss Suggs and ducked her head. "I'm sorry, Miss Suggs."

"That's all right." Almira's mouth opened again, but she remained quiet.

Celia wasn't sure what to say to the schoolteacher, and the silence soon grew awkward. Finally, Lizzie left to join friends who beckoned her to join their huddled whispers beneath a nearby shade trees.

Almira took out her handkerchief and dabbed at her lips.

It seemed best to change the subject. "I hope my mother will be herself again soon and Will and Lizzie will be able to get back to school."

"Yes, that would be good. I hope so too." Almira nodded, gratitude in her smile. "Education is so important." Again, her eyes took on a faraway look.

"So many people feel women should be confined to household chores and shouldn't pursue education—or business. I'm an oddity, I suppose, since I don't intend to be imprisoned in such a way."

Almira's eyes sparkled. "Amen and pass the gumption."

They both laughed. Celia was going to like Almira.

～

TRUETT'S HEART BEAT FAST AS HE CROUCHED BEHIND A BUSH IN James's father's back yard. Through the darkness, Truett could just make out the little wooden shack Cato Burwell shared with his brother Ben. The structure leaned to one side and smoke rose from a crooked chimney. A lamp shone through the curtainless window.

About a hundred yards from the house, his black gelding Colonel waited in the woods. Truett couldn't risk him being closer, lest someone recognize his horse.

He didn't have to wait long. Sheriff Suggs rode up with another man, possibly his son, Curtis. He couldn't see their faces, but he recognized the sheriff by his rotund shape. Since there were only two of them, he could handle those odds.

Suggs banged twice on the back door, then flung it open. They stepped inside.

Truett drew his two Colt revolvers and made his way across the back yard, past the hen house and the garden, past the outhouse, the clothesline, and the root cellar. The back door was open. He eased inside without making a sound.

The smoky kitchen was empty, but male voices drifted from the next room.

Truett sneaked through the open passageway, then stopped and stood against the wall just outside the living room.

Curtis was holding the two black men down on two straight back chairs, one hand on Cato's neck, the other squeezing his brother Ben's. Fear widened Cato's clouded gray eyes as he faced toward Truett, unseeing.

"Where is he?" the sheriff demanded, bending from his six-foot height to glare at Cato.

"He's gone."

"I know he's gone. Tell me where, or you'll get the worst beating of your life." The sheriff lifted his fist over James's father's head.

Truett's blood thumped in his temples. He stepped forward, pointing a revolver at Curtis, who was facing him, and stuck the barrel of the other Colt against Sheriff Suggs's back.

"Hands in the air," Truett said, his voice lowered to a gruff rasp.

Truett tucked one revolver under his arm. He reached over Suggs's shoulder and took the gun from his hand. He set it on the floor and kicked it to Ben, who bent and snatched it up.

"Who are you?" Suggs growled.

"Get out," Truett rasped. "If you ever touch these men again, you'll get worse than a beating."

He shoved the sheriff toward the back door. Curtis closed his mouth and glared. He began walking toward the back of the house. Truett followed, his gun at Sheriff Sugg's back. He noted the bulge of a pistol at Curtis's right side.

"Hands in the air." Truett pressed his gun harder into the sheriff's back while keeping his eye on Curtis. Finally, they reached the back door. Curtis pushed it open and stepped onto the top step.

"You won't get away with this. The sheriff is the law here, and—"

"Shut up, boy," Sheriff Suggs grunted at Curtis.

"Keep walking, unless you want me to blow your sheriff into the next county."

They kept walking across the yard toward the horses. Truett veered to the left, still keeping his guns trained on the two men. He made it to the pen where Cato and Ben kept their hunting dogs as Ben came out the back door.

Ben gave a shrill whistle. The dogs became frenzied. Truett unlatched the gate to the pen and opened it wide.

"Sic 'em!"

The dogs threw themselves into the open, charging toward Suggs and Curtis. The hounds bayed and snarled as they ran. Sheriff Suggs and Curtis raced for their horses. They flung themselves into their saddles a bare moment before the dogs reached them. The animals snapped ferociously at the men's ankles. The Suggs men lit out at a full gallop toward the road and didn't stop once they got there.

Truett shoved his guns into his hip holsters and took off at a fast trot through the woods to find Colonel. Ben and Cato shouted after him, "Hey! Hey!" But Truett didn't look back, not even when Cato Burwell shouted after him, "Much obliged to you!"

CHAPTER 7

Celia dragged the slop bucket down the steep hill to the pig sty. As she moved close to their fence, the big sow and her piglets hurried over to the trough, already grunting and snorting in their eagerness. Celia heaved the bucket over the top of the four-foot high split rails and dumped the slop. She watched the pigs for a moment, but then noticed there was one pig that hadn't come to the trough. Instead, it lay on its side, completely still. On closer inspection, she noted flies buzzing around it.

"Oh, that's just what we need."

Celia trudged back up the hill toward the house and entered the back door to the kitchen. "Where's Will? Another pig has died."

Lizzie barely glanced up from the stove. "He went hunting with Truett."

Celia rolled her eyes. What right did Truett Beverly have to come and get her brother before sunup and take him to shoot at turkeys and rabbits and squirrels?

She knew it was good for him to have a man around to do

things with, but now, thanks to Truett Beverly, she'd have to deal with the dead pig herself.

Celia huffed. Bad enough she had been awake in the middle of the night soothing Tempie after her nightmare.

Lizzie used a cloth to open the oven door and pull out the biscuits. "Will and Truett should be back soon."

Lizzie was interrupted by Tempie's too-familiar scream, coming from outside.

Celia burst back out the door to find Tempie making her way across the yard. The little girl wailed between shallow, shuddering breaths. She held her arms stiffly out from her sides. When she saw Celia, she extended her hands toward her.

Celia lifted her skirt and ran to her. "Are you hurt? What's wrong?" She bent down to examine the child's tear-streaked face.

"Dirty!" Tempie held up her hands, thrusting them in Celia's face. "Dirty!"

"Dirty?" From the child's screams, Celia thought at the very least she had been stung by a bee. She stared at the child.

"Tempie doesn't like to be dirty," Lizzie's wry tone came from the doorway.

Celia sighed, took Tempie's hand, and led her to the basin that rested on a stool by the back steps. She washed Tempie's hands and then dried them with a cloth. "I thought children liked getting dirty."

Tempie stared up at her with shimmering eyes and poked out her lip.

Celia smiled and kissed her cheek. "It's all right, sweetie. All clean now."

Tempie sniffed. "I want my dolly."

"Go on, then." As Celia dried her hands on a cloth, Tempie scampered into the house.

Celia rubbed her face. How could a person be so tired before breakfast?

"Hey, Celia! Look what I killed."

Will and Truett strode toward her across the yard, holding up two brown rabbits by their hind feet.

Harley clasped his slingshot in front of him as he jumped up and down in front of Celia, begging, "I go hunting with Truett and Will next time!"

"No! Absolutely not."

Harley set up a howl that echoed through the woods behind her. "I want to go too!" He turned toward the house and yelled, "Lizzie!"

So, he would appeal to Lizzie, as if she was his mother. Celia sighed. He had little choice, she supposed, if he wanted to find someone to overrule Celia.

"We'll see, Harley," Celia soothed. "Let's talk about it later, all right?"

"I don't think Harley is old enough," Will said softly after Harley ran inside to talk to Lizzie. "We saw a rattlesnake."

She shuddered, then glared at Truett. "Is this true?"

"We stayed still until it slithered away."

"But he could have been killed!" Celia covered her mouth as her lip trembled. She really was tired.

Truett stood looking at her with his mouth open. Finally, he said softly, "I would have shot the snake before it could have bitten Will. I'm watching out for him, I promise."

Why did Truett always have to be hanging around Will, as if he was part of their family?

She knew her thoughts were unkind, but she couldn't seem to cast out the anger that lodged in her chest like a boulder.

She could see the proud tilt of Will's shoulders. She took a deep breath and forced a smile. "That's impressive, Will. Can we eat them?"

"Yep! Truett's going to show me how to skin them."

"Good." Celia turned to go, then remembered. "Another pig

has died. We should probably get him out of the pen as soon as possible."

"Having trouble with your pigs?" Truett asked.

"This is the third one to die," Will answered. "You reckon they'll all die?"

Truett frowned and pushed up his hat with the back of his wrist. "Can't say for certain, but it doesn't sound good. A lot of diseases that affect pigs run rampant in these parts. They often take out the whole herd in a few days."

Celia's heart sank. With no money for food, she'd counted on the pigs to provide winter meat for the family. "What can we do? Is there some kind of . . . I don't know . . . tonic we could give them?"

"Not that I know of." Truett smiled and she suddenly wished she hadn't said anything. For pity's sake, she sounded as desperate and dependent on him as the rest of her family.

"That's all right. We can just slaughter the healthy ones now."

The smile was replaced with a more serious lifting of his eyebrows. "I wouldn't recommend that. The meat wouldn't keep in this heat, and it might not be safe, depending on what the pig died of. But Will and I'll get that dead one out and bury it."

"Don't worry, Celia." Will chimed in. "We'll get rid of that dead pig."

"Thank you. I would appreciate that."

Celia went inside to help Lizzie set the table for breakfast. The window provided a great view of Will and Truett hard at work. First they lifted out the dead pig, and after burying it, skinned the rabbits in the back yard. She did her best to avoid seeing the blood and guts. And to think, some men expected their wives to do the skinning.

Celia, Lizzie, and Tempie ate breakfast in silence, except for Tempie's prattling speech to her doll. Mama was still in bed.

After Celia and Lizzie cleaned up the kitchen, they took their baskets to the garden. As they passed where Will and Truett were skinning the rabbits, Celia called, careful to keep her eyes focused just to the left of them, "Whenever you're ready, go on in the house and help yourselves to some breakfast."

"Thank you kindly," Truett said. She saw his smile from the corner of her eye.

Celia stood between the rows of pea plants and listened as Lizzie showed her how to tell which peas were ready to pick.

"See this one?" Lizzie held out a green and purple mottled pea pod. "You can feel the grown peas inside, making these bumps. The ones that are still flat aren't ready yet."

They picked steadily for an hour in the bright morning sun, then picked the tomatoes, squash, and okra. Truett must have helped them plant the garden. How else would they have known what to plant or how?

She suspected they owed Truett Beverly a lot. According to Lizzie, they would hardly have survived without his help. She should be nice to him, and should probably thank him for all he and his family had done for them. Truett's mother had come over and showed them how to operate the stove and explained to Lizzie about canning and pickling the extra produce from the garden they weren't able to eat.

Celia straightened and pushed her hand into the small of her back. Her hands itched and stung from the tiny, hair-like prickles on the okra plants. Her toes were wet from the morning dew, and she could hardly wait to sit down.

She carried her basket into the kitchen and found Truett and Will still sitting at the table, with Mother in the corner looking droopy-eyed and half asleep. Harley sat in Truett's lap, playing with two wooden soldiers on the table.

Lizzie stepped in just behind Celia.

"Truett, you're still here." Lizzie's voice was so sunny it brightened the room. At the same time, Celia cringed to hear her address an adult male with such familiarity.

"Lizzie, it's impolite to call him that." She smiled to soften her words. "He's Dr. Beverly."

"That's all right, Miss Celia. I don't mind if she calls me Truett. I'm here so often, the little ones probably think I'm family." As if to prove his point, Tempie attempted to crawl into his lap. He boosted her up with one hand, balancing her on his other leg. Harley immediately tried to shove her off, but Truett gently pulled the little boy's hand away.

The picture he made, sitting there with both children on his lap, was ridiculously homey.

Celia let out the breath she was holding, then bit the inside of her lip to stop herself from speaking. But the words popped out anyway. "Don't you have patients to tend to?"

He looked up, his eyes wide and his brows raised. "It's Saturday. I don't go in until noon—unless there's an emergency."

Celia tried not to frown.

Truett and the boys soon went outside while Tempie went to play with her dolls. Truett was helping Will dig a root cellar in the back yard for storing potatoes. Lizzie and Celia sat and shelled peas. After a while, Mother sat up straighter and said, "Let me help."

Lizzie fetched her a tin dishpan and gave her a handful of pea pods. She shelled slowly but steadily until they had finished them all.

Celia went outside to fetch a bucket of water to wash the peas. As she let the bucket down into the well, she saw Truett coming toward her, fairly covered in dirt.

"Would you like some water to wash your hands?"

"You read my mind." His smile showed white teeth against sun-browned skin. When he smiled at her like that, she felt she could hardly breathe, as well as a bit too . . . what was the word?

Feminine?

Ugh. No, she wouldn't think about his smile or how it made

her feel. His presence was just plain unsettling. Did he have to be so helpful? Her family loved him way too much.

He silently stretched his hands out in front of him. Celia hefted the bucket, holding the handle with one hand and tipping the bottom with the other. She poured a steady stream of water over his dirt-encrusted palms. They were large and callused, not the hands of most doctors, surely. They were gentle but masculine hands. He rubbed them together briskly, then turned them over as she continued pouring.

"Thank you kindly."

She stopped and he held them by his sides to drip dry.

He captured her eyes with his. With light brown hair framing his face in small curling wisps at his temples and below his ears, his jaw cut a firm, masculine line. Did he know how appealing he was?

She had a feeling he did.

She turned away to draw more water. Suddenly, he reached over her arm and took the bucket from her hand. She jumped back.

"Sorry." Truett's face was only inches from hers. He drawled in a deep, soft voice, "I'll get that for you."

His eyes were so near, so blue. She stepped away from him to break the spell. "You certainly don't have to."

"But isn't it a man's job to make a woman's life easier?"

Hackles rose on the back of her neck. "What do you mean by that?"

"Men do the heavier work, and women's work is lighter." A smile of amusement played on his lips.

"Oh, is that so?" Was he *trying* to make her angry?

"Of course. A man likes to feel that he's doing the heavy tasks, the ones that are too hard for the women."

Celia folded her arms across her chest and glared at him. He stood there with the full bucket in one hand.

"Isn't that just so typical?" Celia's voice rasped. Her face grew warm and her dress was suddenly too tight around her diaphragm. "Men think they're the 'lords of creation,' with that smug attitude that their 'little woman' couldn't live without them. Well, that's just a load of manure!"

Truett stared a moment, his mouth falling open, then he let out a guffaw and bent forward.

Her face burned. "Maybe some women think they can't live without you, but I'm not one of them. For your information—"

Celia searched for what to say next, hardly certain what she had just said. She should just stop before she said something she would regret, but words tumbled out of her mouth anyway.

"Not all women are like my mother." Her voice was a rough whisper. "I am perfectly capable of taking care of myself, and so is every other woman who isn't too silly and stupid to realize it. And if you think you're so needed around here— The only person around here who needs you is Will!"

She stomped back toward the house with a sinking feeling that she'd just made a fool of herself—and spoken unfairly to Truett Beverly. *Oh, no.* Was that Will standing at the edge of the yard? Had he heard her?

What had she said anyway? Oh, what was it about this man that made her lose control of her temper and her tongue? Better to have bitten her tongue off than to be unjust to a man who had been so good to her family.

She slunk through the kitchen door. Lizzie stared at her as if she'd turned purple. Celia walked past her, straight into the bedroom, and closed the door behind her.

Oh! Why had Truett provoked her so with his smug grin and arrogant words about men being stronger than women?

Still, she really shouldn't have said those things. She suspected her anger had little to do with him or what he said. And everything to do with how upset she was at . . . truly, she hardly knew.

All she could think was, *Daddy, why did you have to bring your family here and then die?*

Celia threw herself across the bed, her heart hammering against her chest. She lay still until her breathing slowed to normal. Tears dripped from her eyes, her face still hot.

Men! They thought they could pull their wife up by the roots and move her to the middle of nowhere, to a backward, nowhere place without even a decent store for miles around, and then up and die. And women were even worse! Maybe they deserved their fate, if they went along with whatever their husband told them to do, never speaking their minds . . .

"Why, God?" Celia whispered against her pillow. "Was that your plan when you created marriage? Well, I will not forget my dream of owning my own dress shop just so a man can think he's the lord of *me*. I won't do it. I can't bear to end up like Mother. She *lived* for Daddy, and he treated her like a servant, not an equal. She had not one thought in her head except to please him. I can't be like that, God. I *won't* be like that."

Celia was thankful no one could hear her except God. He knew what she thought anyway. Hadn't she begged God, since she was twelve, to not let her become like her mother? There was just something terrifying about the way her mother never seemed to have any interest in anything but housework and her father's every whim or wish.

Celia loved so many things—sewing new dresses, creating dress patterns, and she also loved reading history books, listening to political speeches, and reading fiction stories. The thought of giving those things up for a husband made her shudder in horror, then anger.

"God, please let me go back to Nashville." She rested her arm over her face as tears ran into her hairline and chilled her. But she also wanted to help Lizzie and her family. If she left, what would happen to Lizzie, Will, Harley and Tempie? She couldn't leave, with no one to look after them except Mother, who barely even noticed they existed. Still, there had to be a way.

God, please help us. Don't make me stay here. In two months, when summer is over, Lord, please let us be in Nashville. Get me back to Nashville, God. Please.

CHAPTER 8

The next day, Celia rode to church clutching her favorite hat to keep the wind from blowing it off her head. Lizzie had tried to get her to wear something smaller, but Celia had refused. She wasn't going to let anyone dictate her sense of fashion. Besides, if she had to apologize—and she had determined she absolutely would apologize to Truett Beverly, even if he laughed at her—she would do it wearing her favorite dress and her favorite hat.

As they drove into the churchyard, Truett was just helping his mother down from his buggy. He turned and met Celia's gaze, stare for stare. Before they even came to a stop, Truett began walking toward them, maybe just a tiny bit less confident and with a less jaunty step than usual.

It soon became clear he meant to get to her first and help her down from the wagon seat. Well, good. She could get this over with now.

Truett held out his hand to her. "Good morning, Miss Celia." She was relieved to see no sign of jocularity in his expression this morning.

She took his hand, swallowed, and forced the air past the tightness in her throat.

"Good morning, Dr. Beverly." Heat crept into her cheeks at the remembrance of what she had said yesterday.

He helped her down.

Celia spoke quickly, while he was still standing so near and no one else was close enough to hear. "Please let me apologize for what I said yesterday, especially the part about not needing you. That was terribly ungracious." She couldn't meet his eyes. She stared at the ground, at her hands, and just past his shoulder by turns. "I'm sorry I sounded so ungrateful, when I truly am thankful you came to my family's aid. You were generous and kind, and I want to thank you and tell you that I'm sorry."

There, she'd gotten it all out without being interrupted. *Thank you, God.*

"I forgive you. But it was my fault. I baited you, and I'm sorry."

What did he mean, he'd baited her? Had he been in jest the whole time? "Well, I—"

She met his intense—and yet sweet—blue gaze and forgot what she was about to say.

He had baited her. Now she remembered the mischievous little smile the day before when he'd said what he'd said. The heat in her cheeks intensified.

"What I said was true, but I said it to tease you." His amused smile returned. "But it is a compliment to you. A man always teases the woman he wishes to impress."

Celia tried to think of a retort, but huffed instead. She turned on her heel and stalked away. *A man always teases the woman he wishes to impress.* Was he saying he wanted to impress her?

Her heart tripped and tumbled, thumping against her chest. *Stop that!* She was beginning to think he was just an incurable flirt. Or someone with an overactive, ill-placed sense of humor.

How in creation could he wish to impress her after her fit of temper? And why did the fact that he did make her heart flutter?

❧

THAT NIGHT, AFTER THE REST OF THE HOUSE WAS ASLEEP, CELIA stood behind Lizzie, brushing her long honey-blond hair. She and Will had taken after their father, while Celia had inherited her mother's dark hair.

"Lizzie, I've decided I'm going to town tomorrow to send an ad to the Huntsville newspaper about our farm."

"What do you mean? To sell it?" Lizzie turned her head to look up at Celia.

"Yes, of course. We don't need to stay here."

"But what about what Mama said?"

Celia was hoping Lizzie wouldn't bring that up. "Mama hardly knows she's in the world. She ignores the twins, she barely eats. Maybe a change of pace and scenery is exactly what she needs."

"But Celia. She already told you she didn't want to move."

"She said she didn't want to move because Daddy wants us to live here—present tense!—as if Daddy is still alive." Celia made an attempt to lower her voice. She certainly didn't want to wake up Will and the twins, especially during this discussion. The less they knew, the better. She took a deep breath and went on, determined to outline her reasons and plan to Lizzie. If she could get her approval, perhaps the others would fall in line.

"There's no reason why we should stay here. I have to get back to my work in Nashville." Celia had to take a deep breath to calm herself again. "And even if I stayed here, the three of us can't run an entire farm, not profitably anyway. No, I think it's better if we sell the farm and move back."

"What if we can't afford to live in Nashville? You're the only one who has a job."

Celia started braiding her sister's hair in one thick braid down her back. "We can live simply, maybe rent a small house, until I can afford something better for you all."

"But what if we can't sell the farm?"

"I don't know." That was Celia's biggest fear. What they needed was a tidy sum of money to get a house while they waited for the farm to sell—in case it didn't sell right away. "Are you sure Daddy and Mama didn't have an account at the bank where they kept some money? Surely they had some money somewhere."

"I never heard tell of it if they did."

Celia tapped her chin. "That's another thing I need to do tomorrow. I'll send an inquiry to the bank in Nashville, to see if Daddy still has an account there, and I'll go to the bank here and see if he deposited some money there." Celia finished braiding her sister's hair.

"All right." Lizzie turned to face her. Her eyes were so wide, innocent, and guileless. Lizzie had taken over so many chores, had taken care of the twins all by herself, practically. But she trusted Celia to take care of them all.

And that's exactly what Celia would do. She would not let Lizzie down. Or Will. Or Harley and Tempie.

Lizzie's forehead clouded a bit. "But what about Mama? What if she gets upset? You know how mad she was at you for mentioning selling this place."

"We can't worry about that." Celia made her face convey more firmness and confidence than she was feeling. "We have to do what's best. Mother isn't thinking clearly—obviously—isn't thinking at all. We have to make the decisions now."

"Will might not understand. He likes it here."

"Will is only twelve. He doesn't have a say, I'm afraid."

～

CELIA WORE HER BIG, FASHIONABLE HAT AGAIN AS SHE RODE TO town on one of the mares.

That's another thing I need to sell. These horses her father bought. The two missing ones would probably never be found. Someone probably caught and sold them. But they still had three that they could sell. Perhaps she could send them back to the breeding farm in Kentucky where her father bought them. She'd have to look into that too.

Celia entered the post office with her letters to both *The Huntsville Independent* and *The Nashville Banner*, advertising their farm for sale. She wouldn't have to pay much for a small ad, less than a dollar, and it would be worth it if it brought a buyer.

After posting her letters and the payment for the ad, she led her horse across the street to The Bank of Bethel Springs.

The door squeaked when she opened it. All the windows were striped with iron bars. The building appeared empty except for a man behind a desk against the far wall. He stood, moved around the desk, and shuffled toward her. His trousers were held up by suspenders and hitched high over a rotund belly. He tucked his chin into his chest, the fat rolling up around his jaws, and looked at her over the top of tiny spectacles.

"Wiley Fordyce," he announced. "What may I do for you, young lady?"

Wiley Fordyce was the owner of the bank. Good. She wouldn't have to go through a clerk. "Mr. Fordyce, my name is Celia Wilcox. My father was William Wilcox."

Mr. Fordyce cleared his throat. "So sorry about your father's death."

But he didn't look terribly sorry. Instead, his eyes fixed her with a steely look.

"I came to see if my father had an account here." Celia's cheeks heated at the blunt question. "He didn't leave a will, you see, and my family and I weren't quite sure about all his affairs."

"I see." Fordyce raised his brows. His small eyes never wavered from her face. "Of course, this information is confidential, but since you're his daughter, and the eldest . . . I'm afraid the answer to your question is no. Your father did not have any money in this bank. Never set foot in here that I know of." He lifted his hand to his mouth. She hadn't noticed it before, but he held a cigar between two fingers. He clamped it between his teeth.

"Oh." Celia's face probably turned a shade pinker. What could she say now? "Thank you, Mr. Fordyce, for the information." She smiled as pleasantly as she could.

"Yes, ma'am. I mean, miss." He grinned at his own blunder, then watched as she backed away.

Celia stepped back out onto the sunny street. So they *were* destitute. *I am the oldest child and sole protector of a family of four siblings and a mother who can no longer function as such, and I have no money and no immediate way to provide.*

She took a deep breath and turned toward the hitching post where she'd left her mare. Truett Beverly stood there, stroking her horse's neck. That man was everywhere. But if she was honest, she didn't mind so much. After the embarrassing confrontation with the impersonal banker, the sight of Truett made her heart lift.

He nodded in greeting. "Everything all right?"

Celia made an effort to smile and look nonchalant. "Of course, Dr. Beverly. Any patients this morning?"

"One. Monday morning's usually pretty brisk, but it slows down in the summer." He quirked one side of his mouth at his joke. He stopped rubbing the mare and stepped toward her. "You know, as I said, I'm sorry for teasing you. If you ever need anything, let me know."

His face was serious. He was probably thinking, *Poor fatherless, unmarried girl, well on her way to spinsterhood, with a crazy mother and four siblings to care for.*

But perhaps he *could* help her. She was desperate enough to ask. "As a matter of fact, I'm trying to find someone to buy our farm."

His mouth went slack. "You are?"

"Yes. And I would greatly appreciate it if you could keep an ear out for anyone who might want it. I've sent an advertisement to both *The Huntsville Independent* and *The Nashville Banner*. Do you have any other advice for me?"

Truett rubbed his chin and looked down. The red dirt covered his boots with orange dust. "I suppose those are good newspapers for getting the word out. You could advertise in a few more papers, perhaps up North. You never know who might be interested."

She didn't know why, but his simple, earnest answer touched her. His gaze caught hers and held it.

"Where will you go? Back to Nashville?"

"Yes, of course. I need to get back to my job."

"You have family there who could help you?"

"No." Celia twisted the strings of her purse in her hands as she thought of their extended family—or lack thereof. "Truthfully, we don't have much family. Daddy had some aunts and uncles in Dyersburg, but we haven't heard from them in years. Mother's family is gone, died before I was born, most of them. But we'll be all right."

She tried to smile, but the weight of the banker's words, his cold stare, and the fact that her father was dead—dead—and would never come back, stole her presence of mind. She had to bite her lip to keep it from trembling.

"We're all right. Everything is fine." She didn't believe her own words. Keeping her eyes down, she hurried forward and brushed past Truett to her horse. She let him help her mount. "Thank you," she whispered, barely able to get the words out. Oh, how could she lose her composure in front of this man—again!

She thanked God that he didn't say anything else as she rode off. If he'd expressed any sort of sympathy, the tears that were damming behind her eyelids would have overflowed, humiliating her further.

∾

TRUETT WATCHED HER GO, GLAD HE HAD REFRAINED FROM TELLING her there probably weren't too many people anxious to move out to the country and try their hand at farming. Not terribly profitable in this day and time. Perhaps her father could have made a good living raising Thoroughbreds, but it would have taken several years. Years he wasn't given.

It was official. He'd lost the wager he had made with himself, since the apology on Sunday had been only a concession of his having helped her family. She still didn't seem to have a very good opinion of him. Or maybe it was men in general that she didn't like? She'd humbled him a bit and made him question his charm. But he didn't hold it against her. As he'd reminded himself many times, he had nothing to offer her, and therefore he shouldn't be trying to impress her anyway. There was a price on his head, and eventually, in such a small town, Sheriff Suggs would discover his secret. Then he'd be hard-pressed to keep the sheriff from killing him.

Besides, he needed to be thinking about how he might be able to help James and Almira be together again.

As for Celia, she'd said she could take care of herself and her family, and he hoped she really could. Because if she couldn't, he knew her well enough already to know it would just about kill her. And there was something about her, her spirit and determination, that made him . . . if he was honest . . . admire her.

Even if she was rather impolite.

~

CELIA RODE SLOWLY TOWARD HOME, TELLING HERSELF THERE HAD to be something she could do for money.

Up ahead, someone squatted by the side of the road up, looking down at the ground. Slowly, he stood and strolled away, still staring at the grass. When he looked up, Celia recognized . . . Griff.

Griff scowled when he saw her, then turned and hurried away into the trees that bordered the road.

When Celia arrived home, Will helped her unsaddle and brush down Old Sallie.

"Will, I just saw Griff. He was wandering around the side of the road, staring at the ground like he was looking for something."

Will grinned and nodded. "Yeah, he's probably looking for the Glory Patch."

"The what?"

"The Glory Patch. Everybody around here looks for the Glory Patch."

"What's that?"

"A patch of ginseng so big it would make you rich for the rest of your life."

"Ginseng? Does that grow around here?" Celia had once read that ginseng was a plant ancient generations of Chinese people valued for its medicinal purposes.

"Sure 'nough. Grows wild in the coves and valleys around these hills. The man who lives in that swampy place below Truett's land, near the creek, he found a few plants, just a few little roots, and sold them to Pettibone at the General Store for fifteen dollars."

Celia swallowed. Fifteen dollars was a lot of money, especially for a few roots.

"Pettibone sells it to some people in Nashville who ship it overseas to China."

"Do you know what it looks like?" Celia should go with Will to hunt it. How many days would it take them to go over all the land they owned?

"The leaves look just like Virginia Creeper, and it has little red berries that will start showing up in late summer. But the root's what's valuable. They look sorta like long white sweet potatoes. I'm looking for a Glory Patch too. I want us to be so rich we'll never have to worry about money again. You could open your dress shop in Nashville, and we could stay here and hire someone to help Lizzie with the housework."

The Glory Patch sounded like a fairy tale. But if ginseng was that valuable and they could find some, they could afford to hire a live-in housekeeper, someone to take care of the cooking and the twins— and Mother, too—with just a small patch of ginseng. Then Will and Lizzie could go back to school and Celia could get back to Nashville. They wouldn't have to find a Glory Patch. A small patch should do. *See, God? I'm not greedy.*

Just desperate.

~

TWO DAYS LATER, CELIA WOKE UP RESTLESS, THE DAWN JUST BARELY showing through the thin curtains. She'd awakened twice during the night from bad dreams. In one, a bad man was chasing her with a knife, telling her he was going to cut off her arms and legs. In the other, she was swimming under water, but when she tried to come up for air, something was holding her, keeping her head underwater. She was choking, slowly drowning, while she stared up at Lizzie and Will, who were talking and laughing on the bank just above her, oblivious to her distress. She awoke gasping for breath.

Lizzie was already absent from the bed. Celia dressed quickly but didn't fix her hair, leaving it braided loosely down her back.

She helped Lizzie prepare breakfast while everyone else slept. Lizzie worked beside her, singing and humming. Her sister hadn't been raised to be content in such a backwoods environment any more than Celia had. But somehow she was able to be joyful. Perhaps there was something wrong with Celia that she didn't feel that same joy.

When they all lived together in Nashville, Lizzie had preferred socializing over anything else. While Celia was in the house making patterns and sewing, Lizzie was in the front yard playing with dolls, having pretend tea parties with her friends, and playing hide and seek. But Celia had always felt driven to succeed at the business she had chosen. It wasn't only that she enjoyed sewing and creating dresses—she wanted to build a successful business. And there was no possibility of doing that in tiny Bethel Springs.

Why was that? Was it because she wanted to prove she didn't need a man? Or did she just want to prove she wasn't going to turn out like her mother?

"Celia?"

She was staring at the white biscuit dough instead of rolling it out. "Sorry, Lizzie." She picked up the rolling pin and applied it to the ball of dough.

She would achieve her dreams. Although, seeing herself in Bethel Springs, her arms covered halfway to her elbows with flour, it was a little harder to believe.

She needed some time with her dress pattern catalogs and Godey's Ladies Books. She'd brought about two dozen with her when she came here, thinking she'd only be separated from the rest of them until she could get back to Nashville—by September at the very latest. But would she be able to get back by then? Even if they could sell the farm, would they have the money in time? It was already near the end of June.

Celia used a tin can, which had been sawed in half for the purpose, to cut the biscuits into perfect round circles. She placed them on the pan, then opened the oven door. As she shoved them inside, her finger touched the hot oven rack. She jerked her hand back and slammed the door.

Celia blew on her finger.

"You burned yourself!" Lizzie grabbed her hand and dunked it into the bucket of water in the sink.

Celia pulled her hand out of the water and stared. Her nails were chipped and uneven. Her fingertips were stained purple and brown from shelling the black-eyed, purple-hull peas, and now she had a red burn on her right index finger. And it still throbbed and burned.

She checked the wood box. It was almost empty. Looking out the kitchen window, she saw the wood pile was getting small as well. It was stacked only as high as her waist. Where was Will? Wasn't it his responsibility to keep them supplied with wood for the stove?

She called down the hallway. "Will!"

"He went back to bed after his morning chores."

"Well, it's time he woke up." She hollered toward the boys' bedroom. "Will!"

Will stumbled down the hallway and into the kitchen, his shirt and trousers rumpled. "What? I already milked the cow and fed the horses."

"We need firewood." Celia blew on her finger, wishing she had something cold to put on it.

"I have some I've been needing to split."

"What are you waiting for? The sun's already up."

"All right, sis. Don't get in such a' all-fired hurry. Here in the country, we like to take things slooowww." Will snickered as he pushed open the back door and let it slam behind him.

He thought he was so funny, teasing her with that exaggerated drawl and colloquialisms. She sighed and started cleaning up her floury mess.

Lizzie said softly, "You could have let him wait until after breakfast."

Celia didn't reply, but the gentle rebuke made her stomach twist. Still, Will was the one who supposedly liked it here. He should know that people on a farm couldn't sleep late. There was too much work to be done.

Will split wood while Lizzie stirred the gravy in the pan on the stove and Celia set the table. Soon it was ready, and Celia called him to come eat. He ate a quick breakfast of biscuits and sausage gravy, then went straight out to split more wood.

Celia was washing dishes at the dishpan in front of the window. She glanced out just in time to see Will bring the ax down from over his shoulder toward the block of wood standing on its end. But his angle was off. The ax glanced off the wood and struck Will in the leg.

Celia stared, expecting to blink and wake up.

Will held his leg and turned toward the house. Dark liquid soaked his pants in an ever-widening circle, the red seeping between his fingers.

"Will's hurt." Celia lost her breath, her face beginning to tingle.

"What?"

Celia grabbed two clean towels out of the basket by the kitchen table and ran out the door. Lizzie was right behind her.

Will stood holding his leg. "Will, sit down." Celia grabbed his leg and held it up, forcing him onto the ground. She pulled his pant leg up to get a better look at the wound. It was pouring blood, dripping through her fingers and onto the ground. She wrapped one towel tightly around it and then tied the other towel over it to keep it snug.

Will moaned and gasped.

Everything began to spin. *Oh, God, help me!* "Dr. Beverly. I'll go get him."

"He'll already be at his office." Will spoke through clenched teeth. "He gets there at 6:30."

Celia's head pounded. She needed to get Will to Dr. Beverly's office. Did she know how to hitch the horses up to the wagon? Will needed to get to Dr. Beverly as soon as possible. "Keep up the pressure to stop the bleeding, Lizzie, and I'll get the wagon."

Celia ran to the barn and led two horses out to the wagon.

Someone was coming up the lane. Ruby Pritchard, her brother, and her grandmother. But at that very moment, Harley and Tempie bounded out of the house toward Will and Lizzie. When Tempie saw the bloody towels around Will leg, she screamed—not once, but over and over. Harley added to the confusion by yelling, "How'd you do it, Will?"

Ruby's brother, who was a couple of years older than Will, ran over to help Celia hitch up the horses. Tears of gratefulness pricked Celia's eyes as he quickly did the job that would have taken her so much longer. *Thank you, God.*

With Nathan's help, Celia picked Will up and placed him on a quilt in the wagon bed. She turned to Ruby. "Can you watch Harley and Tempie while we take Will to the doctor?"

"Of course. We'll take good care of the little rapscallions."

Ruby's grandmother called, "You just take Nathan here with you to Doc Beverly's, if you need him."

"Thank you, Mrs. Pritchard. We'll manage." Celia climbed onto the seat and took the reins while Lizzie scrambled into the back with Will, holding a fresh towel.

Not wanting to jar Will around too much, Celia set out at an easy but steady speed. Every moment her brain screamed at her that they needed to hurry, but when she turned to look at him, his face was so pale and tight with pain, she forced herself to keep the horses at their slower pace.

It seemed to be taking so long to get there, she began to wonder if the town were moving away from them. Every muscle in her limbs was tense, as if straining to get there faster. Finally, they rounded the bend that brought the town's main street in view. She shuddered with relief and glanced back at Will. "We're here. How are you holding out, Will?" Her breath hitched in her throat at his quivery attempt at a smile.

"Not too bad, sis."

"Are you sure? Because you look . . . scary." The light-headed feeling was back. *Oh, God, take care of my brother. I couldn't bear it if he lost his leg.*

Celia pulled the wagon up in front of Truett's office. She jumped down from the wagon and ran toward it. Truett was already coming out to her.

The relief of seeing him there, looking so strong and capable, made the air rush back into her lungs. "Will's hurt. He's in the wagon."

Truett was striding to the wagon before she could blink. He jumped onto the spokes of the wheel and reached over the side. He hefted Will out and carried him past Celia as she held the door open.

"What happened?" Truett laid Will on the table, which was covered with a white sheet, in the small examination room.

Lizzie sat down in one of the chairs along the wall. Celia hovered beside Will.

"He was splitting wood and the ax came down on his leg."

Truett removed the towels around Will's leg.

"We were trying to stop the bleeding." Celia was unable to take her eyes off what Dr. Beverly was doing, even though the blood-soaked towels and trousers made her stomach turn over sickeningly. It was Will's blood, blood that he spilled obeying her grouchy order to split wood.

"You did well. It looks like the bleeding has stopped." The doctor leaned closer to the wound.

Celia leaned away, her face beginning to tingle again.

What was wrong with her? She wasn't one of those silly girls who fainted at every little thing. She'd never fainted in her life, and she didn't plan to start now. But she wasn't sure how to get rid of this strange feeling. She tried taking a deep breath, but that seemed to make it worse.

She had to be here for Will. She took his hand from where it lay beside him on the table. He squeezed slightly. He was half-sitting, propped on his elbows, staring at Dr. Beverly as he gently probed the wound. Celia wondered how either of them could stand the sight of the ghastly open flesh and fresh blood.

Oh, God, why did I send Will to split wood this morning? This never would have happened if she hadn't been in such an irritable humor. Why did she always have to be so grumpy and irritable in

Bethel Springs? Will never complained, never sulked, never refused to do what she asked. What if his leg got infected, turned gangrenous, and had to be amputated?

Celia tried to keep her eyes off the wound, but they were drawn like moths to a candle. *Poor Will. You didn't deserve this.*

Celia's vision began to cloud and then spin. The room grew hazy. "I think I better sit down." She let go of Will's hand and concentrated. *I will not faint. I will not faint.*

Through her clouded vision, she saw Dr. Beverly looking at her. *Don't look at me. Take care of Will . . . Oh, God, don't let me faint. It would be too humiliating.* But the dark edges closed in on her. She felt herself being lifted, and then she didn't feel anything.

CHAPTER 9

Truett felt around, making sure the bone wasn't chipped or broken. Then he noticed the weak sound of Celia's voice. He glanced up from Will's wound.

Celia was pale as a ghost. *She's going to faint.*

Truett stepped toward her just as her body started crumpling, reaching her just in time to catch her and lifted her into his arms.

Her eyes were closed, but though all the color had drained from her face, she was still beautiful. She fit perfectly in his arms, her head resting against his shoulder.

He wouldn't have pegged Celia Wilcox, of all people, as a swooner, but she had fainted at the sight of Will's bloody leg.

"Celia? Oh my! Is she all right?" Lizzie peered over his arm at her.

"She'll be fine. I'll just lay her down in the other room."

Lizzie stayed beside Will while Truett carried Celia into the back room, where he kept a couple of cots. He wished he could just hold her, cradling her against his chest for a few moments. This exasperating, high-strung woman did strange things to him, and he didn't know why. She was more fascinating than other woman he'd ever known. He'd called on a few back in New York, and escorted some to parties or dances, but they always either disappointed or bored him after a while. But Celia . . . she was different.

His conscience smote him. It was surely wrong to feel this warmth that was seeping all through him like hot molasses.

Besides, he had to get back to Will.

Carefully, he lowered her to the cot and slipped his arms from underneath her. She stayed completely still. Her hair had come loose from her braid. He reached down and smoothed it back, brushing several strands off her cheek. She looked so pale. He checked her pulse. It was steady.

He had to close Will's wound. Celia had only fainted and would be fine, he reassured himself. He'd come back in a few minutes to check on her.

～

Celia opened her eyes and glanced around the strange room. She could remember standing beside Will, watching Truett . . .

Think, think. The last thing she remembered was everything going black and the feeling of someone lifting her.

Her stomach dipped. "I fainted." How humiliating!

"Celia? Are you all right?"

"Lizzie?" Yes, Lizzie. In the doorway. With Truett.

"How are you feeling?" Truett's brows drew together. If he even smiled she would die of embarrassment.

"Where's Will? Is he all right? Please go back to Will. I am fine." Will was the one who needed the doctor's attention!

They both stepped inside and came toward her. She wanted to sit up, but her head weighed a hundred pounds.

"Will's all right." Lizzie picked up Celia's hand and held it.

Celia focused her eyes on Truett. "Where is he? What did you do? Did he just need stitches?"

Truett smiled. Was he laughing at her?

"I stitched up the wound. The cut wasn't too deep. If there's no infection, he should be as good as new in a few weeks. For now he just needs to stay off his leg."

Celia placed a shaky hand over her heart. "Thank goodness."

"What about you?" Lizzie leaned over her. "You're so pale. Is something wrong?" She turned to Dr. Beverly. "Is she all right? What made her faint? She never faints."

"I'm fine. There's nothing wrong with me." Celia was determined to show them both that she was all right. She pushed herself into a sitting position, with Lizzie helping her. The room pitched and rolled like a ship in a storm.

"I think she's all right." He picked up her hand and held two fingers against her wrist. "How do you feel?" Truett's intense blue eyes focused on hers. If she'd seen the least bit of amusement there . . . But he only looked concerned.

"I'm fine. I'm not a fainter. I guess I was worried about Will."

"Had you eaten this morning?"

"Yes. I'm all right." She started to get up, to prove she was fine, but her legs shook like a newborn foal's.

Truett placed a hand on her shoulder. "Why don't you sit for a few more minutes. You don't want to go fainting again." He raised his eyebrows.

Inside, he was probably laughing at her. Of course, why wouldn't he? After she'd said she could take care of herself, vowed she could take care of her whole family as well as any man, she'd fainted like those silly, giggly girls she'd always held in such contempt. It was too much.

She stuck her finger at him. "Don't you dare laugh at me."

He raised his brows again and held out his hands. "I'm not laughing. I was worried about you. Fainting is an involuntary response. You couldn't have stopped yourself."

She remembered the sensation of being lifted. Truett must

have picked her up and carried her, must have held her in his arms. The thought made her dizzy again. She put her hand over her face as a flood of embarrassment made her cheeks hot.

"People can faint for any number of reasons. You can't control it, so it's nothing to be embarrassed about."

"I just don't want you to think of me when Will is the one who's hurt. Shouldn't you check on him?" She couldn't bring herself to look him in the eye.

He backed toward the door. "I will if it will help you rest. You stay there. Please." He pointed at her as he turned and left the room.

"Oh, Celia." Lizzie's eyes were lit up like Christmas morning. She whispered, "You should have seen the look on his face when he swept you up in his arms and gazed down at you. Oh, it was so sweet. I think he's in love with you!"

"Hush! Please don't let him hear you say that," Celia whispered back. "Besides, that's ridiculous. He couldn't possibly think of me as anything but a silly, stupid, fainting girl." Tears stung her eyes.

Lizzie was imagining things. But she did wish she could remember how it felt to be held in his arms.

Lizzie was rubbing off on her, apparently.

Celia sat up, holding her sister's arm, and waited as her vision gradually stopped spinning. With Lizzie's help she got up from the bed and walked into the examination room.

Truett was cleaning up his tools and putting them away, while Will reclined on a pillow on the examining table, looking wrung out but alert.

"Oh, Will. Are you all right? I'm so sorry." Celia squeezed her brother's hand. His leg still had traces of blood smeared over it, with tiny black stitches criss-crossing it.

Will grinned. "Don't be sorry. I wasn't watching what I was doing. But it'll make a great scar, don't you think? I can't wait to show the fellas."

She had meant she was sorry she had fainted while he was

getting stitched up, but she also wanted to tell him how sorry she was for being so grouchy that morning, how horrified she had been at the thought of him being seriously injured. But rather than saying all that in front of Dr. Beverly, she decided to wait until they were home.

"You're such a boy," Lizzie said, and she and Celia both laughed, though Celia's was a bit shaky. Thank goodness he wasn't upset with her—his bossy grouch of a sister. *God, from now on I promise not to be grouchy with Will or anyone else, ever again.* She only hoped she could keep her promise.

Truett soon finished and turned to Will. "Ready?"

Will nodded. Truett picked him up and carried him out to the wagon, laying him on the quilts. Lizzie climbed into the back beside Will.

Truett focused his gaze on Celia, standing next to the wagon seat.

She looked away, needing to express her gratitude for what he had done for Will, but embarrassed at her silly fainting spell. He continued standing in front of her. She lifted her eyes to his. "Thank you . . . for what you did for Will." She bit her lip and murmured, "And I'm sorry I fainted."

"Nothing to be sorry about." His voice was soft. "You couldn't help it, and you were just worried about your brother." His throat convulsed slightly as he swallowed, his eyes never straying from hers. "It was my pleasure to be of help."

Not a flicker of humor passed over his face, as he held her gaze with his, his lips slightly parted.

She turned toward the wagon seat. His hands clasped her waist and he hoisted her up.

As she sat on the wooden seat and collected the reins, their gazes locked again. She quickly turned away and urged the horses forward.

Lord, what just happened here? She could still feel his hands around her waist. A warm tingling spread through her.

What was wrong with her? Perhaps she had just spent too much time away from her sewing. As soon as she got back to the house, she planned to pull out whatever material she could find and create the most intricate, detailed dress she'd ever sewn.

If that didn't drive Truett Beverly out of her thoughts, nothing would.

~

TRUETT COULDN'T CHASE CELIA WILCOX FROM HIS THOUGHTS. Especially the way she looked when she fainted, so pale and helpless. It had turned his insides to mush to see her that way. But he certainly liked the way she felt in his arms, soft and warm and . . . perfect.

He shouldn't be thinking this way. After all, she had gotten mad at his teasing and yelled at him, telling him her family didn't need him, then stalking off. But then, she had apologized. She was easy to forgive.

He had promised himself he would write her off as uppity and irritable if she did not think well of him after two weeks. But the unfortunate truth was, he still couldn't quite forget about her. Whether she knew it or not, she and her family did need him. And now that he knew what she felt like in his arms, he wanted to feel that again.

But she wasn't likely to faint in his arms again anytime soon.

However . . . the Fourth of July was coming up, which meant his mother was probably organizing a dance. A dance would afford a perfect opportunity to get her in his arms again.

If he had any sense, he'd forget about Celia. She didn't even like him.

Although, she hadn't exactly looked at him with hate in her eyes after he sewed up Will's leg. As he recalled, she had looked quite grateful when she thanked him so prettily just before he lifted her onto the wagon seat.

It had taken more than two weeks, about three, in fact, but maybe she was coming around. And maybe he was plumb addled, but he still wanted her to admit she was wrong about him, that she had completely underrated him—his abilities and his charm.

CHAPTER 10

The next morning, Celia's eyes flew open. A *thunk* seemed to come from the back door. She didn't hear anyone stirring in Will and Harley's room. Lizzie was still beside her. And Tempie and Mama never got up this early.

Carefully, to avoid waking Lizzie, Celia eased herself out of bed. She grabbed her robe off the hook on the wall and put it on. Only the barest gray light was visible through the windows. The clock on the mantle showed a quarter past five.

She tip-toed through the hallway to the kitchen and peered out the window, her breath catching at the sight of a man striding across the yard, milk bucket in hand. He disappeared into the barn.

Was this man trying to steal their cow's morning milk? Well, he couldn't have it—not unless he at least asked first!

But the milk might only be the beginning of what he wanted. Perhaps he was a drifter and would kill them all in their beds. Her heart pounded inside her chest. She'd read a newspaper account of that very thing happening somewhere in Kansas.

Should she go outside and confront him? Not in her nightgown and wrapper! But with his hurt leg, Will was in no condition to face an intruder. Nightclothes or not, if anyone faced the man, it should be Celia.

She padded softly into the breezeway and found her father's old hunting rifle hanging on the wall on two wooden pegs. If only they had a smaller gun. But she'd have to make do with what she had. Good thing Daddy had taught her how to shoot all those years ago.

Still, it had been a long time since she'd held a gun.

Celia hitched the rifle up to her armpit as she stared out the kitchen window again. She quickly pushed the window up and propped the end of the gun barrel on the window sill, aiming at the barn. When he got close enough, she'd demand to know who he was and what he was doing there.

She waited, propping her hip against the sink as she kept her eyes trained on the barn door. The gun grew heavy in her arms, and the sky lightened even more. The rooster crowed, as he normally did around 5:30, but the man still had not emerged. Was he out there? Had he left without her seeing him?

Finally, the man, wearing a blue chambray shirt with sleeves rolled up past his elbows, came out of the barn carrying the milk bucket. He strode across the yard toward her and the house, but his eyes were trained on the ground as he walked. Celia leaned forward. Unless she was mightily mistaken, the man was Truett Beverly.

Her heart thumped double time as he approached the back door. He set the bucket on the top step and, without looking up, turned and strode back toward the barn.

She slumped against the counter and relaxed her grip on the gun.

Soon, Truett exited the barn again, this time pushing a full wheel barrow. Had he mucked the stable? After dumping that, he sauntered over to the wood pile, picked up the ax, raised it above his shoulder with practiced precision . . . and brought it down on the block of wood, splitting it in two.

Tears sprang to Celia's eyes. She blinked several times to clear her vision. She wasn't given to tears any more than she was given to fainting spells. Now, it seemed she was losing control at every turn—especially when Truett Beverly was around. It must mean that she was still sad about her father's death. After all, she hadn't allowed herself to cry very much when he died—besides that embarrassing display in front of Truett Beverly when he'd told her Daddy was dead. Crying didn't help anything, and it wouldn't bring her father back.

Truett set another block of wood on the broad stump. He lifted the ax and swung it down, splitting it with the first swing. Then he set up a much larger block of wood on the stump, tapping an iron wedge into the wood with the flat end of the ax. He then picked up the sledge hammer and brought it down on the wedge, which sank into the wood. He swung the hammer again and the block of wood split in two.

Celia had seen men split wood before, but never was she so fascinated before. His shirt was clinging to him, and it was already darkening with a patch of sweat down the middle of his back. She really shouldn't be watching the play of muscles around his shoulders as he swung the sledge hammer.

"Who is that?"

Celia jumped and spun around, her hand over her heart as she gasped for breath. "Oh. Lizzie." A guilty burn crept up her neck and into her cheeks.

Lizzie gave her a quizzical look. "Why do you have that gun?"

"This?" Celia had forgotten she was still holding Daddy's rifle. "Oh. I heard someone outside and didn't know who it was. But it's just Dr. Beverly." She stepped away from the window, trying to look nonchalant. "I'll go put it away."

"What's he doing?"

"Splitting wood." She shrugged, as though the town doctor splitting wood in their yard was the most ordinary thing.

"Oh, that is so sweet." Lizzie peeked out the window.

Yes it was. Very sweet.

She put away the gun and then came back to help Lizzie with breakfast. She knew how to make the dough for the biscuits now, so she started getting out the flour and butter while Lizzie built a fire in the stove, but she had to force herself not to look out the window.

She tore her gaze away. Again. What would Lizzie think?

Celia finished mixing the biscuit dough, but when she turned to get the rolling pin, which was only inches from the window, she looked out.

Truett brought the ax down on a smaller piece of wood. The pieces flew in two directions. He leaned the ax against the wood pile and wiped his forehead with the back of his hand. Then he bent over and began gathering the pieces of wood. When he started to turn in the direction of the house, she whirled away from the window, forgetting the rolling pin. She had to scrunch down and snake her hand across the counter so he wouldn't see her through the window—if he happened to be looking.

"Celia?" Lizzie wrinkled her nose. "What are you doing?"

"Nothing."

Lizzie frowned.

"I just don't want Truett to see me."

"You don't want him to see you staring at him, you mean." Lizzie laughed. "Celia Wilcox, tell the truth. You like him."

"Lizzie, stop. I don't"—she dropped her voice to a hiss— "like him!" She finished the statement as an angry whisper. Then her conscience smote her. "All right, maybe I like him, just like you and Will and Tempie and Harley like him. We all like him. Now will you please stop talking about it?"

"Whatever you say, Celia."

Lizzie grinned. Celia huffed at her. There was no use arguing. Besides, her feelings for Truett Beverly were nothing she wanted to discuss, even with herself. She was going back to Nashville, and the sooner the better.

"But I do think you should go offer the poor man a dipper of water." Lizzie was turned toward the stove so Celia couldn't see her expression.

"I'm not even dressed!"

"Well, go get dressed. You don't want him to see you in your nightgown, do you?"

"Of course not!" Celia yanked her wrapper tighter around her waist. She turned and stomped to the bedroom to get her clothes. Just to prove to Lizzie that she didn't care, she picked out her ugliest work dress.

Should she really go outside and offer Truett water? Part of her thought it was the nice thing to do, but part of her just couldn't do it. He would think she was flirting with him! Wasn't it Rebecca in the Bible who snagged herself a husband by offering to draw water? She was sure Truett had read that story, too. No, Lizzie was just trying to play matchmaker again. He could get his own water.

When they finished preparing breakfast, Lizzie stood in the back door and called out to Truett. "Will you come in and eat with us?"

Celia stood back as far as she could from the window. Truett straightened and looked back at Lizzie. His hair was dark with sweat and curled against his temples. "Thank you, Lizzie, but I'll grab a bite at home. I'm about finished up here. I need to get to the office." He smiled and his eyes sparkled in the sun.

"I'll wrap you up a biscuit anyway. Celia makes good biscuits."

Lizzie slipped back inside, grinning from ear to ear. Celia wanted to snap, "Why should it matter to him if I make good biscuits?" But she held her tongue.

A few minutes later, Truett came to the back door. Celia stood back as Lizzie went outside and begged him again to come in and eat something.

"No thanks, Miss Lizzie, but much obliged anyway."

She handed him a cloth bag with three biscuits with butter and plum jelly. He thanked her. As she leaned toward him to give him a hug, he clasped her shoulder.

"No, you'll get yourself all sweaty."

Celia had to at least thank him. But the picture he made standing there, his hair damp on his forehead, his work shirt clinging to him, and his face ruddy and handsome, like David in the Bible . . . she wasn't sure she could even speak.

The very idea.

Celia stepped forward until she was standing in the doorway. "Thank you for all the work you did for us this morning."

Truett gave her a friendly nod. "My pleasure, Miss Celia."

His eyes lingered on hers and the corners of his mouth quirked higher before he finally turned away. Her stomach fluttered as she gazed after him.

~

LATER THAT MORNING, CELIA STOOD BY THE STOOL AT THE BACK door, washing Tempie's muddy foot.

Her little sister hadn't wanted to be left behind when Harley crossed the creek to chase after a lizard. But as soon as her bare foot encountered mud, she started screaming. Celia heard her all the way from the kitchen.

"Tempie, sweetie, please don't go near the stream again. It's always muddy around there, and you hate mud. Besides, I don't want you to get on a snake."

"Truett said his dog got bit by a rattlesnake and died." Tempie poked out her lip. "Poor puppy."

And if one of those rattlesnakes bit you or Harley . . . Her breath caught in her throat. She didn't want to scare the child, so she said, "Just please don't go out of the yard. Wouldn't you rather play with your dollies than go traipsing through the woods?"

Tempie's eyes held a frown, her lip poking out even further.

Celia steeled herself against the coming tantrum, but instead, Lizzie burst through the back door.

"Mrs. Beverly and Griff are coming up the lane!"

Celia dried Tempie's feet with her apron. "There, all clean."

Tempie ran off to greet their visitors.

Celia's worry about Griff being unsafe was the only thing that kept her from being glad of the distraction. Visitors were about the only thing that broke the monotony of life in the country. She still daydreamed about the shop she wanted to own in Nashville, but somehow sewing didn't hold the same charm it once had. She supposed it was because she was always so tired from taking care of Tempie and Harley, the gardening, cooking, cleaning . . .

Celia took off her apron as she went into the house and smoothed back the wisps of hair that had escaped from the tight bun on the back of her head. Her brown gingham dress wasn't exactly the height of fashion, but she figured it hardly mattered out here. All she needed to fit in perfectly was a matching gingham bonnet.

She watched out the window as Lizzie greeted Mrs. Beverly on the porch, while Griff, who stood head and shoulders taller than his mother, lurked behind her on the steps. Celia shuddered, remembering Griff with the huge gray boulder over his head, preparing to throw it at his petite mother.

Mrs. Beverly's smile lit up her entire face and changed her appearance so that she hardly looked like the same person who had cowered in fear before her son. Griff's appearance was also greatly altered. His mouth hung open and he had the look of a shy little boy, which contrasted oddly with his manly size.

Mrs. Beverly hugged Lizzie with one arm, a basket hanging from her other arm. "Oh, you sweet little darlin'! Where's that precious boy with the hurt leg? I brought him a peach pie and some blackberry jelly."

Will hobbled into the room behind her and sat down on the couch, propping his leg up on a stool.

Lizzie came in the house, followed by Mrs. Beverly, Tempie, and Griff. Lizzie accepted the cloth-covered basket from Mrs. Beverly and a basket of strawberries from Griff and took them to the kitchen.

Mrs. Beverly bent to hug Tempie, who was clinging to her skirt. "Tempie! What have you been at, you sweet thing?" She straightened and, her arms open wide, came to hug Celia. "And here's the older sister, as beautiful a young lady as we've ever seen around Bethel Springs. How are you, dear?"

Celia smiled. "I'm very well, thank you. Won't you sit down? Can I get you a cup of tea or coffee?"

"Oh, no, dear, don't trouble yourself." She ignored the chairs and grasped Celia's hand. "I want to apologize for not coming by sooner. I'm your neighbor and it was remiss of me not to welcome you." She wrinkled her forehead. "You don't know how sorry I am about your poor father, the dear man. And now your mother's health . . . Well, if you need any blessed thing you just call on me. And I mean that."

Mrs. Beverly's eye caught Will lying on the horsehair couch. "Oh, Will. You precious thing. Just look at that leg." She went to him and patted his cheek and peered into his face. "Your color is good. Any medicines you want, you just let me know and I'll get them from Truett. I'll make sure he checks on you regularly."

Mrs. Beverly sank down on an upholstered chair. Griff, seeing his mother wasn't going anywhere, turned with slumping shoulders and shuffled back out the front door. Through the window Celia watched him sit on the edge of the porch where Harley was playing with some wooden soldiers and horses. Harley gave Griff some of his men and horses and they started playing.

Tempie skipped to her dolls and tea set in a corner of the room and talked quietly to them, taking up the little chipped plates then setting them out again in front of her inanimate friends.

Lizzie came back in and sat on the other side of Celia.

"Sweet little Lizzie." Mrs. Beverly reached out her hand, and

Lizzie hurried over and gave her another hug. "She's such an angel, the way she took over the household after your father, bless his soul, went to heaven. Don't you think so, Celia?"

"Yes, ma'am. I admire my sister and brother very much." Lizzie and Will had shown a lot of maturity. *Unlike me, who stayed away at my job and let the full burden fall on my younger siblings.* Was Mrs. Beverly thinking the same thing?

"And you, my dear, giving up your employment and dream of opening a dress shop to come and take care of your family . . ." She smiled sadly at Celia, then shook her head.

Celia shifted in her chair. Should she try to explain to the woman that she hadn't given up, that she still intended to go back? But that was uncertain now, although Celia was still hoping to find a way.

Mrs. Beverly continued. "We all must make sacrifices for our families. You may not know this, Miss Celia, but Mr. Beverly, ever since the war, has been living with his brother in Columbia, Tennessee, helping him run his brick manufacturing business. You'll meet Mr. Beverly. He comes home every so often. Mr. Beverly and his brother, William Beverly, both have good heads for business, which is fortunate for us, I suppose. After the war, things were so altered."

Mrs. Beverly frowned almost imperceptibly, then flashed a wide smile. "But 'all things work together for good to them that love God.' And Mr. Beverly comes home whenever he can, bless him." She lowered her voice. "Griff doesn't like to make the trip to Columbia. It quite unsettles him. So we make out with Truett's help. Families do what they have to do to take care of each other."

Celia peeked out the screen door for a glimpse of Griff. He was still sitting with Harley as they played with their toy men and horses. Griff's voice drifted through the door to Celia. She listened to try to make out what he was saying.

"It's the hooded horseman! Bang, bang! Take that, mean old sheriff!"

Harley's voice answered with, "I'll get you, hooded horseman! You can't get away from me! Bang, bang! You're dead!"

"And how is your mother, the poor dear?" Mrs. Beverly said, drawing her attention away from Griff and Harley.

"She is well in body, I believe, though not so well in mind. Speaking of Mother, let me go get her. She's sitting in the kitchen. I'm sure some company will do her good." Celia went hurrying through the hallway to the kitchen. In a coaxing voice, she urged her mother to get up and come to the parlor to visit with Mrs. Beverly. They made their way as quickly as her mother's shuffling, slippered feet would take her into the room. Celia sat her in the most comfortable chair, and then took her place again. Mrs. Beverly went over and spoke kindly to her, holding her hands as she patiently re-introduced herself, repeating her name. Then she came back to her chair near Celia's.

As effusive as Mrs. Beverly was, Celia sensed a sincerity in her that was not unlike her son's. She couldn't help but like Truett's mother.

Mrs. Beverly spoke quietly. "I'm so sorry. I do hope she will learn to cast her sorrow on the Lord. It is hard." Mrs. Beverly nodded and a faraway look came into her gaze. "I lost two sons in the war. I don't know if you knew. Truett and Griff had two older brothers. But they're gone now." Her voice became thin and quiet as she spoke the last sentence.

"I'm so sorry for your loss." Celia's heart clenched. Truett couldn't have been more than twelve years old, Will's age, when the war ended.

"You know," Mrs. Beverly brightened, smiling again, "Will reminds me so much of Truett at that age. He even has the same blond hair and blue eyes. So handsome. Truett was such a good boy, always looking after Griff. Griff is actually older than Truett, but Truett's always had to watch out for him, ever since the accident."

Mrs. Beverly clasped one hand over her chest. "Listen to me, jabbering on. I'll be forgot what it was I came to tell you."

She paused and smiled, looking first at Lizzie and then at Celia.

Lizzie leaned forward. "What is it?"

"Just something for you young folks." She leaned forward, too, whispering conspiratorially. "We're having a dance at the big cotton warehouse in Bethel Springs next Saturday. Won't that be fun?"

"A dance! Hurray!" Lizzie jumped out of her seat and laughed.

Celia raised her eyebrows. Lizzie had never been to a dance before, and Celia wasn't so sure she was ready for one now, at only fourteen.

"Don't worry." Mrs. Beverly smiled at Celia. "Our country dances aren't so formal as the ones in Nashville. Children of all ages come and have lemonade and cake and pie and play games. The older ladies watch over them. It's all very proper. More like a picnic, actually."

"Oh. But Mother is still in mourning. Are you sure it's proper?"

Mrs. Beverly squeezed her hand. "It's been six months. No one would think anything of you young people coming to the party. And of course, your mother must come, too, to watch the little ones."

As a widow, Mama's full mourning period lasted longer. For at least a year she would be expected to wear black, with a veil covering her face in public, and would not be expected to attend social events. But apparently Mrs. Beverly felt the Fourth of July dance was an exception. Or perhaps formal mourning practices were not as adhered to in the informal setting of Bethel Springs.

"Now the dance is going to be July third, that's a week from this Saturday. The Fourth of July is on a Sunday this year, so we're just going to celebrate The Glorious Fourth a day early."

Lizzie clapped her hands and Tempie joined in, squealing with laughter, even though she probably had no idea what she was clapping about. Even Will was smiling.

Mrs. Beverly rose from her chair. "I'd better run along. I need to go tell Mrs. Prichard and Ruby and, oh, just a whole host of people that I haven't told yet. I'll see all of you there." She chucked Tempie under chin on the way out, making the child giggle.

$\sim$

THAT EVENING IN THE LAMPLIGHT, CELIA SAT AT THE DESK IN THE corner, penning a letter to the horse farm in Kentucky where her father had bought the four broodmares and one stallion, asking if they'd buy three of the mares back. One mare was still missing. And the stallion that had kicked Daddy. A cold chill slithered down her spine just thinking about that horse. She was glad he was lost, since she'd rather not have to look on the creature that had killed her father and caused her family so much grief.

Having finished her letter, Celia took out her sewing. The fabric was a fine muslin, striped with a pattern of tiny flowers. She imagined the lady who would wear it someday.

"Celia?"

She looked up at Lizzie, who sat nearby with her embroidery in her lap. She had stopped stitching and was staring at her with a tiny smile. *Uh-oh.* What was she thinking about? From the look on her face . . .

"What did you think of Truett's mother, Mrs. Beverly?"

"I thought she was the most effusive, most demonstrative woman I've ever met."

"Oh, Celia! How could say that?" Lizzie's look of horror rebuked her. "She's very sweet. I love her. She's good and kind and always thinking of others. Admit that you liked her." Lizzie's voice was stern—especially for Lizzie.

"I never said I didn't like her. In spite of her effusiveness, she was sincere and sweet. I liked her. Satisfied?"

"Yes." Lizzie smiled, a bit too smugly. She took up her embroidery again. "Mrs. Beverly would make a wonderful mother-in-law, don't you think?"

Celia sighed. "I do like Mrs. Beverly and I'm thankful she's been so kind to all of you, but I'm tired of you talking to me about Truett." Celia stood and walked to the window and looked out. There was nothing to see, and it was dark anyway, so she paced back to stand near Lizzie.

"He may be a good man and might make a good husband, if I were after one. But you know I could never be content sitting home, waiting for my man to come home so I could cook for him. I couldn't bear to listen to him tell me all his opinions just so I could adopt them." She gestured at the ceiling, wishing she could make Lizzie understand the churning inside her. And yet, perhaps it was best she didn't. Perhaps if Lizzie knew how she felt, she might not like her anymore. But something compelled her to keep trying.

"And I don't want to live here. I'd go crazy! I miss the noise of town and the people hurrying around me. Here, no one hurries. There's nowhere to go! Can you honestly see me married to a doctor, living out here, fighting with Mrs. Beverly over who was going to give Truett the first kiss when he arrives home?"

"Oh, Celia!" Lizzie threw her head back to look at the ceiling. "You're impossible!"

"Maybe I am, but I just don't want to be like Mama. She was happy and content to take care of the house and hurry to the door the moment Daddy came home. I'm just not made that way. I don't want my life to be over when I marry. Or have my husband die and wish I was dead too."

Part of her longed to be married and to have that closeness, but then she imagined being married and something happening to her husband, a sudden illness or accident, sending her into the mental state Mother was currently in. Why would she do that to herself, when she could be doing what she really loved—creating new dresses, designing new patterns, setting up her own shop, keeping the books—succeeding! Why would she want to end her life before it had begun? Why were men the only ones who should strive for success?

Her heart was pounding. She pressed a hand to her eyes and took a deep breath.

"All right, Celia," Lizzie said quietly. "But don't blame me when you end up a lonely old maid."

Celia pursed her lips. "Look here, Elizabeth Wilcox. I have nothing against marriage. I will probably get married someday. But I have things I want to do first, exciting, significant things."

"That's fine. But will you come to the dance next Saturday? Will you dance with someone if they ask you? It won't endanger your *plans* if you dance a few times."

Celia looked through lowered eyelashes at Lizzie. "For your information, I like to dance. But maybe nobody will ask me. Young men never asked me to dance at home."

She didn't really like talking about this, but she *would* like to know why she'd never been popular with the young men of her family's acquaintance. Other girls—some rather homely—garnered half a dozen marriage proposals by the time they were Celia's age. She'd never had one.

"Mother always said I intimidate men, scare them off. But maybe I'm just not pretty enough."

"You're beautiful!"

Men did seem to stare at her on the street when she passed them, and young men sometimes became tongue-tied when they were first introduced to her. But they never came around to court her. Not one.

"I think Mother was right." Lizzie sat up straighter. "You do scare them off. But not because you're not pretty. It's because you're beautiful and smart, you know exactly what you want. And they know it's not them. You don't make them feel important, and men like to feel important."

"Listen to you, so wise." Celia smiled. "And only fourteen."

Lizzie threw a ball of embroidery thread at her.

Celia laughed. "I mean it!"

"Well, I mean it, too. I know you don't want any man who'd be afraid of you. But Truett Beverly isn't afraid of you, is he?"

"Fine." It could never be, wasn't meant to be, so she wished Lizzie would stop talking about it. "If you'll stop pushing Truett Beverly at me morning, noon, and night, if he asks me, I'll dance with him. All right?"

"All right." Lizzie looked down, but Celia could see she was smiling.

Why did she feel like she'd just been tricked?

CHAPTER 11

Celia arrived at the dance with Lizzie, Harley, Tempie, and Will, who was using a crutch to walk.

The cotton warehouse was little more than a large shed, with only one side enclosed. It was decorated with colored paper lanterns, though the sun was still up and bathing everything in a summer evening glow. Fresh cut lilies, gladioluses, daisies, and purple bachelor buttons rose high out of butter churns decorated with yellow and pink ribbons. Bright red and blue cloths covered the refreshment tables, which were laden with fruit pies and pitchers of lemonade.

Lizzie followed the children over to the food table and helped them each get a slice of pie and a cup of lemonade. They went to sit under a shade tree, where quilts had been spread and several other children were eating, squealing, and laughing.

A bandstand stood at the enclosed end of the large, open-sided building. The players tuned their instruments—three fiddles, a banjo, and two guitars.

"Celia!" Ruby Prichard hugged her, catching her off guard.

"Hello, Ruby."

Ruby, who was Celia's age, had visited them a few times with her younger sister, Olean, Lizzie's friend.

"I'm so glad you're here, Celia. I get so nervous at these kinds of things. You'll keep me company, won't you?"

"Of course." Celia allowed Ruby to link her arm in hers.

"Don't you look beautiful! Did Lizzie do your hair? I have to get her to show me how to do that. And your dress is right pretty," Ruby said, glancing down.

"Thank you. So is yours." Celia had let Lizzie talk her into wearing the white muslin with the pink flowered pattern and a dark pink ribbon around her waist. The dress was a bit out of style, but it was more festive than her other fancy dresses, and her only dress that wasn't black, dark blue, green, or a half mourning color—lavender, gray, or mauve. Celia had never noticed that about her wardrobe before. And since she didn't have a hat to match, Lizzie had also talked her into wearing her hair curled and decorated with wildflowers, with two bouncy curls hanging down on either side by her ears. When she looked in the mirror, she almost didn't recognize herself. The less formal style seemed to soften her features, and she had to admit, she liked the way she looked.

Ruby wore her hair in curls down her back, and her dress was similar in style and pattern to Celia's, only with yellow flowers.

Ruby squeezed her arm. "We should have dances more often!" She giggled, then pointed and waved to Beulah Pettibone, who was just alighting from a carriage in the yard.

"That's Beulah," Ruby whispered confidentially. "Her daddy owns the general store. She thinks she's so rich." Ruby rolled her eyes, and Celia let a small burst of laughter escape. *I must be nervous, too.*

Beulah pranced toward them, holding up the skirt of her frilly, ruffled pink dress. "Am I late?"

"Oh, no." Ruby smiled in a friendly way, but she didn't take

Beulah's arm and didn't let go of Celia's. "You're just in time. It sounds like the band is getting ready to start. I can hardly wait!"

"Me, too." Beulah smiled a cat-like smile. Celia remembered her as the girl who was talking to Truett her first Sunday in Bethel Springs. The doctor and the daughter of the town's only successful merchant. What a perfect match.

Celia's stomach sank and she quickly dismissed the thought.

The band struck up a lively tune. People trickled forward, settling at the edge of the dance floor, tapping their toes and nodding in time to the song.

Practically every style of dress was represented. Some men wore suits, complete with vests and double-breasted tailcoats. Others were in shirtsleeves in the hot July weather. The older ladies wore gingham dresses buttoned all the way to their chins, along with cotton bonnets to shield them from the sun.

Ruby stared longingly at the dance floor. "I hope someone asks me to dance."

Celia tapped her toes to the music. She'd missed the last two dances at home in Nashville because no one had asked her to go. It had seemed a waste of time anyway. But here in this sleepy little place, time seemed to take on a different dimension, as if there was more of it.

Too much.

A father and little girl started dancing at one end of the floor, the girl laughing as her Daddy stomped his feet so fast she couldn't keep up.

Celia's father had danced with her when she was about that size.

Tears sprang to Celia's eyes. Never again would she dance with Daddy. Never again would she see him, ask his advice, or bask in his approval.

She blinked rapidly, keeping her gaze away from the father and his daughter and trying to focus on a fiddle player who sawed the bow across the strings of the instrument while rapidly jerking his body in time with the rhythm. In contrast, the banjo player stood stock still, all except his thumb and fingers, which buzzed over the banjo strings like bees in search of nectar.

Her heart slowed as she brought her tears under control. Why did she have to miss her father at such odd times? She concentrated on the music while Ruby turned her head this way and that, trying to catch sight of everyone present.

The song ended as people began to crowd around the dance floor. A gangly young man approached them. His Adam's apple bobbed as he swallowed, his eyes focusing on Ruby. "Miss Ruby, will you dance with me?"

"It would be my pleasure." Ruby's face beamed as she unhooked her arm from Celia and followed him to the dance floor.

Celia was alone now. She caught sight of Truett Beverly's head and shoulders. His mother handed him two pies. He and another man, an older version of Truett and Griff, carried them toward the refreshment table. Ah! That must be Truett's father, home for the holiday.

Truett turned his head and she looked quickly away, not wanting him to catch her watching him.

"Miss Celia Wilcox." Curtis Suggs closed the gap between them with two long strides and grinned down at her. "Will you honor me with this dance, Miss Celia?"

"Of course."

The dance was announced as a quadrille, and the couples lined up opposite each other. Curtis's grin struck her as cocky and predatorial. Celia was thankful it was a lively dance, with little opportunity for talking.

The men bowed and the ladies curtsied as the dance began. Soon they were skipping in a circle, exchanging partners with the three other couples in their square.

Curtis's hand was clammy and cool, and she had to clasp it often—but only briefly, thank goodness. He had been very polite when she'd met him before, but if she wasn't mistaken, she smelled whiskey on his breath. Drinking could certainly change a man's personality.

Middle-aged and young couples, single and married alike took part in the dance. Celia's heart lightened at the smiles on every face and the brisk movement of the dance, in spite of her growing aversion to her partner.

The dance ended and Curtis Suggs took Celia's hand. His eyes, the way they were clamped on her, made her feel intruded upon.

"Miss Celia, might I say, you look particularly beautiful this evening." He practically smacked his lips as his gaze slid down her figure.

She had a sudden urge to slap him but settled for snatching her hand away. "Excuse me. I'm going to get a cup of lemonade."

She spun around before he could say another word and headed to the refreshment table. How dare he come to this party drunk and look at her that way? Her hands and knees shook. She kept her gaze straight ahead and focused on the pitchers of lemonade. She let one of the ladies pour her a cup and stood sipping it, concentrating on slowing her breathing.

"May I say, you are an excellent dancer, Miss Celia."

"Nothing out of the common way, I'm sure." She turned around and faced Truett Beverly. The way he was looking at her—respectful and humble, so unlike Curtis Suggs—set her at ease, and she remembered her promise to Lizzie to dance with him.

~

TRUETT SPOTTED CURTIS COMING THEIR WAY, FIRE IN HIS EYES. "Don't look now, but Curtis is coming over here." The hound dog no doubt wished to ask Celia to dance the Virginia Reel with him.

Celia's eyes opened wider, a look of panic in them. Curtis was closing the distance quickly.

Truett bowed and said, "Miss Celia, will you dance with me?"

She visibly relaxed, and her smile looked relieved. "Why, yes I will."

His heart gave a little leap at her gratifying reaction.

Curtis reached them and narrowed his eyes. He stopped just behind Celia and glared at Truett.

"Evening, Curtis." Truett gently took Celia's elbow. "Have some lemonade."

Truett forced himself not to laugh at Curtis's confounded look.

He focused on Celia as they walked toward the dance floor. Her hair looked softer and prettier, not pulled back in her usual severe, spinster-ish bun. In fact, she looked prettier than he had ever seen her. Should he tell her? He didn't want to say anything that wasn't proper.

He was nervous, and he hoped he didn't start to sweat. She'd already seen him sweaty. When he was splitting wood it was all right, but at a dance it seemed like a bad thing.

She was gazing up at him, straight into his eyes. Could she tell that he was drawn to her, that he wanted to make her smile so badly it made his mouth go dry?

They were almost to the dance floor. The band was talking over the music. Other partners were beginning to line up.

"You look beautiful tonight, Miss Wilcox." He led her to her place.

"Thank you, Dr. Beverly."

She smiled up at him. He was sure his heart stopped for five whole seconds. A soft, feminine smell, like lilacs and roses, wafted up from her hair, filling his head and making his heart skip.

"Please, call me Truett."

She raised her eyebrows but didn't reply.

He realized he was still standing beside her, holding her elbow. He moved to his place opposite her and the music began. The men bowed and the women curtsied. He and Celia met in the middle and linked arms, dancing around in a circle, then held hands as they spun around again. She smiled at him so warmly he wondered if he was dreaming.

They changed partners two times, then came back together to hold hands and skip down the line of dancers and back again.

"You look like you're having a good time."

"I am having a good time." Her dimple deepened. He hadn't noticed it before. Probably because he'd never seen her smile so big.

His lungs seemed to swell to twice their normal capacity. They might as well have been the only two people in the room, because hers was the only face he saw. *Lord, let the next dance be a waltz.*

The music ended. Her cheeks had turned a healthy pink, which heightened her appeal and made him wonder how soft her cheek would feel against his fingers.

"Shall I get you some lemonade?"

"No, let's dance again."

His heart soared, and the band leader granted his wish, announcing a waltz. She placed her right hand in his left. Afraid of breaking the spell, he gently laid his right hand on the curve of her waist. Then she placed her left hand on his shoulder. He searched her eyes, trying to read her thoughts. Was she at all affected by his touch?

Someone tapped his left shoulder. Celia let go of him, but he kept his right hand on her waist.

He turned his head and saw Curtis Suggs glaring at him with narrowed eyes.

"I'm cutting in."

"Why don't you ask the lady who she wishes to dance with."

Curtis's cheeks flamed red. His eyes flashed fire. He turned to Celia. "Miss Celia, would you do me the honor?"

"I'm dancing with Dr. Beverly now, thank you." Celia didn't smile.

Truett turned his back on Curtis. If the varmint didn't get the hint from Celia's unfriendly look, Truett would have to give him a message he couldn't mistake.

He focused again on his lovely partner, and the smile returned to her lips. They clasped hands again, and he was highly aware of every one of her fingers touching his hand and his shoulder.

The music started and they began to move in rhythm. The curls hanging by each of her cheeks swayed as she moved, caressing her face, then flowing backward to brush her ear. Her eyes sparkled as she gazed up at him. He tried not to stare at her lips, he truly did, but the way they turned up at the corners was irresistible.

～

CELIA LET THE MUSIC OF THE WALTZ AND TRUETT'S ARMS CARRY her around the floor, her feet gliding as if on ice. She found it hard not to stare at him. He was so handsome, with his hair combed back, the slight cleft in his strong chin. His sun-tanned skin contrasted nicely with his white shirt. Her eyes kept slipping to his chest, so broad, reminding her of the way his muscles had rippled when he wielded the ax. His cologne, which smelled of bergamot and rosemary, wafted over her as they danced.

His bright blue eyes stared back so intensely, it made her heart flutter like the wings of some great bird trapped inside her chest. She was powerfully aware of his nearness and the feel of his hand on her waist and the other clasping hers, the hardness of his jaw and fierceness in his eye when he'd forced Curtis to let her choose between them. He hadn't taken his eyes off her face since.

When the song ended, it came almost as a shock, the time went by so fast.

As the other dancers slowly moved away, she and Truett simply stood still. Finally, he asked, "Would you like to dance the next one?"

"Yes." She sounded out of breath, though the waltz had not tired her at all.

She couldn't stop staring as images of him went through her mind—of him jumping onto the wheel of the wagon to lift Will out, of him crashing into Griff to stop him from hitting his mother, of him reciting poetry the day he drove her home. What had she called him? *Truett Shakespeare.*

"What are you smiling about?" he asked.

"Oh, I was just remembering your gift for reciting poetry."

"As I recall, you weren't very impressed."

"Perhaps I was but didn't want to show it."

"I suspected as much."

"You did, did you?" Celia tried to give him a reproving look, but with the smile on her face, she probably looked flirtatious instead.

"Shall I recite something else for you? Your beauty inspires me."

"All right." She was aware that they were now alone on the dance floor, and everyone was staring at them, but the advantage was that no one could eavesdrop on their conversation.

A twinkle came into his eyes, but he otherwise grew serious.

"SHE WALKS IN BEAUTY, LIKE THE NIGHT
  Of cloudless climes and starry skies;
 And all that's best of dark and bright
  Meet in her aspect and her eyes:
 Thus mellowed to that tender light
  Which heaven to gaudy day denies."

CELIA'S HEART HAMMERED AGAINST HER CHEST. HER EYES WERE locked on his. He continued in a low, deep voice.

"One shade the more, one ray the less,
  Had half impaired the nameless grace
Which waves in every raven tress,"

His gaze strayed to her hair.

"Or softly lightens o'er her face;
Where thoughts serenely sweet express
  How pure, how dear their dwelling place.

"And on that cheek, and o'er that brow,
  So soft, so calm, yet eloquent,
The smiles that win, the tints that glow,
  But tell of days in goodness spent,
A mind at peace with all below,
  A heart whose love is innocent!"

No one else had ever recited poetry to her before, and it took her breath away. Did he really feel that way about her, that her beauty reminded him of a clear night sky? That her heart was full of innocent love? If she were able to speak, she would tell him she was impressed, that the poem was very fine and his recitation equally fine. But her heart seemed to have lodged in her throat.

Just then the musicians announced the Barn Dance—a Schottische.

Truett leaned toward her and let his gaze fall to the floor, breaking the spell. "That was Lord Byron, by the way, lest you think I wrote it myself."

Celia managed to find her voice. "I knew that, though I'm sure you could write something just as lovely. Truett Shakespeare." She gave him a coy look out of the corner of her eye.

She was surprised at herself—flirting, actually flirting, with a man.

She'd never had so much fun in her life.

They had to stand side-by-side for the next dance, holding hands. Several other couples joined them on the floor. Celia reveled in the warmth of his hand holding hers in a firm grip. Never had she felt this way. It was disconcerting and exciting at the same time. Perhaps she should stop herself now. After all, where was all this attraction and flirting and dancing taking them? Wherever it was, it wasn't in her plan.

Celia's palms started to perspire. What if she got herself into something she couldn't get out of? She was starting to care about Truett Beverly. This must be how it had started between her mother and father. A dance, a touch of the hand, attraction to a kind, intelligent, handsome man. The next thing you know, you're trapped for life.

The music began for the Schottische. She had to push these thoughts away and concentrate on the dance steps or she'd end up falling or tripping or otherwise embarrassing herself. She'd have to think through this situation after this dance was over. Perhaps she could get away by herself, use the excuse that she was fatigued.

The dance was her favorite, and soon she was twirling in Truett's arms. She couldn't remember what she was even thinking about before, only how warm his hand felt on her back, guiding her through the steps of the dance, whirling her around again and again.

At one point in the dance, they had to briefly change partners, and Celia found herself dancing with Curtis Suggs. Her back went rigid the moment he touched her. He smirked and asked, "Are you having a good time?"

"Yes, I am." She stared him in the eye and dared him to look down.

She was so happy when she returned to Truett's arms that she almost laughed out loud.

When the dance was over, Truett held her hand and led her to the outside edge of the dance floor. If she was out of breath before, she was much more so now. She concentrated on slowing her breathing.

Wasn't she supposed to do something when the dance was over? Truett's smiling eyes and strong grip sent a tingle down her back. She couldn't remember.

Truett's features grew sober. "If Curtis Suggs bothers you, you let me know. I'll take care of him."

Celia shook her head. "He wouldn't dare."

"I just don't want anyone frightening you . . . although it's hard to imagine that anyone could." One corner of his mouth lifted in a half-smile, then his gaze focused on her lips.

Celia found herself staring at his lips, too. How would it feel to kiss him?

She turned her head away and gulped a deep breath of night air, clearing her head of the slight but distinct smell of his bergamot and rosemary cologne. Had anyone seen them staring so brazenly at each other? Did they know what she was thinking? Her cheeks grew hot just thinking about it.

Blushing. Another thing to add to her list of things she never did before she met Truett Beverly.

"Shall we get some lemonade?" Celia gently extracted her hand from his.

He nodded. She took his arm as they strolled toward the refreshments.

Darkness had overtaken the lingering sunset, and now their only light was from the lanterns.

Truett handed her a cup and she looked around for the rest of her family. Will stood propped on his crutch talking to some boys. Lizzie was huddled in a tight knot with her friends, giggles erupting every few seconds. Her mother sat on a blanket, with

Harley and Tempie racing several other children in a crazy course that wound around trees and groups of standing adults. Mama was looking around at everyone with a slightly confused expression. At least she wasn't staring off into space.

"Is everyone all right?" Truett drank from his cup.

"Yes, they all seem to be having fun. Except Mother. I probably should get her and the twins home before much longer." She frowned ruefully, her heart sinking at the prospect of leaving.

Just then, Mrs. Beverly approached them where they stood in the shadows near the refreshments. "Oh, Celia, don't you look lovely! I've never seen your hair so fetching." Then she turned to the man who was striding up behind her. "Celia Wilcox, I want to introduce you to my husband, John Beverly."

Celia smiled. "How do you do Mr. Beverly?"

"Miss Wilcox, it's a pleasure to meet you." He squeezed her hand and smiled pleasantly.

Celia took note of how handsome Truett's father was, for all his gray hair and creases around his eyes. He resembled Truett but lacked a certain gentleness of expression that graced his son's countenance.

Mrs. Beverly turned to her son. "Truett, darling, I believe your father, Griff, and I are going." She squeezed his forearm. "You stay here with Celia and escort her and her family home, won't you?"

"Are you sure you don't need me?"

"Of course not, son. You just have a good time."

"I'll help you clear out some of your pies and things." Then he turned to Celia. "Please don't run off. I'll be right back."

Her heart fluttered and she stared at his retreating back, so broad . . . Why was she thinking about such things? She was demoralized to find out she was so weak and worldly about men. She'd never been so before!

Now she remembered what she was supposed to think about —what this crazy attraction was leading her to. Was she falling so in love with Truett that she would forget about her dream and stay here in Bethel Springs? She shuddered, a sick feeling twisting her stomach. After she'd worked so hard, prayed so hard, wanted it so badly, could she give up on her dream of opening her own shop? Could she forget that her family was depending on her now to provide for them?

She wouldn't, couldn't forget that. But Truett was from Bethel Springs, had come back here after finishing medical school. People like that were very attached to their hometown. He would never leave. Besides, his mother needed him, with his father away most of the time, to help her with Griff.

It was clear. She had to stay away from Truett Beverly. If she didn't, things would only get worse. He was already ruining her peace of mind, making her act like the silly, giggly girls she always scorned. She had to put a stop to it. She'd resolve to do it now, while he wasn't standing right beside her, because she seemed to lose her mind when he was near.

But his face. The timbre of his voice and the soft warmth of his eyes. How it made her feel when he recited the poem by Lord Byron . . . His voice sent tingles down her spine.

But I don't even like poetry!

Studying poetry in school always seemed a waste of time. Now, the first man who quoted a bit of Byron had her swooning like a ninny. Was she going to allow herself to become emotional over a country doctor who still lived with his mother?

She set her jaw, and just in time, too, as Truett had finished loading his mother's wagon and was striding her way.

CHAPTER 12

Truett smiled as his family piled into the wagon. Now he was free to return to Celia.

On his way, he passed Sheriff Suggs and Curtis with their heads together. They looked up to level a glare at him. Had they figured out his secret?

Not even the prospect of future trouble with the sheriff and his son could dampen Truett's spirits, not after the way Celia had been responding to him, smiling, flirting, dancing with him, letting him hold her hand. But the look in her eye was the best of all. He could almost believe she was as enamored of him as he was of her.

His heart tripped over itself.

He'd been unable to tear his eyes off her. Holding her and dancing with her had been better than he imagined. How he had wished they were alone so he could kiss her. She'd looked so inviting, sweeter than he'd ever seen her, and with such an expression of longing on her face. Perhaps tonight, when he took her home . . .

But when he met her eyes, the look on her face sent a sense of foreboding through him.

She sure didn't look like she would kiss him now. She looked like she'd just bit into a green persimmon.

Was it something he said? His first impulse was to say something teasing, but that hadn't gone over well in the past.

They stood facing each other. "Is something wrong?"

"Why do you ask?" The words jumped from her like the crack of a whip. She folded her arms over her chest.

Because you look like you just snuggled up to a cocklebur. "No reason."

Coolly raising her eyebrows, she said, "I believe my family and I are almost ready to go home. I'm going to talk to Ruby, then I'll be ready."

"All right." But she was already moving away, giving him the cold shoulder.

His head was spinning. One moment she was hanging on his every word, warm as an August afternoon. The next moment she was as cold as a January snow storm.

Celia walked toward Ruby, but before she could reach her, Grady Skidmore approached the other girl, briefly spoke, and then led her to the dance floor.

Celia stood still. He couldn't see her face, but her back looked rigid. Then she walked over to the edge of the dance floor. She appeared to make eye contact with Worley Till. The man's face registered shock. He straightened his shoulders and crossed over to Celia, obviously asking her to dance. She let him lead her onto the floor for the rest of the waltz that had just started.

A hard knot formed in Truett's throat. Had he misunderstood? Had she never been as interested in him as she'd seemed? He watched her face now as she danced with Worley.

Worley was tall and lanky and not exactly the most graceful dancer, but he managed to keep from stepping on her feet. Celia's smile seemed tight, and she seemed to be holding herself as far away from him as she could, much different from the close and friendly way she had danced with Truett. He couldn't have imagined it.

When the dance was over, she gave a slight curtsy to Worley, then moved to Ruby's side. Ruby's eyes were as big as saucers. She turned in Truett's direction, but Celia wouldn't look at him. He would have given quite a sum to hear what the two of them were saying.

Ruby squeezed her arm and giggled, then turned away. Celia went to round up her family.

His thoughts still churning, he walked over to offer his assistance. Tempie was asleep in her mother's lap, so he squatted beside her and lifted the little girl in his arms. He carried her to their wagon and lay her on a quilt. Next, he helped her mother up onto the seat.

"Oh, Celia, you and Truett were the best dancers on the floor!" Lizzie bounced with enthusiasm on the back of the wagon. "And you looked like you were having so much fun! I've never seen you looking so happy."

Truett risked a glance at Celia. She glared at Lizzie, as if trying to silence her sister.

Celia helped Harley into the back of the wagon, and he sat beside his sleeping sister. There was just enough room on the seat for Truett, Mrs. Wilcox, and one more person. Everyone else was seated, so he held out his hand to Celia. She took it, holding up her skirt to sit by her mother, and he helped her up, but she didn't look at him.

When they were all in, Truett climbed onto the seat and set the horses in motion toward home.

All the anticipation and enjoyment had gone out of him, as Celia's mood had clearly changed toward him. Was she angry with something he had done? But he couldn't think of anything that might have offended her. When he'd walked away from her to help his mother, she'd looked perfectly amiable. But when he came back, her attitude was just the opposite. It didn't make any kind of sense.

But he wouldn't let her get away with this sudden change. No, he would force her to tell him what he'd done. He couldn't have been mistaken about the warmth he'd seen in her eyes.

He relived the way she'd gazed up at him, friendly and smiling.

Twenty minutes later, he turned the horses into the Wilcox place. He was decided. It might not be strictly the gentlemanly thing to do, but he couldn't let her get away tonight without at least trying to get out of her some sort of explanation.

~

CELIA SMOOTHED HER FACE INTO COOL LINES. SHE WOULD THANK Truett for escorting them home—without looking him in the eye —and bid him good night. She would refuse to even glance at him, since she wasn't confident that she'd otherwise be able to keep up the frosty façade.

She wouldn't let him ruin her plans. If she ever wanted to leave this place without breaking her heart, she had to focus on getting back to Nashville.

The wagon stopped and Celia scrambled down from the wagon seat before Truett could come around and help her. She hurried to the back of the wagon and gently slid Tempie's sleeping form to the end so she could pick her up.

Oh no! Harley was asleep too. She couldn't carry them both. If only Will could take Harley, but Will was still hobbling around on his crutch, and while she stood there trying to decide what to do, Will and Lizzie and Mama were already walking toward the house.

She bit her lip and carefully lifted Tempie, hoping she could get her little sister to the house before Truett—

She almost bumped into him when she turned around.

She held Tempie, refusing to look at him. "I can carry them

both into the house. You can unhitch one of the horses and ride home."

Truett grunted. She looked up, and the moonlight showed his expression—his lips a grim line, his eyes almost fierce.

She should have kept her promise not to look him in the eye.

He brushed past her, climbed into the wagon bed, and lifted Harley in his arms. He lowered himself to sit at the end of the wagon, then got down, still holding the sleeping child against his shoulder.

Standing beside Celia, he seemed to be challenging her, waiting to see if she would try and stop him from carrying her little brother inside.

Come on, Harley, wake up. Insist he let you down so you can walk. But the child didn't stir, and Celia was forced to let Truett carry him. She turned and walked toward the house.

Truett followed her up the steps, across the porch, and through the front door.

She stepped around a doll on the floor. She could feel Truett's eyes on her but didn't turn to look. She stood in the door of Will and Harley's bedroom. Pointing with her head at the bed against the opposite wall, she whispered, "You can lay Harley over there."

She continued on to Mama's bedroom and lay Tempie on the bed. Mama was already putting on her nightgown and barely glanced at Celia as she closed the door behind her.

The house was completely quiet. Where were Will and Lizzie? She peered down the hall that led to the kitchen but saw no light from that direction. The other way led past her and her siblings' bedroom—and Truett. Had he already left?

She tip-toed softly and peeked inside Harley's room. Truett was bent over Harley's bed as he pulled the sheet over the little boy, tucking it gently under his chin and around his arms and legs.

Celia's stomach flipped at the tender way he treated her little brother.

He turned around and saw her watching him. Her face went hot. She had to let him know there was nothing between them.

He moved toward her, each step slow and deliberate.

She turned and scurried across the parlor toward the front door to see him out. She clutched at her throat. Why was she practically gasping for air?

Truett was still only halfway across the room, his face unreadable in the dark.

Celia's heart beat faster. She had to get control of herself. She straightened her shoulders and wrapped her hands around her arms. Just a few more seconds and he would be out the door and she could breathe again.

As he drew nearer, she opened the door for him and willed her voice to steady. "Thank you, Dr. Beverly, for escorting us home."

Her cool dismissal of him sent a pang of guilt through her. But she couldn't think like that. She must do whatever was necessary. It was for his own good, wasn't it? She had to be honest with him, to let him know there could never be anything between them.

He kept coming until he stood face to face with her. He was so close she could make out the blue of his eyes in the dark room and smell the now-familiar scent of bergamot and rosemary. "Celia, I'd like to speak with you on the porch."

"Oh, I can't. I have to—" Her voice sounded breathless as her throat tightened again.

"Please." But the word sounded more like a command. "It will only take a minute."

"Well." Celia lifted her chin, trying to appear offended and hide the fact that her heart was racing.

He held the door open for her and let her precede him onto the wooden planks of the porch. The screen door shut behind them. He faced her, his arm brushing hers, and bent his head. His lips were so close she could feel his breath on her forehead, sending a delicious tingling sensation all through her. *Sweet heaven. I'm losing my mind again.*

"Celia, what's wrong?" His voice was much softer than before. "Did I do something?"

"What do you mean? Of course not. It was late. Time to go home. Thank you for escorting us—"

"I'm not leaving until I find out why you suddenly gave me the cold shoulder." He widened his stance, planting his boots in a decidedly stubborn way.

"What are you talking about? I did nothing of the kind. It was a dance. Aren't I allowed to dance with whomever I please?"

"That's not what I'm talking about and you know it."

"Then just what are you talking about?" She crossed her arms, giving her a bit of a barrier to his masculine frame just inches away.

He sighed. It was too dark to see his expression.

"Come here. Please." He took her arm and pulled her toward the edge of the porch. They could see each other now, the moon shining full on their faces. "Can you honestly tell me you don't care for me?" His voice lowered, softening. "That you don't want me to court you? Because I would like to court you."

Celia's mouth dropped open. She never expected him to be so blunt. "I . . . as a matter of fact . . ." She swallowed. *Oh, Lord, give me words!* Aiming her gaze beyond his shoulder, she forced herself not to look at him. Finally, she managed to draw in a deeper breath. "I appreciate the help you've given to my family. You're a good man, but in fact, I don't want you to court me."

There, she'd said it. Her future was safe.

"Won't you even look at me?" His fingertips brushed her cheek, as if to turn her face toward him.

A pleasant warmth was stealing through her from his touch, snaking down to her stomach, where she had apparently swallowed a dozen butterflies.

She looked into his eyes before she could stop herself. The tenderness she saw in his expression brought tears to her eyes. This was harder than she imagined.

She whispered hoarsely, "I don't want you to court me."

The hurt that flashed through his eyes twisted her insides. His hand fell from her cheek to his side.

She'd flirted with him, enjoyed his arms and his dancing, then coldly rejected him. If he'd been rude or crude or looked at her the way Curtis Suggs had, she wouldn't feel these pangs of guilt and regret. Inside she was so torn. He had been nothing but good and kind. And now his eyes were wide with pain.

Somehow he'd never looked more handsome. His hair was a bit mussed, curling over his ears. The moonlight and shadows seemed to bring out the slight cleft in his chin and give his cheekbones and jawline a hard, chiseled appearance. And her heart ached to take her words back. Her arms fought to slip around him. Her cheek tingled, imagining being pressed against his chest.

Mad. She was completely insane.

"All right, then. You don't owe me an explanation, of course, but I do wish you would tell me if I did something wrong."

Her heart fluttered. Now what could she say? She was as much in danger as ever. "Well, I . . . a lady doesn't have to have a reason. And no, you didn't do anything wrong."

Uh-oh. From the look on his face, she was not conveying the proper sternness.

"Is it because you don't like me?" A bit of a smile played around the corners of his lips.

And what perfect lips they were, too.

"I don't have to answer that." She looked past his shoulder again. "I don't dislike you."

"Then you do like me."

"I didn't say that."

"Then you're afraid I'll keep you from going back to Nashville."

"Well . . . yes." Her eyelids fluttered as she struggled to break free from the hold of his intense blue eyes. Her gaze slipped down, but she encountered his broad chest, which only made her imagine again how it would feel to press her cheek against it and hear his heart beating.

"Celia, I—"

His hand was coming toward her face. She took a step back. When she did, her foot went off the edge of the porch.

"Oh!" Celia flailed her arms. She was falling! He grabbed her, but it was too late. They both fell the three feet off the porch into the flower bed below.

CHAPTER 13

S
he was lying on top of him, he on his back. Somehow he had managed to place his body between hers and the ground as he took the brunt of the fall.

Celia scrambled off of him and pushed herself up, propping on her elbow. A daisy lay across his chest, its long stem crumpled and its white petals askew.

"Are you all right?" Truett asked, also pushing himself up to look into her face.

"Yes. Are you hurt? I'm so sorry." When he didn't say anything, she asked again, "Are you hurt?"

He moved slowly. "I don't think so."

She managed to get to her feet in the middle of the crushed patch of daisies and bachelor buttons. She bent and tugged on his upper arm, the muscles as hard as rock

Once he was standing, he straightened his back. He carefully flexed his left shoulder, the one he had fallen on, wincing as he did so.

"You're hurt, aren't you?"

He nodded.

"Where does it hurt?"

Truett frowned and closed his eyes for a moment. Then he pointed to the left side of his chest.

His heart.

"Oh, for pity's sake. You're just teasing me, Truett Beverly." Celia slapped lightly at his arm.

A lock of brown hair had fallen over his forehead and hung down over one eyebrow. She considered reaching up and brushing it back.

He was staring at her again too. "Now, don't fall backward this time. I'm not going to hurt you."

"I'm not afraid."

"Then hold still."

Her heart jumped into her throat as he slowly raised his hand to her face. With his palm, he brushed back some curls that were clinging to her sweat-dampened cheek and pulled a beat-up daisy from her hair.

"You want it?" he asked with a playful smile.

She shook her head and he dropped the limp flower to the ground.

She stood on her tip-toes and pulled a dead leaf out of his hair, her fingertips brushing his forehead.

Truett's eyelids fell to half-mast.

Oh no. Her heart hammered against her chest. She quickly pulled her hand away, rocking back on her heels. She looked down at her feet. "I have to go in now." Her voice sounded breathless.

She turned toward the steps, which were just beyond Truett's right shoulder. She waited for him to step aside, but he didn't. She was so close to him she could feel the heat emanating from his body and smell the dirt they had just fallen into and were probably still covered with.

"Celia?"

She lifted her head but found herself closer than she'd

expected. In fact, his face was barely two inches from hers. Her gaze slipped from his eyes to his lips . . . the gap closed . . .

And then they were kissing.

His lips were warm and soft and firm at the same time. Her heart seemed to melt all the way into her toes. Truett Beverly was kissing her. And she was letting him!

His hands were on her back, pulling her closer.

Her first kiss. She never imagined it could feel this way, gentle and eager at the same time, making her knees weak. She shouldn't like it, should she? A lady shouldn't allow a man to kiss her this way. She should push him away, run up the steps, and slam the door on him.

She dismissed the thought as the most disagreeable one she'd ever had.

~

TRUETT POURED HIS WHOLE HEART INTO THE KISS, AFRAID THAT AT any moment she would tear herself away from him.

Her hands pressed against his chest, and then they slipped up and around his neck.

The back of her head fit perfectly in his hand. Her lips were warm and yielding, but she wasn't responding.

The thought made him pull away and look down at her. Her eyes remained closed and her lips parted. She didn't move as she exhaled a fluttery sigh.

His pulse leapt. He bent and covered her mouth with his again. This time, she kissed him back.

Celia did like him. She did want him to court her. She could hardly deny it after letting him kiss her like this. This moment was perfect. She was everything he wanted—determined, but with a soft, tender side hiding just behind the independent façade she showed the world. And he could save her and her family from their poverty-stricken circumstances, at least in a modest way.

If only she would let him.

Truett pulled back. Her eyelids fluttered open, her lips plump and red and more tempting than ever. He murmured, "You're so beautiful." He so wanted to kiss her again. The way she was staring at him, with that sweet, dazed look on her face, he didn't think she would mind.

He drew her closer, but her eyes opened wide and she pushed against his chest.

∾

CELIA'S MIND CAME BACK TO HER WHEN SHE REALIZED HE WAS going to kiss her again. For the third time. What was she doing? Behaving like a wanton trollop!

She pushed herself out of his arms, and he let her. He was so sweet and kind . . . generous . . . handsome . . . his blue eyes, his tousled hair, his perfect lips . . . No.

"I'm going in the house now." She focused her eyes past him, on the front door. She mustn't look at him.

"Celia, wait—" He reached out and touched her arm.

"No!"

She clapped her hand over her mouth. Did she want the whole family to hear her? Pointing her finger at his chest, she kept her eyes from straying north. She lowered her voice and hissed, "You stay away from me!"

"You're not mad at me again, are you?" There was more amusement than worry in voice.

"Your behavior was not that of a gentleman, kissing me like that."

"But you're the one who kissed me." A grin tugged at the corners of his mouth. Truett shrugged. "I was just standing here, minding my own business . . ."

Heat stung her face. Her mouth fell open but no sound came out. Finally, her voice returned with a squeak. "Me?"

Had she really been the one to initiate the kiss? She tried to remember exactly what had happened. She was standing in front of him, saying she had to go inside. When he didn't move and let her pass, she lifted her face and looked into his eyes—and then they were kissing. To be honest, she wasn't sure who had kissed whom, but it was sooooo lovely.

No, she mustn't think like that! She must stick to the point here, and the point was that she . . . she had melted at the look on his face. She couldn't resist lifting her lips to his.

No, no! The point was that she had to get him out of here, tell him his kiss meant nothing, that he wasn't to ever let his lips come near hers again.

"Listen, it's high time you left, Truett Beverly, so stand aside and let me pass."

"You're right. I should go."

He sounded so contrite, she couldn't help but look up at him. But the look on his face was so hopeful and sweet . . .

"Will you let me court you?"

"No!" The answer burst from a place of desperation deep inside her. She looked away and stomped past as he stepped aside. "You may not court me." She hurried up the steps, whispering. "I'm . . . I'm not ready for that."

She closed the wooden door and locked it with the key. Then she leaned back against the door. She pressed the back of her hand against her mouth, where she could still feel his lips against hers. Her heart fluttered at the memory.

"Oh, what have I done?"

∿

LIZZIE TRIED TO PRY SOME INFORMATION OUT OF HER THAT NIGHT in bed. "Are you and Truett courting now?" she asked.

"No, we're not courting. Go to sleep."

"Why not, Celia? He likes you, I just know it."

That's a fair guess. He probably wouldn't kiss a girl he didn't like. "Go to sleep, Lizzie."

"And you like him. I can tell."

He could probably tell, too—*right before I ordered him to never come near me again.*

"You didn't chase him away, did you, Celia?"

"Listen, I told you I'm not looking to marry Truett Beverly, or anybody else, so please leave me alone about him."

"All right, all right, but you're gonna spoil everything."

No, she was trying to save them—and get them out of the country and back to town. She just had to wait for someone to respond to her ads in the newspapers, someone to make an offer on their farm, and they were leaving Bethel Springs forever—it and every last one of its populace.

But maybe Lizzie was right. She had spoiled everything. She'd told Truett she wanted nothing to do with him, but it wasn't true. Part of her really wanted him to hold her and kiss her every day for the rest of her life.

Celia lay awake long after Lizzie's rhythmic breathing told her she was asleep. She tried not to ruminate on what Truett must think of her. First she'd flirted with him and made loving eyes at him. Then she'd treated him coldly and rudely for no reason. Finally, she'd let him kiss her. And enjoyed it! She wondered if he could tell.

But of course he could tell. Her face burned as she remembered how she'd behaved—besotted and wanton! Never would she have thought herself capable of such behavior. But she'd enjoyed his company at the dance. The dancing, the poetry—he had completely befuddled her brain. And as soon as they were alone together, he'd taken advantage of it and kissed her.

Well, that wasn't exactly true. Truthfully, she'd wanted him to kiss her, had even been thinking about it when they were dancing. And then she hadn't exactly tried to stop him. And as for his teasing accusation that she'd kissed him—it was simply mutual—she as much to blame as he.

But what was she to do now?

She could probably go to him tomorrow, when she went to the post office to fetch the mail, apologize for her hot-and-cold behavior, and tell him he could court her after all. Then she'd be able to look forward to more time with him, more hand-holding, and even more kissing. He might even try to steal a kiss tomorrow, in his office.

Celia's heart skipped a beat at that exciting thought.

But then tears sprang to her eyes. No, she couldn't do that. She couldn't ever let him kiss her again. Courting led to marriage, and she couldn't get married. Not now, not until she was able to earn enough money to open her shop.

Besides, marriage did things to girls. Her mother had only been seventeen when she married her father, and what had she become? Mrs. William Wilcox, not even entitled to her own name. She had to be called Mrs. William Wilcox, as if she ceased to matter and had taken on her husband's identity. And therefore, who was she when her husband died? Nobody. The former Mrs. William Wilcox, she was so despairing she couldn't face life. She was quite literally a ghost of her former self.

But perhaps she was overreactive. No one else she knew seemed to feel this way. Perhaps it was only because she was so distraught at what had happened to Mama. Or because she'd been criticized one too many times for wanting to own her own business. But Celia had seen other girls, soon after their marriage, disappear from society. Sometimes they were too sick from pregnancy to leave their houses, or too burdened with the responsibility of running a home and trying to satisfy the demands of their husbands to even venture out of doors to enjoy a conversation with friends. What was their life for except to cater to their husband's every desire?

Celia's temples pounded. Cold fingers closed around her heart, making it beat erratically.

Daddy had always treated her like an intelligent person, telling her she could be anything she wanted, be it a teacher or historian or business owner. He seemed proud and flattered that she wanted to own her own business, and he seemed to take it for granted that she would never marry. He had told her that most men wouldn't want to marry someone with ambitions such as hers. Celia hadn't minded. She's always had a fear, a horror, of becoming like her mother.

Mother had never understood her, never understood her aversion to becoming a wife. If her mother knew how she felt, she would resent Celia's feeling that "wife" was synonymous with "controlled." Owned. Beaten down.

Tears streamed from Celia's eyes, wetting her pillow. But what good were tears? Action was the answer to her problem. She must stay strong and keep herself from falling in love with Truett Beverly, or anyone else. Although no one else had ever given her any trouble. Truett was far above anyone else she'd ever known, in character, and every other way.

No. She wouldn't start thinking about him again.

She mustn't.

CHAPTER 14

The next day was Sunday, and they all slept a little late. When Celia went out to the barn to do Will's chores of mucking the stable and milking the cow, she found that Truett had already been there and done it.

Celia got dressed for church slowly, not even bothering to try to hurry the twins until Lizzie began to get frustrated with them. Then Celia helped distract them while Lizzie buttoned Harley's shirt and Tempie's dress.

They arrived at church late, just as Celia had hoped, since she wanted to avoid Truett if at all possible. They sat in the back.

Almira Suggs sat across the aisle from her, fanning herself with a square piece of cardstock. Celia had taken an instant liking to the young schoolmarm, and she hoped to talk with her after the sermon.

She tried to pay attention, but the preacher's words droned in such a monotone, she found that when her eyes blinked, they didn't want to open up again. Besides his lulling tone, his message was almost exactly the same as it had been every Sunday since she had been there—and this was her fourth!

She frowned at the remembrance of her first Sunday. She'd

thought the preacher's message interesting and was impressed with his memory of Scripture. Little did she know that she would also have the same Scriptures memorized herself in four weeks.

At first she hadn't even seen Truett anywhere among the congregation. But with some shifting in seats, he was revealed near the front, sitting next to Mrs. Beverly and Griff. She recognized the back of his head instantly. He was as familiar as if she'd known him all her life.

Where did that silly thought come from? She hardly knew the man.

A movement caught her attention from the left corner of her eye. Almira Suggs stood up, her face as pale as milk. She made a dash for the door and was gone.

No one else seemed to take notice. Lizzie had told her that the poor girl's mother died when she was very young. No one followed her out. Celia quietly went after her.

Once outside, Celia didn't see anyone. She stood on the bottom step and listened. The muffled sound of retching came from around the side of the little white church building. She followed the noise and found Almira bent over in the knee-high grass that edged the clearing at the rear of the church.

She didn't want to embarrass her, but she wanted to at least offer help. She walked closer. "Miss Suggs?"

Slowly Almira shook her head. "I'm all right."

"Are you sure?" Celia drew closer and put her hand on the young woman's shoulder. "Can I do anything for you? Fetch someone to take you home?"

"No, I'm well." Almira stood a little taller and gave a wan smile. "Just a bit of female weakness."

"Being sick isn't 'female weakness.'" She gently took her arm. "There's a bench over here. Why don't you sit for a minute?"

Celia led her over to the wrought-iron bench and sat down beside her. When Almira didn't speak, Celia said, "You look awfully pale. Do you need to see a doctor?"

She instantly regretted her words. The last thing she wanted to have to do was fetch Dr. Beverly.

"No, please don't worry about me." Almira's eyebrows drew together. "I'm fine. Truly I am. I have a tendency for stomach ailments." She looked Celia in the eye. "Please don't tell anyone I was sick."

"Of course, if you wish it."

"I do. Thank you, Celia. You're very sweet." She smiled, but it seemed a sad smile.

Celia sensed a loneliness in her that she could understand more than she cared to admit. A tug at her heart drew her toward Almira. "I'm still getting to know people around here. Why don't you come over for tea some time? You don't live far, do you?"

"No, just the other side of the Prichards' from you."

"Perhaps we could swap books. I had to leave most of mine in Nashville, but I do have a couple of novels you might be interested in."

"I would like that very much." Almira's face brightened and most of the color seemed to come back into her cheeks.

"Then I'll expect you . . . Thursday?"

"Oh, yes, I could come Thursday."

"Good."

The collective sound of voices raised in song told them the church was singing the final hymn before being dismissed.

"Are you well enough to make it home?" Celia asked.

"Oh, yes. I am well, don't worry." And she did look much better than before.

"We can take you home in our wagon."

She shook her head. "I rode my mare. She'll get me home. I'm all right."

Celia was anxious to round up her siblings as quickly as possible in case Truett wanted to talk to her. Her cheeks grew warm just thinking about coming face to face with him again so soon after their kiss. She watched the door of the church as people trickled out to shake the preacher's hand. Truett came out before any of her family. She looked away from him, but still kept him in the corner of her vision. He didn't even look around for her. He went straight to his horse, mounted, and rode away.

Her heart sank in disappointment. *Ugh.* Of all the ridiculous reactions . . .

He must be respecting her command for him to stay away. But it hurt, in spite of her telling herself it was what she wanted. Honestly, she wasn't sure what she wanted. No, that wasn't true. Her irresponsible heart wanted Truett. But she could not let it have him.

∼

THE NEXT DAY, CELIA FOUND TWO MORE PIGS DEAD IN THEIR PEN and the rest, including the sow, swaying unsteadily on their short legs and acting lethargic. *Lord, what will we do if they all die?* They would have no meat this winter and no money to buy any.

Celia helped Will dig the holes for the pigs' graves, then followed through with her plan for the morning, which was to ride to town to check their mail.

She asked for her mail through the little barred window. The postmaster handed her two letters, one from the Circle W Horse Farm in Kentucky, and the other from the Planters Bank of Nashville.

Her heart beat in her throat. She tore open the letter from the bank as soon as she stepped outside the train station, which also served as city hall and post office.

Dear Miss Wilcox, This letter is to inform you that your father, Mr. William Earnest Wilcox, withdrew his assets and closed his account with The Planters Bank of Nashville on the 4th day of August, 1879. We have had no further dealings with him.

Celia crumpled the paper in her hand. Then it was true. They had no money, except for the seven dollars in the coffee can behind the flour sack. How long could that last them?

Next, Celia tore open the letter from the Kentucky horse farm. She glanced through its contents, her eye catching "*sum of $40 per broodmare and $80 for the stallion*" and "*a man required to travel on the train with the horses.*"

Forty dollars each was much less than her father had paid for the mares and not nearly enough to do them much good. And of course, they no longer had the stallion.

She'd have to be desperate for survival to accept such a paltry amount for those broodmares. Perhaps she could sell them by advertising in the newspaper. But who would pay her the actual worth of the horses? In these times, in Alabama, who actually needed Thoroughbred broodmares? They were too valuable to be used as work horses on a farm.

Celia leaned a forearm against Old Sallie and rubbed her temple where it had started to ache. What would happen to them without money? Celia didn't want Harley and Tempie to grow up without proper clothing, shoes, and food. She didn't want Will and Lizzie to have few or no prospects for the future, too poor for any sort of private education.

Her heart heavy, Celia mounted the horse and started through town.

A piece of paper nailed to a hitching post caught her eye. It was a wanted poster, rustling in a hot gust of wind. The reward especially drew her attention—$500. That was enough money to hire someone to take care of her siblings *and* get Celia back to Nashville, even if they weren't able to sell their farm.

She drew closer to the piece of paper and saw that the reward was for "the hooded man" who had "thwarted justice" in Madison County. The $500 was for anyone who could give information as to the identity of the black-hooded horseman who had fired his gun at a lawman.

Five hundred dollars was the largest reward Celia had ever seen for a local criminal, an enormous sum for someone who hadn't committed murder. What had the hooded man done to draw such a reward? Celia had heard that he had prevented the sheriff from arresting a black man, Truett's friend, James Burwell. But it was also rumored that this Mr. Burwell was innocent and that Sheriff Suggs had attempted to hang him without a trial. But would a sheriff blatantly defy the law by lynching a man who hadn't been tried?

Either way, Celia would like to have the reward. She should let the authorities take care of it, since it was none of her affair, but five hundred dollars! That would answer all her prayers, for herself as well as her family. But of course, she didn't know who the hooded horseman was, or anything about him.

As she passed Truett's office, she couldn't help glancing his way. Was he inside? What did he think of her now, after she refused to let him court her? After all he'd done for her and her family, he probably thought her cold and heartless. She certainly wouldn't fault him for it if he did. He couldn't know how heavy her heart felt every time she thought of how she'd treated him.

She looked away from the doctor's office window. What was done was done. Besides, she couldn't have reacted any other way. It was either hurt him now or break both their hearts when she had to leave and go back to Nashville.

Besides, when he learned all about her "manly ambitions," he couldn't possibly want her for a wife.

~

TRUETT WATCHED CELIA THROUGH HIS OFFICE WINDOW AS SHE TORE open first one letter then the other. Her hair was pulled back in that severe way of hers, not a wisp hanging free. But she was still pretty, especially her eyes . . . Would he ever be able to look at her again without thinking about their kiss?

But she had been adamant about not wanting him to court her. He shouldn't think about her at all.

Celia stared at the letter, then wadded it in her fist. The way her mouth went slack and her shoulders wilted, it must be bad news.

Truett stepped back from the window so she wouldn't see him.

Would she look his way? Could she be that cold, to come to town and not even think about him or even turn her eyes toward his office?

She stood beside her horse, holding both letters in her clenched fist. She rubbed her forehead as though trying to gather her thoughts. Pursing her lips together, she mounted, then swung the mare toward home.

She paused to look at something—the wanted poster. *His* wanted posted.

Finally, she continued down the road. As she passed his office, she bent her head and covertly turned her gaze toward his office. His heart stopped. Had she changed her mind about him? After a moment, she focused her eyes on the road ahead and urged her horse into a trot.

Truett let out the breath he was holding. So it was to be this way. Perhaps it was for the best.

He watched Sheriff Suggs talking with Aubrey Pettibone earlier as they stood on the sidewalk. Then Suggs had looked all around, to see if anyone was watching them, and the two had gone inside Pettibone's store. Something was afoot, and he had a feeling it had to do with the new store a black man had opened a few miles from town. The store was only a few miles on the other side of the Wilcox place, near Killingsworth Cove, and would surely take away business from Aubrey Pettibone's general store.

A farmer interrupted his musings, coming into his office to get the stitches out of the gash Truett had sewed up the week before.

Truett went to work on the stitches, but he was still

wondering how he could find out what Suggs and Pettibone were up to—without raising suspicion.

Anything was worth doing if it kept his mind off Celia.

～

CELIA RUMINATED ON THEIR MONEY PROBLEMS ON THE WAY HOME. Her mother clearly had no plans to provide for them. It was up to Celia to figure out what to do and how to provide for her family.

She drew near the last bend in the road before they reached home when Old Sallie began limping. Celia dismounted and finally coaxed the horse into lifting her back leg. Sure enough, she'd lost a shoe.

Celia heaved a sigh. Taking the reins, she set out on foot, leading the horse down the dusty red road. At least they were almost home.

A voice drifted to her, coming from somewhere down the road, singing.

A little girl appeared around the bend. Her hair hung in several black braids that were tied with red ribbon, a bow by each ear. Her skin was smooth and dark brown. The basket on her arm swung gently back and forth as she walked. Her face broke into a wide grin when she saw Celia. "Morning, ma'am."

Celia opened her mouth to say "Good morning" back, but her eye at that moment caught sight of a brown diamond-patterned rattlesnake, coiled in the middle of the road, facing the little girl.

"Stop!" Celia could barely get the word out. "Don't move!"

The girl looked down at what Celia was staring at and let loose an ear-piercing scream, clutching her basket against her chest.

Old Sallie whinnied and reared, pawing the air. Celia held on to her bridle.

She'd heard that a snake wouldn't strike if you held perfectly still, but the girl was not holding still. She slid her feet backward, clutching at her arms as she hugged the basket tighter.

"Don't move!" Desperation made Celia's voice shrill.

The snake raised its head higher, shaking its tail. The snake's rattles sounded like hundreds of tiny feet, marching, coming for them. The hair on the back of Celia's neck prickled at the sinister warning.

The snake's body was coiled, its head facing the little girl only two feet away, well within striking distance. If the snake bit the little girl, she could die.

A steely calm entered Celia's veins and steadied her hands. She had to act quickly to save the girl.

She picked up a rock and threw it with all her strength. She purposely made it hit the ground a foot shy of the snake's coiled-up body. Just as she'd hoped, the snake jerked its head from the girl's direction to the rock, lunging and striking at it.

Celia yelled, "Get back."

The poor girl sobbed, tears streaming down her cheeks, as she crept backward down the road, back in the direction she'd come.

Celia looked around for something to use to kill the snake, now that it was facing in her direction. Old Sallie snorted and pulled backward on the bridle.

Celia couldn't let the snake frighten her horse into charging. A long stick lay at the edge of the road. She bent and grabbed it. The outer layer crumbled. The stick was rotten. She threw it down.

The snake uncoiled itself and began to move toward Celia and Old Sallie. She only had a few seconds before the snake would be close enough to strike.

Fear tightened her chest and made her breathing shallow. Desperately, she looked around for something else. She spotted another stick lying farther off the road. She pulled Old Sallie after her as she stepped off the road and stretched her arm to reach it.

She grabbed hold of the sturdy limb. The snake continued its menacing pose, its forked tongue darting in and out, its beady eyes now trained on Celia, and its rattles shaking at her.

"I'm going to kill you, snake." Celia's voice trembled in spite of her bravado.

The little girl stood a safe distance away, sniffling. "Please don't let that snake bite you."

The rattlesnake slithered toward Celia. The girl screamed.

Celia got in front of Old Sallie and let go of the bridle. Clutching the stick in both hands, she brought the end of the limb down hard.

Thwack!

Oh no! She'd missed the snake altogether and hit the ground beside it, instead.

CHAPTER 15

Vibrations shivered up Celia's arms, almost causing her to drop the stick.

The snake lifted its head, coiling itself in a striking pose, and Celia brought the stick down again, this time hitting the snake, but still missing its head, her intended target.

Though the blow made a tiny dent in the snake's body, its head pivoted toward her stick. The snake's glittery, diamond-patterned length coiled tighter, getting ready to strike.

Celia brought the stick down a third time, and this time she hit the head. She brought the stick down again and again, hitting the head several more times, and yet the rattles continued their tuneless racket. Finally, as she continued her assault, the snake's rattles went limp on the ground.

Her hands trembled and her knees went weak. She couldn't seem to take her eyes off the creature.

"Oh, miss!" The little girl stepped cautiously forward. "I never seen nobody kill a snake with a stick before." The child came closer. The evidence of tears still shimmered on her cheeks, but they were smiling now. "You must be the bravest lady in Madison County."

Celia laughed nervously. If she was so brave, why was she shaking like a leaf?

A strange step-shuffle came from around the bend just before Will appeared, hobbling toward them with his rifle in one hand and a crutch in the other.

"Will! You shouldn't be out here." She realized the futility of her statement and another shaky chuckle erupted from her throat.

Her horse nickered behind her, and she threw down her weapon and went to retrieve Old Sallie from thirty feet away, from where she'd shied to.

Will bent over Celia's handiwork. "Shoot-fire and brimstone, Celia! Did you kill this rattler?"

"She sure did." The little girl spoke up, her cheeks crowding her eyes as she grinned. "She wasn't a bit scared neither."

"I wouldn't go that far." Celia rubbed the side of her neck with a trembling hand.

"She beat that old snake into the ground!" The little girl shook her head. "I was never so glad to see something get dead."

"He sure is a big old fellow. Got seven rattles!" Will picked up the stick that Celia had just bludgeoned him with and used it to lift the snake into the air

The little girl jerked backward with a little squeal and Celia sucked in quick breath through her teeth.

"For pity's sake, Will, do you have to touch the thing?"

"Six feet long," Will said, a hush in his voice.

The girl was gradually edging toward Celia. Who was the little girl, and where was she going? Finally, their eyes met.

"Miss or ma'am, I don't know which it is, but you done saved me from that snake, and I'm much obliged."

Tears stung her eyes and, impulsively, Celia put her arms around the girl, bending over and hugging her tight.

Celia drew back. "It's miss." She sniffed, her heart full. It wasn't hard to smile at the precious little girl. "Celia Wilcox. And this is my brother, Will. What's your name?"

"Annie Hartley. Pleased to meet you, Miss Celia."

Annie was shorter than Will, and Celia guessed she was at least two years younger. She had such a sweet smile.

"Pleased to meet you too, Annie. Would you like to come in for some tea? Our house is just around this bend."

"Thank you, Miss Celia. That snake done scared me so bad, I feel like I need to sit down. My heart's pounding right out of my chest."

"Mine, too." Celia took a deep breath and let it out.

Will carried the snake draped over the stick.

"Throw that thing down." Celia shuddered.

"I want to take it home, show it to Truett when he comes over."

"All right."

"Where were you headed?" Will asked Annie.

"I came down the road today to tell folks about my Daddy and uncle's new store."

"Oh?" Celia raised her eyebrows. She hadn't known there was any store around except Pettibone's General Store in Bethel Springs. Both Tempie and Harley would need new shoes come fall, and the General Store's prices were scandalous compared to what they were in Nashville. And the Lord knew they didn't have any money to waste.

"Oh, surely, Miss Celia. It's just up the road towards Killingsworth Cove, where my family all lives. In fact, your house is the closest one down this road."

Killingsworth Cove was a little community on the opposite side of their farm from Bethel Springs.

"We've got everything you might need, Miss Celia. Do you need some eggs? I got a basket full right here." Annie lifted the red and white checked cloth covering her basket.

"We have chickens and plenty of eggs, but I do need some thread."

Annie stuck her hand in the basket and pulled out a spool and held it up triumphantly. "You need white thread, Miss Celia?"

"Why yes. How much?"

"Just four cents." She leaned closer as they walked along the lane to their house. Cupping her hand around her mouth, she whispered, "That's one cent cheaper than at the Bethel Springs store."

Celia smiled. "Then you've just sold a spool of thread."

She knew there were people who would frown upon her doing business at a black folks' store, but she didn't care about that. She'd always believed in putting herself in others' shoes and empathizing with their situation, and she certainly wouldn't like it if someone slighted her just because of the color of her skin. It wasn't Christian. And besides, she needed to save every penny she could if they didn't find a buyer for their farm.

But of course they would find a buyer. They had to.

"My Daddy let me take these things and go out and let folks know about our store."

The three of them talked as they made their way into the house and sat down at the kitchen table while Celia made a pot of tea and got the four cents to pay Annie for the spool of thread.

Tempie showed Annie her dolls, and after playing with the younger girl for a few minutes, Annie got up to leave.

"We'll come by the store real soon," Celia assured her. The girl smiled and waved as she left.

Celia watched her go and, feeling a strong kinship with Annie, she prayed a silent prayer that the little girl's dream of seeing her father's store prosper would come true.

~

WILL WAS ABLE TO DO ALL HIS MORNING CHORES AGAIN THE NEXT morning. When he was done, he came and told Celia, "Bad news. The pigs . . ."

"They're dead?"

He nodded, frowning, his eyebrows rising apologetically. "All of them."

A pang went through Celia's midsection at what the loss of the pigs meant. But there was nothing to do but bury them. She was too afraid of getting whatever disease the pigs died of to think about butchering one and eating it.

She felt an entirely different pang, but equally awful, thinking about the fact that Truett Beverly had stopped coming around. She had no chance of seeing him in the back yard anymore now that Will's leg was healed enough that he could do the chores again. Not that she usually saw Truett anyway, except for a glimpse as he left the barn.

The memory of his kiss, unfortunately, popped up at all times of the day and night. Her thoughts forced her to relive it again and again—though, if she were honest with herself, she didn't mind. But she should never have allowed him to kiss her. She could never let it happen again, and yet, she experienced a sinking, hollow feeling in her stomach at what he must think of her, of the pain he might be experiencing because she had rejected him.

She was a mess. And all because of a country doctor in Bethel Springs, Alabama. She must never let herself get near Truett Beverly again. Truly, it was demoralizing to admit, but she couldn't trust herself with him.

In the meantime, there was plenty of work to do on the farm, and now that they had no meat to get them through the winter, she felt the pressure even more. She set to work cleaning their harvest of yellow squash and slicing it, preparing it to be pickled. She also washed and cooked some tomatoes, which she poured into heated glass jars, to be stored for the winter. They couldn't afford to let any of their vegetables go to waste, and Mrs. Beverly had shown Lizzie how best to preserve each kind of vegetable and fruit.

As Celia dried her hands on her apron, someone knocked on the front screen door and called, "Celia? Lizzie? You here?"

Celia hurried down the hall from the kitchen. Crowded around the screen door stood Olean, Ruby, and their grandmother, Granny Lula Mae.

"Come in." Celia pushed the door open for them.

"Why don't we just set out here on the porch where it's cooler?" Granny Lula Mae sat down in the rocking chair on the front porch. Ruby helped Celia carry two more straight back chairs from the parlor to the front porch.

"Where's Lizzie?" Olean peered through the screen door.

"She's out back somewhere with Will and the twins. I think they were picking corn."

"His leg must be better." Olean lifted her eyebrows. She tried to look indifferent, but Celia knew she was sweet on Will.

"Oh, yes, his leg is healing nicely." She smiled, wondering if, when he saw they had company, he would climb up the porch steps and show off the scar on his leg.

"I'll go let Lizzie and Will know we have company." She went back through the house to the back door and hollered out at Will and Lizzie, who were in the garden. They waved at her, and Celia hurried back to the front porch. "Would anyone care for something to drink?" Celia asked. "We're out of coffee at the moment." And probably would be out of it until their farm sold.

"Oh, child, what would we want with coffee on a hot day like today? Don't even mention it." Granny Lula Mae fanned herself with the homemade fan she'd brought with her. Then she leaned over and spat into a tin can lined with an old handkerchief.

Celia forced herself not to let her expression show her disgust at the snuff-dipping habit. Why would anyone want to put that smelly brown powder inside their mouth so that it distorted their face, and then have to carry a cup around all day in which to spit the foul-smelling juice?

"Celia, any news about the notices you put in the newspaper?"

Ruby asked. "Has anyone come to buy the place?"

Just then Mama came to the door. Its hinges screeched lazily, and she stepped out onto the porch.

"News? No." Celia squirmed on her hard wooden chair and gave Ruby a pointed look. She shook her head. *Please change the subject.*

Ruby stared at her, then Mama.

Mama's hair stood out from her head like she hadn't brushed it in days, which she probably hadn't. She stared blandly at their guests, then sat down in the remaining empty chair.

"Hey there, Mrs. Wilcox. You're shore looking good today."

Granny Lula Mae's pitying, sing-song greeting gave Celia a sinking feeling along with a pang of guilt at the realization that perhaps she should pay more attention to her mother and at least brush her hair for her.

"How're you feeling, honey?" Granny Lula Mae reached over and patted Mama's arm with a wrinkled, age-spotted hand.

"Fine." Mama nodded, a slightly puzzled look in her eyes.

"Now don't you be worried. You got a fine boy in Will, and you're still young. You might marry again."

Celia's heart stopped. Would Mama start crying? Would she scream at the old woman? But Mama simply gave Granny a slightly annoyed look, folded her hands in her lap, and stared out across the front yard.

Ruby must have seen it as a good time to change the subject, because she said, "Celia, have you seen the wanted posters? The ones with the hooded horseman on them?"

"The hooded horseman? Oh, yes, I saw one."

"I've heard tell that he stopped a group of men from hanging a black man. He cut the rope with a rifle bullet and they both escaped from a dozen men, all armed."

Celia leaned forward, feeling intrigued in spite of herself. "Why would he do that?"

"Didn't want them men to hang him, I reckon." Ruby shrugged.

"But if you ask me, he should have let them hang him."

"But what if he was innocent?" That's what Truett believed. "A man shouldn't be hanged if he hasn't had a trial. It's against the law."

Ruby's eyes were big and round. "I heard it was the sheriff who was hanging him. Should a man keep the sheriff from hanging a black man if he's a mind to?"

"Well, yes, if the sheriff hasn't made sure the man had the benefit of a trial." Celia sat straighter in her chair when she realized Ruby thought the sheriff should be able to do anything he wanted. "A sheriff is entrusted to uphold the law, not invent it. That's against federal statutes."

Ruby's mouth hung ajar as she stared at Celia with a mixture of surprise and confusion.

"The sheriff shouldn't set himself up as the judge, jury, and executioner. It isn't right. What if the man was innocent and it could be proven in a court of law?"

"Well, I reckon you're right, Celia, but don't let anybody hear you say that about Sheriff Suggs."

"If the Negro's guilty," Granny Lula Mae spoke up, "he ought to be hanged, says I."

"That's for a judge and jury to decide." Celia tried to keep her voice at a respectful level and tone, since Granny Lula Mae was her elder and Celia didn't want to offend her. But who might the hooded horseman be? Was he simply someone who didn't want this sheriff to get away with killing a man who hadn't had a fair trial? Or did he know the man in question and want to save him because he was innocent?

Celia's mind flashed back to the day she'd arrived in Bethel Springs. She'd sat on Truett Beverly's buggy seat, seen fury flash in his eyes when he told her that James Burwell was his friend and would never hurt a woman. Truett wouldn't have allowed the sheriff to hang James Burwell. He would have stopped him.

Was it possible . . .? Was Truett Beverly the hooded horseman?

CHAPTER 16

Celia's blood roared in her ears. Surely she was being silly, jumping to a ridiculous conclusion. How could Truett Beverly, the town doctor, be this notorious hooded horseman? But she couldn't get the thought out of her head.

Celia swallowed. "Who was the colored man they tried to hang?"

"James Burwell."

She knew that already, but hearing the man's name seemed to confirm her suspicions.

Ruby leaned close again. "And the woman he supposedly tried to force himself on was the sheriff's own daughter, Almira Suggs. Our schoolteacher. That's what the sheriff don't want everybody to know."

Had Almira been molested? She did indeed look like a woman with some sort of trouble on her mind. But if she'd been attacked, how could Truett defend the man? None of it made sense. Surely Truett wouldn't risk his life to save a man like that.

And surely Almira wouldn't falsely accuse anyone of such a crime.

"And folks say," Ruby went on, "that the hooded horseman attacked Sheriff Suggs and Curtis while they was trying to get James Burwell's daddy to tell them where he went to."

Purely gossip. Hearsay.

But some of it had to be true, or else there'd be no wanted poster and no five hundred dollar reward for a hooded horseman.

She knew for a fact that Sheriff Suggs was looking for James Burwell and that James was accused of assaulting a woman. She'd heard the sheriff with her own ears.

Could Truett be mistaken about his friend's character?

She cleared her throat. "No matter what, it's wrong to hang a man without a fair trial. 'Vengeance is mine, saith the Lord.'"

"Look-a here, missy." Granny Lula Mae shook her bony finger at Celia. "Back during the war, there weren't no fair trials. If a man attacked or murdered somebody, it was up to the men of the community to make sure justice was done and decent folks was protected.

"The Yankees controlled this whole place, from the Tennessee line to The Tennessee River south of Huntsville, and do you think for one minute the Yankees was gone hang a man if he weren't a Southerner? No, sir, they never done it. Why, Captain Frank Gurley hisself went and got a man out of the jail what had killed a whole family, mother, a grown girl, three little girls, and a little boy."

Granny fixed her narrowed eyes on Celia, reminding her of a hawk, with her crooked nose and thin lips. "Captain Gurley made shore justice was done. He sneaked up to the jail, got around them Yankee guards, and took that prisoner out. The jailer, he was a good Christian man from Killingsworth Cove, and he didn't give Captain Gurley no lip. He was glad to give up his prisoner to him. His wife even went and found the rope and give it to Captain Gurley. He took that man out to the woods and hanged him. And we was all grateful."

Her face was bland as she rocked back and forth in the wooden rocker.

Celia said quietly, "There's no war going on now. Life is more civilized, and we should allow the justice system to do what it's there for. We have no need of taking the law into our own hands now."

"That be true enough," Granny Lula Mae said softly.

Celia was pleasantly surprised to hear the old woman agree with her. She didn't want to come across as disrespectful—or get the rough side of Granny Lula Mae's tongue.

Celia was afraid to ask, but asked anyway. "Does anyone think they know who the hooded horseman is?"

Ruby's eyebrows lifted. "It's a mystery. Don't you think it's exciting? The most exciting thing that's happened in Bethel Springs in a long time."

"Yes, a mystery." Her mind went back to Truett. If he was the one thwarting the sheriff, what would happen to him? He'd be caught, sooner or later. She remembered how he had pretended to the sheriff to be genteelly outraged at the thought of someone molesting a woman, spouting poetry at the sheriff. But when the sheriff was out of earshot, he'd adamantly defended the suspected perpetrator, James Burwell, saying he'd never hurt a woman.

It was Truett. She was sure of it.

"Celia, are you all right?" Ruby stood up and leaned over her. "You look pale. Should I fetch you some cool water?"

"No, I'm fine." Celia forced her stiff lips to smile.

Ruby trotted to the well to get her a dipperful of water anyway.

"This heat will shore 'nough wilt you down." Granny Lula Mae went on fanning and rocking.

Ruby ran up the steps, holding the dipper in both hands while a few drops spilled over the sides and onto her bare feet.

"Thank you." Celia drank some of the water then handed the

dipper back to her. Ruby drank the rest. Olean took it back to the well and hung it on the hook.

"What about Almira?" Celia couldn't resist asking. "Have you asked her what happened?"

"Not me." Ruby shook her head, her braids flapping wildly. "She was my teacher up until last year. Maybe you could ask her."

Yes, maybe I will. If Truett was risking his life, Celia wanted to know if it was for a worthy cause.

"Don't let's talk about this no more," Ruby said, her eyebrows drawn together. "Something more pleasant would perk us all up." Her face broke into a smile. "Has Dr. Beverly been to see you lately, Celia?" Ruby grinned so big Celia saw a hole where a tooth should have been in the back of her mouth.

Celia swallowed. Not exactly the change of subject she'd hoped for.

"No, he hasn't." Lizzie answered for her as she walked up the steps. She carried Tempie on her hip, with Harley trailing behind.

Olean hugged Lizzie then took Tempie out of her arms, cooing over the child.

"Lizzie." Celia gave her voice a tone of warning.

"Well, it's true." Lizzie shook her finger and glared at Celia. "He hasn't been to see her once since the dance. She must have hurt his feelings."

Celia glared back. *Hush your mouth, Lizzie,* she wanted to say. Like the grouchy big sister she was.

"Aw, don't get riled." Lizzie waved a dismissive hand at her sister and then turned to Ruby, frowning and shaking her head. "Celia doesn't like to talk about Truett Beverly."

But Ruby had no lack of things to talk about, and Celia was relieved when she changed the topic. She gossiped about who was courting who, and who was in the family way, and about how exciting it was to have a mysterious hooded horseman running around saving people.

Celia sat back and tried not to speak or attract attention to herself as she ruminated. And when Granny announced it was time to go, Celia was able to give them all a genuine smile, as Granny got up from the rocking chair and took her spit cup with her.

But her smile was short-lived, because as the hooded horseman, Truett was in danger.

~

ALMIRA SUGGS CAME AT NINE O'CLOCK ON THURSDAY MORNING, bringing five of her favorite books. Celia rarely read novels, preferring to read history books and collections of essays or sermons. But she was so caught up in Almira's enthusiasm for a novel called *Persuasion* by British authoress, Jane Austen, that she promised to read it.

"It's about a girl," Almira explained, "whose friend persuades her not to marry a man because her family disapproves of him. After a few years he comes back a successful sea captain."

Later, as Celia walked Almira down the lane, she was still trying to work up the courage to ask what had happened between Almira and James Burwell. As they strolled slowly, Almira said, "Just like the heroine, I'm in love with someone my father disapproves of."

"Oh?" Her heart leapt.

Almira smiled wanly. "I'm not so sure it will work out as well for me as it did in Jane Austen's novel. But I shouldn't talk about it." She shook her head, tears welling in her eyes. She stopped and faced Celia. "I'm not sure I'll be able to teach this year. The school needs a teacher. Would you be willing to take over for me?"

"Me?" Celia stared back at Almira, disappointed in the abrupt change of topic. "I don't think so. I'm planning to go back to work —in Nashville—in September. Isn't there someone else who could do it?"

"Perhaps." A deep crease brought Almira's eyebrows together.

Celia suspected something was worrying her besides simply who was going to take her place as the town's teacher. She laid a hand on Almira's shoulder. "Are you in trouble? I promise I won't tell a soul if you wish to confide in me."

Almira nodded. Tears swam in her eyes, then slipped down her cheeks.

"I'm in love with James Burwell. My Daddy accused him of raping me and even tried to hang him, but James would never do such a thing."

Almira covered her face with her hands and cried while Celia kept her hand on her shoulder, hoping it comforted her.

When Almira lifted her tear-stained face, she pinned Celia with a fierce look. "My father should be proud to have a son-in-law who is a scientist, don't you think? James is a botanist, an inventor. A man who is good and kind. But because his skin is the wrong color—" her voice broke on a sob.

"I'm so sorry, Almira. It doesn't make sense to me, either. Society is cruel. But you're right. A man's skin color shouldn't matter. God judges the heart."

Almira leaned her head on Celia's shoulder as Celia slipped her arm around her. "Thank God you understand." Tears continued to drip from her eyes. "There is something worse, and if you turn away and never speak to me again, I will understand. But . . . I think I may be pregnant."

Celia bit back the gasp that rose into her throat. Her face prickled at the thought of being with child and unmarried.

"And if I am, and if my father finds out, not being able to teach school will be the least of my worries."

Celia had to work to keep her expression neutral, telling herself to react with compassion instead of judgment. She had heard of unmarried women having children, but she'd never known any personally. And it wouldn't help Almira to see her looking shocked.

"And now my father has forced James to flee for his life. I don't know where he is, and I miss him so much."

Celia kept her arm around Almira's shoulder. Celia had never been in a situation in which she could imagine being tempted in such a way. Before her kiss with Truett Beverly, she'd never understood. How was a man able to persuade a woman to give away her virtue? But Truett's kiss had stirred feelings inside her that she could imagine leading to something much beyond a few kisses.

No, she shouldn't condemn Almira any more than Jesus had condemned the woman caught in adultery and thrown at his feet.

"Is there any way I could help?"

"There's nothing you can do." Almira shook her head and wiped her eyes with her hands.

Celia handed her a handkerchief.

"Thank you." Almira laughed nervously. "I must have forgotten mine." She wiped her face and nose. "There is one thing you can do for me. If I'm unable to teach, you could step in for me."

"I'm not sure I'll be here, but if I am, I will do it for you."

"I must be going. I've bothered you with my troubles for too long."

Celia's heart swelled against her chest as she stared at Almira. The girl had no one, no mother or siblings, only a father, and he hated the man she loved. What would her father do if he found her pregnant? Celia shuddered.

"If you need anything, Almira—and I mean this—please come to me. I'll do whatever I can. If you need a place to stay or anything else."

"Thank you. That means so much to me." Almira threw her arms around her. "I've only known you for a short time, but I treasure your friendship, Celia." She pulled back and smiled a tremulous smile. "I'll go now, but thank you for the books and for listening to me."

"You're welcome."

They waved good-bye.

Truett was right. James hadn't forced himself on anyone. She tried to picture Truett Beverly putting on the black hood and riding out to save his friend. Brave, indeed. Maybe crazy. And a little romantic too, like a story in a book. But then, he did love to spout poetry.

The more she thought of Truett Beverly, the harder her heart pounded. She had to tell him to be careful. If she had figured out that he was the hooded horseman, surely others would too. Truett was too good to die at the hands of an evil sheriff like Suggs. She'd never met anyone like Truett before—handsome, kind, brave, and good.

But she mustn't think this way. Look what had happened to Almira.

It was best if women stayed away from men.

But she had to warn Truett to be careful and not to don the hood and cape again. If she had a chance to warn him but didn't take it, she'd never forgive herself if he was killed.

CHAPTER 17

Truett slapped the new medical journal closed in disgust. It had arrived in the morning mail, but he couldn't concentrate on reading when his mind kept bringing the thought of Celia Wilcox between him and the page.

Why couldn't someone get violently ill, or split their head open? Anything to give him something to do. Not that he really wanted to see anyone hurt, but he'd already straightened his shelves, dusted the jars of tonics and elixirs and remedies, and looked over his inventory of medical supplies. He needed something to do.

He wished he'd never laid eyes on Celia Wilcox.

Well, that wasn't entirely true—which was the whole problem. Every time he saw her he was sorely tempted to forget his promise to himself to stay away from her. Even at church—especially at church—the memories would appear before his mind's eye, memories of the Fourth of July dance, the way she felt in his arms, and their kiss. How was he ever going to get her out of his mind? Obviously, she was completely unaffected by him.

Although, remembering the way she reacted to his kisses . . .

No, he mustn't remember. *She* had obviously forgotten.

The longer he stayed away from her, the more difficult it became to think on anything but her. He was like a drunk wishing for that next drink, longing for it. Maybe if he could talk to her one more time, let her insult him and tell him she didn't care for him, he'd start to dislike her. Then he could quit these confounded, Celia-induced delirium tremens.

Truett growled and tossed the journal aside. Sure, he could face down a bunch of armed men and risk his life, but one disagreeable, unpredictable young woman had sent him reeling.

But she wasn't disagreeable, not really. She had come here, a place she didn't want to be, to help her family. No, she was vibrant and beautiful and intelligent, with a mind of her own. And yet, he'd seen her be vulnerable and sweet too. There was so much there that he wanted to explore, and he wanted her to want to know him as well.

Truett was tired of these thoughts. He grabbed his hat and coat. A ride to clear his head, some fresh air—that was what he needed.

He burst out the door, heading for the livery to get his horse.

~

CELIA HOED BETWEEN THE ROWS OF PURPLE-HULL PEAS, CHOPPING and leveling the little shoots of green grass that sprouted here and there between the leafy vegetable plants. It had finally rained, which their plants needed, but now the grass was threatening to take over.

She still hadn't worked up the nerve to talk to Truett, and two weeks had passed since she'd sent the notices to the Huntsville and Nashville newspapers about their farm and horses for sale. Still no response. A week ago, out of desperation, she'd sent the advertisement to a newspaper in Birmingham and one in Decatur, but still nothing. Even though it only cost a few cents to run the ads, especially in the weekly newspapers, she couldn't keep using up the family's money on newspaper notices. They were down to their last five dollars. She lay in bed at night, unable to sleep for thinking about their situation. Things were looking desperate. She might have to give up her savings for the family's survival.

Celia slashed at another weed, then grabbed one that was as high as her knee. She tugged until it gave way, its roots snapping and sending her backward a step.

Her breath came fast, but not fast enough to satisfy her lungs. Perhaps it was the humid heat stifling her. She stopped to rest. Leaning on her hoe handle, she wiped her forehead with a handkerchief.

Would she end up as Bethel Springs's next schoolteacher?

Perhaps it was the heat that made her feel so sick she wondered if her breakfast biscuit would come back up. But the thought of facing a roomful of children of various sizes and ages frightened her more than she cared to admit. Harley and Tempie were handful enough. They were too young to go to school for at least another year. She loved the little twins. They were her brother and sister and she was barely able to handle them. What if she had to teach two dozen Harleys and Tempies? She'd almost rather face a road full of rattlesnakes.

She looked up. Lizzie stood at the edge of the pea patch, pausing in her picking to patiently wipe Tempie's hands while the child sniffled back her tears. Harley stood nearby, squealing about a toad he had caught.

Celia bit her lip. She loved her family and had come to help Lizzie out of love, but she wasn't the "cheerful giver" her sister was. Lizzie never complained, but if Celia was completely honest with herself, there was a bit of resentment alongside the love that had made her give up her job in town because her Mama was sitting around grieving herself to death.

Was it right to feel animosity toward her own mother for taking her father's death so hard? *Maybe I'm just not a very good person.* All Celia did was fuss and fume. She didn't even like her own company these days.

Tears stung her eyes. She wanted to cry, to break down and sob out her frustration at feeling trapped, and the shameful realization that she wasn't the "good" person she always thought she was. Lizzie was sweet and generous and uncomplaining, while Celia was grouchy and ambitious.

She blinked to keep the tears at bay as she scraped at the stubborn green weeds, making miniscule progress down the long row of their garden. What was the use anyway? The grass and weeds would never stop growing, never stop plaguing the garden, fighting and choking the life out of everything.

"Celia! I've got the mail!" Will waved a letter in the air from the edge of the back yard.

Perhaps it was good news for a change. She dropped the hoe and ran. Of course it was good news. God would not leave them here, would not make her stay. He'd made a way for her to get back to Nashville.

Will handed her the envelope and she tore it open. She read quickly, her eyes scanning the words. The writer of the letter was a man offering her an amount for the farm based solely on the acreage, but the amount was pitiful. Barely one-fourth the price her father had paid for the farm. The offer wasn't even enough to pay rent for a decent house for two years, much less buy a house outright.

Celia looked away from Will's hopeful expression.

Tears pricked her eyes as she clenched the letter in her fist.

"What does it say?" Will stared up at her, his blond hair messy after his ride to town.

She wanted to scream, but tears rose faster and drowned the urge. She placed the wadded letter into Will's hand and stalked away, her head high, her shoulders straight, hoping no one knew she was about to break into sobs.

When she was out of sight of the house, Celia ran. She ran up the hill to her father's grave, fell to her knees, and let out her fury in sobs.

"Stupid man. Who does he think we are? That we would take such a paltry sum for the only home we have." She pounded her fists on the hard ground by Daddy's headstone until shards of pain shot through her hand. She leaned forward, staring at her father's grave.

"Why, Daddy? Why did you have to die? I'm so angry." The sobs started again, shaking her shoulders. They finally stopped and she clenched her fists. "You should never have brought them here. You should never have left us. Now what can we do?"

She looked up at the silent tree branches, tears still dripping from her eyes. She shouldn't complain, shouldn't rail at her poor father. It wasn't as if he'd chosen to die. And it was the utmost foolishness to blame God and accuse Him of not caring. But why was He letting this happen? Her plans of a year ago seemed to have been burned to ashes, all but hopeless. How could things have changed so quickly? *God, why?*

Her father's gravestone seemed to mock her, whispering that her mother had wasted the family's money on the white marble obelisk. She had to get away from it. She didn't want to see it anymore or think these thoughts.

She scrambled to her feet and began walking, she wasn't sure where. She walked toward the woods along the ridge, which was mostly covered in grass and pale broom straw, her hatless head absorbing the full heat of the sun.

She made her way down the side of the ridge, toward the trees and the shade. Then she wandered aimlessly through the heavily wooded area. She wasn't even sure if she was still on her family's land, or if she'd wandered onto the Beverlys' wide-ranging acreage. She kept her mind off thoughts she didn't want to think by concentrating on the varying trees and their different-shaped leaves, the wild blackberry vines and their thorns, or the textures of the trees' bark. Gradually, her heart was soothed and her tears dried, making her skin feel tight.

Celia took deep breaths, inhaling the freshness of nature. Here there was no pungent manure to assault her nose, no children crying or screaming or demanding to be fed or washed or left alone. Here, she didn't have to see Lizzie working harder than any fourteen-year-old they'd grown up with in their city-bred world, or Will limping on his hurt leg. Here, Mother didn't sit around looking as if she had abandoned them mentally, emotionally, and for all practical purposes. Here, none of those things left her feeling guilty or sad or desperate.

She lifted a branch and stepped under it. Just then she noticed a dark opening hid in the side of a little hill.

A cave!

She couldn't remember Will or any of the children mentioning it, perhaps because they were supposed to stay on their own land and not wander onto other people's property. Did anyone else know about it?

Celia had heard of Indians in the area using caves for storage and shelter. Could there be something interesting inside, some old pottery or perhaps pictures, painted on the walls? She went inside.

The hollow sound of dripping water greeted her. The floor of the cave was solid, but bumpy, its walls rounding up into an arch over her head. Several yards away, light streamed in from above, probably from a hole in the cave ceiling. Cautiously, she proceeded. A few wet spots showed where water continually seeped through the rock walls.

She soon reached the hole in the ceiling. On the floor beneath it were a few sticks and dirt and debris from the outside world. Farther in, the cave narrowed and the ceiling lowered, so that she had to bend down to keep from bumping her head on the rock. Then she came to what seemed like a little round room, and there the cave ended.

As she turned to leave, her eye caught sight of a black bundle lying on the floor, tucked against the wall in the little cavern. She bent over to pick it up. Carrying it closer to the light streaming in through the hole, she realized it was two things. When she lifted them, she gasped..

In one hand she held a black hood, complete with eye holes. In the other, a long black cloak.

The hooded horseman's disguise.

The longer she stared at them, the more her hands shook. Her first impulse was to throw them down and run away. But she forced herself to take a deep breath.

Perhaps there was a clue as to who owned these things. Maybe they didn't belong to Truett after all.

She carefully looked over the material, but what was she looking for? It wasn't as if she would find his name sewn inside. She tried to imagine Truett wearing the hood.

Suddenly, she knew how to find out if it was Truett's or not. Before she could change her mind, she pressed the hood against her face and breathed in its scent.

The memory of kissing Truett flooded her senses as she inhaled the bergamot and rosemary cologne mixed with the scent that was uniquely his.

She held the hood against her cheek and closed her eyes, breathing in his smell. More images of Truett Beverly floated before her. She could almost feel his arms around her.

"God, please don't let Sheriff Suggs kill him. Please help me talk to him." The urge to protect him gripped her. Perhaps he wouldn't have need of the hood and cloak again. But what if he did? She couldn't live with herself if something happened to him and she didn't tell him that he should not be risking his life like this.

She couldn't be seen with the incriminating items, so she balled them up and left them where she'd found them, then scurried out of the cave to find Truett.

~

C ELIA RODE TOWARD TOWN ON O LD S ALLIE. H ER HEART BEAT FAST as she contemplated what she was about to do. She'd hardly slept at all last night thinking about what might happen if he rode out again to try to thwart Sheriff's Suggs' evil actions. It was only a matter of time before the sheriff would catch him.

If only she didn't have to face him. Truett must still be angry with her, and she couldn't blame him. It had been over three weeks since the night of the dance and their kiss. They had both worked hard to avoid each other.

She had to ask him to be careful, but how much should she tell him? Should she be vague and just say he should be careful? That wouldn't make any sense. He wouldn't know what she was talking about. She would have to tell him she knew his secret. And to tell his secret, she would have to get him alone, completely alone, where no one else could hear their conversation.

Old Sallie whinnied and bobbed her head up and down. Her own nerves were making the horse nervous.

She had to get the mail anyway, and then she would go to Truett's office and speak with him. But as she came into sight of Main Street, she saw him helping his mother down from her buggy, with Griff standing nearby.

Now how was she going to speak to Truett privately with his mother around?

She couldn't avoid them. Mrs. Beverly was already looking up.

"Well, if it isn't Celia Wilcox!" Mrs. Beverly let Truett place her on her feet.

Truett glanced up, his eyes going wide at the sight of her, then closing for two full seconds.

Celia tried not to dwell on his reaction.

"Mrs. Beverly! How are you today?"

"Oh, I'm very well, you darling thing. Come over here and tell us the news."

Celia hopped down off her horse before Truett's mother told him to go help her dismount. She smiled her brightest fake smile at them.

Mrs. Beverly took her hand and held it out, looking her up and down. "My, how pretty you are, Celia!" She gave her son a sly look out of the corner of her eye. "Doesn't she look pretty, Truett?"

Truett did not smile. "Yes, she looks very pretty."

A stab of pain pierced her heart at his grudging monotone. But she had to keep her mind on her plan.

"Thank you, Dr. Beverly." She flashed her smile at him, then turned her attention back to Mrs. Beverly. "How is your garden faring in this hot weather?"

"Oh, honey, it's wilting like a plucked violet. This July heat is bad, but August is usually worse. But then it'll be winter before you know it and we'll all be complaining about the cold." She laughed and clasped Celia's hands. "You must come up to the house and see me. I told Lizzie I would show her how to make a pie crust. She says hers never turn out right. And I'll come over and bring you some of my blackberry dumplings. Truett here says they're his favorite, the best thing I make."

Mrs. Beverly's mouth smiled but her eyes seemed to drill right through Celia, no doubt trying to figure out if Celia cared for her son or was just being heartless. Her cheeks began to burn. Truett scuffed his feet, coughed, and cleared his throat.

Obviously the conversation was over, but Celia was determined to speak to Truett. Since his mother was standing there waiting for her to leave.

"Thank you, Mrs. Beverly." She spoke quickly while edging away. "You're very sweet to us. Good day, Mrs. Beverly. Dr. Beverly."

A frown tugged the corners of his mouth down. She'd displeased him by calling him Dr. Beverly, no doubt. But surely he couldn't expect her to address him by his first name in front of his mother.

As they started to turn away, Celia had an idea. "Oh, Truett—I mean, Dr. Beverly—Will was wondering if you could come by this evening and help him." Her face burned hotter at the way he and his mother were looking at her. They must see right through her ruse to get Truett to her house. *But I'm only trying to save him!*

"Will has been trying to figure out what kind of animal has been stealing the eggs in the henhouse, and last night it killed one of our hens."

"Probably a possum." Truett stared back at her.

Celia waited for him to say he would come by, but when the silence stretched a few seconds, she added, "So you'll come and help Will?"

"Of course." He nodded, his eyes only a little less suspicious than before.

He loved Will. He would come for Will's sake.

"Thank you so much. Will's been missing you. He'll be so glad to see you. Good-bye."

Celia hurried away, her face burning.

She took a deep breath as she tied Old Sallie to the hitching post and walked inside, hoping the postmaster would think her red cheeks were simply from the heat.

An uncomfortable heaviness settled in her chest when she thought about how obvious Truett had made it that he no longer liked her. He probably considered her a cruel flirt. No wonder he didn't even smile at her. No wonder his mother was trying to read her thoughts, to find out if Celia was going to hurt her son. Again.

She couldn't stand to think about that.

Celia asked for her mail.

"None today, Miss Wilcox. Sorry."

She nodded, then turned and walked out. Her disappointment at getting no mail was thrust to the back of her mind as she passed Truett's office. But his mother was inside. No opportunity to warn him now. She'd have to try again tonight.

CHAPTER 18

Truett arrived after supper. He didn't come inside, only came to the back door and asked for Will. Will ran out and they walked around the back yard in the fading light.

Celia watched them out the back window, trying to wash up the supper dishes. Truett and Will talked, walking around the henhouse, disappearing from sight for several minutes at a time.

All right, I've got him here, God. Now how am I going to get him alone to talk to him? Somehow she had to get him in the house, or on the front porch. No, the front porch might remind him of their kiss. He'd really wonder what she was up to. First she kisses him, then she tells him he can't court her, then she avoids him for weeks, now she wants to talk to him alone?

He'd think she had lost her mind, or worse, that she was a tease. And that was the last thing she'd ever wanted to be known as.

But she had to speak to him. She had to convince him there were other ways to make sure the sheriff didn't hurt innocent people. There had to be a way, a due process of the judicial system that would force the sheriff to uphold the law and not break it. She had to convince Truett that what he was doing was foolish and was going to get him killed.

Just like Father.

Will opened the back door and stepped into the kitchen.

"Where's Truett?" Celia's voice sounded breathy and desperate. She tried to wipe the anxiety from her expression.

"Went home." Will picked up an apple from the bowl on the table and bit into it.

Celia closed her eyes, her stomach twisting. Had she really lost her chance to talk to him and warn him? Perhaps she should run after him.

"But he'll be back tomorrow night."

The breath rushed out of her in a sigh of relief. She'd get another chance.

"He's going to help me catch that mean old possum. Said it must be a huge one." Will crunched into the crisp apple again.

This time she'd make sure she took advantage of her opportunity. She wouldn't let him get away again without talking to him.

~

CELIA AWOKE IN THE MIDDLE OF THE NIGHT, SHAKING ALL OVER, even though she'd escaped the horror of her dream.

Truett was riding his black horse wearing the hood and cloak from the cave. He rode into the forest until he reached a clearing. Sheriff Suggs stood with several men. They led a horse and its rider toward a giant tree, where a noose hung from its lowest branch. Sheriff Suggs slipped the rope over the person's head and around their neck. Then Celia saw the victim's face.

Annie. The little girl Celia had saved from the rattlesnake!

She wanted to scream, *"No! Stop!"*, but the paralysis of dreaming would not let her intervene.

Truett rode directly to the men with white hoods and Sheriff Suggs raised a gun, pointing it at Truett.

The gun fired once, twice, three times.

Truett jerked backward and tumbled to the ground.

He lay on the ground, three holes in his chest.

Sheriff Suggs walked over and yanked the black hood off. Truett's eyes were closed and his face was ashen.

Celia shuddered, squeezing her eyes shut against the memory of the dream. Each breath came hard and fast, and her heart raced like mad inside her chest.

"Celia?" Lizzie stirred beside her and opened her eyes.

"I was only dreaming," Celia whispered. "Go back to sleep."

She tried to calm her breathing, but the image of Truett's face wouldn't go away. She lay back down, but every time she closed her eyes, she saw Truett's face again, looking as gray as her father's had at his funeral.

Pain throbbed in her chest. She didn't want to admit it, even to God, but she cared so much about Truett that she was afraid it would kill her if something happened to him.

Was she destined to become like her mother? A walking dead woman, simply because her husband had died?

And Truett wasn't even her husband.

Celia shivered and clutched the blanket tighter. She was a coward either way she looked at it. She was a coward for being afraid to love Truett, and a coward for being so terrified that she would turn out like her mother if he died.

She pressed her hand against her heart, trying not to disturb Lizzie. She should probably just get up, since there was no way she'd be able to sleep anymore with these thoughts churning inside her head. She was also too hot and sweaty. Maybe she was sick?

Thunder rumbled in the distance. A storm was on the way. No wonder the air seemed so heavy and hot and oppressive.

Soon, flashes of lightning illumined the sky outside the

bedroom window. It was probably almost morning, but the coming storm would keep them from seeing the sun for some time yet.

A loud crack erupted, seeming to come from just outside the window. A rumbling boom followed.

Lizzie woke up. Celia hugged her, feeling comforted by her sister's arms.

"Oh, Lord, save us from the storm outside." *And save me from the storm inside.*

$\sim$

TRUETT FROWNED AS HE WALKED TO THE WILCOX PLACE. THE storm had knocked over a length of fence around their cow pasture, but he had fixed that fairly quickly.

He wished he didn't care how the Wilcox farm had fared, but he did. He tried to tell himself he cared only because of Will and Lizzie and the twins. They needed someone to look out for them. But he grudgingly admitted he cared about Celia too. Even if she was cold and unfeeling, then maddeningly flirtatious. Fickle creature.

If he was truthful with himself, he didn't believe she was cold and unfeeling. But why did she not want to allow him to court her after she had kissed him the way she had?

None of it made sense. And yesterday she had kept standing at the window and staring out at him while he and Will had talked over what to do about the henhouse thief. He had pretended he didn't notice her, but why was she staring at him?

He should forget about her.

He'd never had much trouble forgetting about any of the other girls he'd known. What was different about Celia Wilcox?

For one thing, most other girls had disappointed him in some way, whether it be through a shallow way of thinking or a lack of character. Celia was neither dull nor shallow and, while she may be fickle, she was not without character.

She'd acted so different yesterday, smiling at him, seeming so anxious to have him come to help Will. It was as if she wanted to say something but was afraid to in front of his mother.

He was probably imagining things. She was only concerned about Will and knew he was missing him.

Well, he wouldn't play the fool for her. Not again.

Truett scowled as he realized, yes, he would play the fool for her again. It wouldn't take much coaxing from her, either.

He neared the house and saw Will at the well. The boy looked up and called, "Hey, Truett! Come see what happened to our tree!"

Tree limbs were scattered all over the yard, but they were small ones. Will led him around the house. The giant pecan tree, whose massive trunk stood only a few feet from the kitchen door, had been pulled up by its roots—but not all the way—by the powerful wind. The tree was leaning, as though one root stronger than the others had refused to break in the face of the raging wind and was holding the tree at a forty-five-degree angle . . . over the house.

Truett scrubbed his unshaven cheek with his hand. "Oh. My."

The tree didn't budge, but in his mind, Truett saw it toppling the rest of the way over and smashing the small farmhouse in less time than it would take to yell "Timber!"

And smashing whoever was inside.

Will spoke up. "How do you think we'll get her down without hitting the house?"

"We'll figure out a way." There were ways to make a tree fall where you wanted it to, but it was tricky and fairly dangerous. Even more so when it was already leaning the wrong way.

Celia hurried out the front door and down the porch steps. Her eyes were big as she stared at him—the prettiest brown eyes —and then walked straight toward him. His heart jumped in his throat at the way she pressed a hand to her chest, smiled, and said, "I'm so glad you're here."

He had to swallow, hard.

He cleared his throat, trying to shrug off the nervous heat crawling up the back of his neck. "Got yourself a little tree problem?"

She looked worried. "Do you know how we can get it down without it falling on the house?"

So . . . Celia Wilcox needed him. He shouldn't think about it that way. It wasn't gentlemanly. "I reckon I can get it taken care of for you."

"That is very kind of you."

She looked quite humble, especially compared to the way she'd looked the time she told him she didn't need him.

"What will you do? Will it take long? I'd hate for you to have to be away from your office for very long."

It would make her feel bad if he emphasized what a long, hard job this was going to be, and how he would have to be away from his office all day. But he would be chivalrous and downplay it.

"We'll take it down. The next stiff wind could send it crashing down on you."

"Oh." She looked appropriately alarmed, her hand clutching at her neck.

"Will and I will ride to town and get some help. We'll pick up some equipment while we're there and have this tree out of your way by nightfall, Lord willing."

Her eyes flitted around like she was thinking hard. Was she that uncomfortable with accepting his help?

"I do want to thank you, Truett. I know it is a sacrifice on your part, and you're so good to help us."

He'd never heard her sound this humble or grateful. He was enjoying it way too much. *Here I go breaking all my promises to myself.* "It's nothing, Miss Celia." Truett tipped his hat as his chest swelled.

"Let's get going, Tru." Will stood impatiently at his side.

"Wait." Celia's eyebrows still drew together, her eyes revealing concern. She opened her mouth to speak, then closed it. Finally she said, "You'll be back?"

He nodded, willing her to speak what was on her mind. After a moment of hesitation, she simply smiled and walked back toward the house.

Truett shook his head at her strange behavior. At least she wasn't giving him the cold shoulder.

Once he and Will were in town, he put a note on his office door that he would be at the Wilcox place all day. Then he went to Greenbrier Lee's blacksmith shop to borrow a winch and some rope. Fortunately, when he explained the situation to Greenbrier and Grady Skidmore, who was passing by, they volunteered to come along and help.

They rode back to the Wilcox place and the four of them set to work on the tree.

~

"CELIA, WHAT'S THE MATTER WITH YOU?" LIZZIE SQUINTED AT HER sister. "You're acting as nervous as a mouse under a cat's paw."

"I am not!" When she realized she was wringing her hands, she clasped them firmly together.

"What ails you lately? If you want to tell Truett you're sorry and you didn't mean whatever it was you did to make him stop coming around, then I'm all for it." Lizzie lifted her chin.

Celia moved away from the window. Lizzie had obviously caught her staring out at the men—well, it was actually only Truett she'd been staring at—while wringing her hands like a ninny.

Lizzie laughed and went off to the root cellar to get some sweet potatoes.

Celia and Lizzie were busy cooking, making a huge noon meal

to feed the men who had come to help them fell the dangerously tipping tree. She'd said a prayer that they would be able to take it down safely and that no one would get hurt, but an even bigger worry was that Truett would get away again before she could talk to him. And she couldn't exactly say anything to him with those other men around. How could she know that they wouldn't betray Truett?

Since Lizzie had gone to check on Mother, Celia allowed herself another peek outside. Truett's hat was pushed back off his forehead and the top two buttons of his blue chambray work shirt were unbuttoned. He hadn't shaved this morning, and the stubble gave him a rough, outdoorsman look that put a catch in her throat.

Truett was taking his turn pulling the long two-handled saw, with Greenbrier the blacksmith on the other handle. They settled into a rhythm.

"I was thinking . . ." Lizzie entered the kitchen.

Celia spun around and dropped the tin cup she was holding. It clattered on the floor as Celia bent and snatched it up. "What?"

"Are you staring at Truett again?"

"Why would I do that?"

Lizzie smirked. Celia cringed inwardly at her sister's knowing look. She feigned an aloof expression.

"As I was saying, we probably shouldn't let Mama see the tree. It might frighten her. We could bring her meals to her room, instead of calling her out. I thought I'd get her a cup of tea."

"Whatever you think, Lizzie. That's fine."

Lizzie walked past her to the screen door and gazed out. "How are they going to make it fall away from the house?"

Celia came to stand beside her. Since Lizzie was looking, she could too, couldn't she?

"The way Will explained it, they've cut a wedge out of the other side, the side they want it to fall toward."

Truett straightened his back and stepped away from the saw to give Will and Grady a turn.

Celia went on. "They tied one rope to the tree and attached it to a winch. Now they're cutting it from this side at a sharp angle. They'll cut all the way through to the wedge on the other side."

Truett walked over to the winch at the edge of the yard.

"Truett is turning the handle to keep the tension as tight as possible. Now he's tightening the other rope, which they wound around that tree, since they only had one winch. When they get the tree cut in two, they'll pull it down using the ropes and the winch."

Lizzie sighed. "Isn't it a blessing to have such kind neighbors?" She turned her sweet, innocent smile on Celia. "Especially one as handsome as Dr. Truett Beverly?"

Celia pursed her lips at her sister.

"You have to admit," Lizzie shook her finger at her, "if it weren't for him, we would have been up a creek."

She bit the inside of her lip. Truett was undeniably a good man. Good enough to work hard all day to help out a family who neither deserved his help nor was able to reward his kindness or return the favor.

Well, he didn't look like he minded. He and the other two men were laughing and slapping each other on the back. Will was having a great time, too. He seemed to have grown two inches with the pride of working alongside the three men, doing an equal share.

"Let's go get them some water." Lizzie's face lit up and she tugged on Celia's arm. "Come on! Show a little gratitude for all they're doing for us."

She let Lizzie drag her outside to the well. They each drew a bucket of cool water, hung a long-handled dipper on the side, and headed toward the men.

Lizzie scurried toward Will and Grady, so Celia started for

Truett, her knees feeling a bit weak. Probably from not getting much sleep.

~

TRUETT LOOKED UP FROM THE WINCH TO SEE CELIA HEADING HIS way with a bucket of water. Then again, it was probably Lizzie who had forced her into bringing him a drink. He couldn't let himself go all soft in the head, although it was difficult any time she was around.

She smiled shyly, which was a first, and said, "Water?"

"Thanks." He took the dipper from her hand. His fingers brushed hers. He forced himself to look away from her mesmerizing brown eyes and gulped down the entire contents of the dipper.

He wiped his mouth with his sleeve and handed her the empty ladle.

She refilled it and held it out to him. He shook his head. "Thank you."

"Truett, I—" She glanced to the left where Greenbrier approached. Her lips twitched ending in a slight frown, that quickly changed back to a bland look. She turned her gaze back to him. "How are things progressing?"

What was going on inside that head of hers?

She handed the dipper to Greenbrier and he drank, spilling half of it down his already wet shirt. She handed him another one, then took a step away from him. Truett forced himself not to laugh.

"It's progressing well, I think."

"Oh, yeah, it's coming along." Greenbrier's voice boomed. Truett had often wondered if the man was naturally loud, or if the ring of his hammer, day after day, had made him slightly deaf. "We'll give it the old heave-ho before much longer."

"We certainly owe you men a debt of gratitude for your help."

She looked as if she really meant it, her head tilted at a humble angle. She glanced up at him through black lashes and Truett's heart did a flip.

"It ain't nothing, miss. I was ready for some fresh air and sunshine after banging away in that smithy!" Greenbrier's guffaw was even louder than his words.

Truett cocked his head at Celia. "Will says you killed a snake, Miss Celia."

Her cheeks turned a pretty pink, but there was pride in the tilt of her chin. "I did."

Greenbrier whistled. "With a gun? A little miss like you?"

"It was with a stick, I heard." Truett grinned.

She turned a half smile up at him.

"A stick!" Greenbrier hooted, drawing Will and Grady over.

"You must be a feisty little thing!" Greenbrier laughed again, repeating the report of Celia's snake encounter for their benefit.

Feisty? Truett allowed himself a rueful chuckle. *I'll say she is. Feisty and beautiful and way too beguiling for anybody's good.*

Will and Grady each had a drink and then wandered away with Greenbrier, still discussing rattlesnakes.

"You are feisty," Truett said quietly, studying Celia's face, "but I'd call it brave."

She shook her head. "I'm not brave." When she met Truett's gaze, a cloud descended over her expression. "You're the brave one."

His heart not only flipped, it flopped like a newly caught fish on a creek bank.

Yep, he was hooked. Again.

Will called out to Truett, "Seven rattles! This big around!" Will held up his hands to show how fat the snake was.

Celia smiled at her brother. And then, without another glance at Truett, began walking back to the house.

"Thanks for the water, Celia," he called after her.

"You're welcome. Dinner will be ready in an hour or so. We want you all to join us."

"We'll be happy to."

And when she smiled, he forgave her all, everything, the cold shoulder after the kiss, and whatever else she'd done.

There was something she wanted to tell him, something she couldn't say in front of anyone else. Could it be she had changed her mind? That she did want him to court her after all? It must be that. What else could it be?

CHAPTER 19

Celia's heart hammered as she walked toward the house. She wasn't sure how a man covered in sweat could look so good. But she was more determined than ever to warn him that his safety—his very life!—was in jeopardy.

When dinner was ready they set up a trestle table outside. Celia and Lizzie served while the men and children ate. The men ate so fast she hardly had time to sit down before they were up and working again.

A couple of hours later, while Celia was getting a blackberry cobbler ready to put in the oven, Will came to the back door.

"Truett says it's best if you all come on out of the house about now while we see if we can get this tree to fall the other way. Just in case."

Celia quickly rounded up Tempie, who was playing with her dolls, and Mother, who was sitting in her rocking chair in the bedroom. She hustled them out the door and stood with Lizzie. Harley was already outside.

Truett and the other men shouted back and forth. Carefully but efficiently, they tightened the ropes, then sawed some more, then tightened again. Already the tree was straightening. In a few more minutes it was leaning away from the house.

Truett paused in the process long enough to tell them all to move farther away, out of the tree's reach, should it fall somewhere other than where they planned for it to go.

Lizzie prayed out loud that God would keep the men—and their house—safe from the tree. Celia joined her silently. *And God, please give me a chance to talk to Truett, alone. Please don't let me seem like a tease.* She added, *And help me get back to Nashville before I fall in love with him.*

It might already be too late for that last request.

Truett pulled on one rope while Will cranked the winch. Greenbrier and Grady sawed until they all heard a loud crack. The two men scrambled out of the way.

"Will!" Truett called out. "Be ready to run!" His voice strained as he pulled on the rope.

Celia held her breath. Several more loud cracks came from the trunk of the tree as it slowly began its descent. It picked up speed and crashed to the ground in the wide expanse between Truett and Will.

The men raised a cheer loud enough to rival the huge tree's crash.

Celia let out the breath she'd been holding. Everyone was safe. The house was safe. *Thank you, God.*

Surely now the men would leave and she could catch Truett and get a private word with him. But they all just stood around, talking and congratulating each other, seemingly unconcerned about getting back to their regular work. Every once in a while, one of the men would cast a glance her direction, probably wondering why she was standing outside watching them. Finally, Celia had no choice but to go inside.

She watched from the window as the men gathered their winch and rope . . . and then lingered a bit longer at the well, getting another drink. Finally, they headed toward Greenbrier's

189

wagon and loaded their stuff on it. Truett was just coming back around with Will when Celia stepped out the back door.

"You're not leaving yet, are you?"

Will said, "He's coming back tonight after supper to help me get that possum."

"Oh. Well, I just—"

"He's got to go get cleaned up."

Truett smiled and quirked an eyebrow at her. He was about to say something teasing, she just knew it. But at least he wasn't mad at her—or worse, indifferent.

"Is there something else I can do for you?" Truett's intense gaze sent her heart to pounding again.

"No, I just—had something . . . to discuss with you."

He and Will both stared at her as if waiting for her to continue. Heat rose up her neck and into her cheeks. Why couldn't Will take a hint and leave? But she couldn't risk saying anything in front of her brother. Or the men who were waiting for him just on the other side of the house. She did her best to swallow her frustration.

"I'll talk with you tonight." Celia retreated back inside the house.

Tonight, Lord, or else I'm riding over to his house and spilling everything I know, even if I have to do it in front of Mrs. Beverly and Griff!

⁓

CELIA KNEW SHE WAS BEHAVING ERRATICALLY DURING SUPPER, BUT she didn't realize Will and Lizzie had noticed until she caught them grinning at each other.

"What?"

"Nothing," Lizzie said, and skittered away down the hall.

Will walked toward her and laid his hand on her shoulder. "It's okay, sis. You don't have to be so nervous. I'm pretty sure Truett likes you too."

It was on the tip of her tongue to ask him how he knew this. She stopped herself just in time.

"Listen here. I—" She halted the tirade she wanted to unleash, lest she humiliate herself further. But she couldn't bear to lose another chance to talk to Truett. If she didn't enlist her brother's help, she might miss her opportunity—again.

Celia took a deep breath. "The truth is, I need to talk to Truett alone tonight, just for a minute."

Will took a step back and held up his hands. "Far be it from me to come between you and your beau."

"He is not my beau." Celia kept her voice low and spoke slowly, hoping the fierceness in her tone would scare the sass out of the boy. "I just need to talk to him, all right? It isn't about me, it isn't about you, but it's important." She leaned toward his face, hoping her brother felt the implication of a threat. "Do you understand?"

"Yes, ma'am, I understand perfectly." But he never lost the silly grin on his face.

He wasn't the least bit afraid of her. And he didn't believe for a moment that she wasn't sweet on Truett.

Could she blame him when she wasn't sure herself?

Someone knocked at the back door. Celia jumped.

Will started down the hall then cupped his mouth and whispered, "Don't be nervous."

Celia glared at him and went to the door. Truett stood there looking much different than he had a few hours before. He was clean-shaven and wore a fresh white shirt. His wet hair was combed back from his face.

Celia coughed to clear her thoughts, then slipped outside to join Truett. "Will should be out soon. He's helping Harley get settled into bed."

~

NOW TRUETT WOULD FINALLY FIND OUT WHAT WAS ON HER MIND.

"Shall we take a little walk?" Truett stepped back to let her get down the back steps and then offered her his arm. When she slipped her hand inside the crook of his elbow a delicious warmth engulfed him.

They wandered slowly across the yard. Night came late this time of year, so the light from the sun still had not completely faded. Already the cicadas' nightly harangue accompanied the chirp of the crickets and the distant song of frogs down by the creek. He let the familiar sounds calm his pulse as he waited for Celia to speak.

They made their way around to the tree they had felled earlier, near the edge of the yard. She let go of his arm and turned to face him. The deepening twilight made her eyes look like polished amber stones he'd seen in a jewelry store in New York, sparkling and brilliant.

Oh, how he was reminded of their kiss. His gaze fell upon her lips, but when he forced himself to focus on her voice, he couldn't help but note the pain and discomfort in her tone, delivering the unwelcome truth that her thoughts were far from where his had gone.

"Truett, I have something to say to you, and I'm just going to say it before we get interrupted." She cast her eyes cautiously toward the house.

"I'm listening." His heart thumped hard against his chest. Was she about to tell him how sorry she was about how she had treated him?

She took a deep breath, then hesitated.

"Maybe I should sit down first." His attempt at a joke did not put her at ease. He decided he'd better, and sat down on the felled tree.

"You must be tired. Thanks for all you did to remove the danger of this tree." Her face softened as she glanced at him then stared off into the black forest.

His muscles had done more work today than in recent

memory, and he was already feeling sore, especially in his shoulders. His legs felt as though they'd been wrung out then hung to dry.

"I was glad to do it for you." Wait. He hadn't meant to say it was *for her*. But the words were out and he wouldn't take them back.

"Oh, Truett, what I want to say is that I'm worried about you." She turned her face toward him and clasped her hands in front of her.

His heart skipped a beat at her look of concern, his breath deserting him.

She spoke in a breathless whisper. "I know you're the one who saved James Burwell from being lynched."

His stomach twisted.

"I know you're the hooded horseman on the wanted posters. You must be careful." The words seemed wrenched from her throat. Her face twisted with fervency. Her brows were creased, making her appear a little afraid.

"How did you know?"

"It doesn't matter how I know. I figured it out."

"You did?" His throat grew tight.

A thrill passed through his gut at the thought that she knew him better than anyone. She had seen him not as a weak poet but as a daring hooded horseman. None of the folks he'd grown up with—not even his mother—had deduced the truth.

But Celia had.

"Don't you see?" She gazed into his eyes. "If I figured it out, someone else will, too. Or they might find your hood and cape in the cave just like I did—"

"Wait a minute. You found a black hood and cape. What makes you think they belong to me?"

She wouldn't look him in the eye and clasped and unclasped her hands.

Was this conversation about to get even more interesting?

~

CELIA BLINKED SEVERAL TIMES, TRYING TO FRAME A RESPONSE THAT would preserve her dignity. If she confessed how she'd pressed the clothing against her face, breathed in his scent, remembered their kiss . . . what little pride she had left would disappear like smoke.

"Are you saying they don't belong to you?"

"I'm not saying anything."

Celia's shoulders slumped as tension left her body. She'd finally got it out. She'd been as taut as a banjo string ever since she'd decided she had to warn him. But she still had to make him see the danger he was in and make him promise to be careful, and to secure the help of someone higher in authority than the sheriff.

"I'd just like to know how you figured all this out."

She sighed, realizing they were in for a long conversation, and sat down beside him.

"Ruby and her grandmother came over and were talking about the hooded horseman. I just got to thinking about you and how fierce you had looked when you spoke of James Burwell almost being lynched—"

"You thought I looked fierce?" Truett raised his eyebrows and smiled.

Celia shook her head at how pleased he sounded. "Anyway, I just realized that it made sense that you were the hooded horseman. They said you also attacked Sheriff Suggs, but I didn't believe that."

"And then you found my hood and cloak. How did you know they were mine?"

He turned his body so that his knee brushed hers where they sat on the big tree trunk.

"I just knew."

"How?"

"I'm not telling you." They stared each other in the eye so long Celia's eyes began to water.

The light had faded until there was little more than a glow in the sky overhead. She could still make out his features, the slight cleft in his chin and the strong, masculine line of his jaw. His intense gaze seemed to search her heart. Could he see that she had been suppressing her desire for him ever since that first day she'd met him, when the compassion in his face had created a longing in her she didn't understand? How she'd held back from admiring him, from trusting him and allowing him to court her?

She pressed her hands against her face to cool the sting in her cheeks, thankful he couldn't read her mind. But the conflict inside her made tears spring to her eyes. The truth was that she was terrified to allow herself to love him. Look what love had done to her mother! Besides, the man was doing a dangerous thing. He would most likely hang sooner or later, whenever Sheriff Suggs found out what he'd done. Then where would he be? Cold in the grave. And where would that leave anyone who loved him? Comfortless and alone.

"What are you thinking?" Truett reached out and touched her hand.

"I'm thinking that you're crazy and you're going to be killed." She could barely see through the sudden pain that was blurring her vision. Her heart twisted inside her chest. She wanted to stop her words, knowing they were irrational, but they spilled out anyway. "What were you thinking when you crossed this sheriff? Did you think you wouldn't be found out? Did you think you wouldn't be killed? What do you plan to do now?" A tear slipped from each eye and Celia swiped at them with her hand. Words were coming out that she hadn't meant to say, things she didn't know she was going to say until she heard herself say them.

"Please don't cry."

"When you get yourself killed, what good will that do? My father got himself killed with his foolishness, now you're trying to do the same thing. There has to be another way. You have to get someone from Huntsville involved, someone who can stop this sheriff from taking matters into his own hands, from lynching people. If you don't, he's going to kill you. I can't let that happen to you."

Celia pressed her lips together, knowing there was nothing she could do to control what would happen to him. Tears were still oozing down her cheeks. She blinked, willing the them to dry up.

She glanced at Truett and immediately tried to look away. But she was caught. The tenderness in his expression pierced her heart. *This man is so good and I'm so selfish, God. And such a coward.* When had she become so fearful?

Truett reached for her hand again. This time she didn't resist. His gentle fingers wrapped around hers. He never took his eyes off her face.

She had revealed too much of her thoughts and feelings. Her mind screamed at her to flee, but she couldn't resist the warmth that was flooding her chest. He was so deserving of everything good, of a good wife. He deserved someone much more perfect that she was. She shouldn't let him hold her hand. Didn't he know he deserved someone better?

They sat in silence for a minute or two. Truett finally looked down at her hand and began to rub the back of it with his thumb. His callused palm pressed against her hand, which, after a few weeks of hoeing and gardening, had a few calluses, too.

How could she fight the way she felt? Did she love him? Should she agree to let him court her?

CHAPTER 20

The way Truett stroked the back of her hand sent tingles up her arm. She shouldn't be enjoying his touch so much.

When he stopped, she opened her eyes. He was no longer looking at her, but was gazing off to the side. "When I was seven years old," he spoke slowly and deliberately, "my father and my two oldest brothers went off to fight the Yankees."

Celia studied his face. He wore a blank expression, but his serious tone made her want to hear every word.

"Father survived, but I never saw my brothers again. They were both killed at Chickamauga." He sighed and shook his head. "I was too young to go fight." He stopped again and they listened for a moment to the frogs croaking to each other from down on the creek bank.

"This whole area of North Alabama, from the Tennessee state line to the Tennessee River below Huntsville, was occupied by the Yankees for almost the entire war. They headquartered in Huntsville and raided this area regularly. Near the end of the war, they burned most of the houses around here."

His hollow expression made the air rush from her lungs. "I

didn't know." She was afraid he wouldn't go on, but finally he continued.

"One day they came, burning every plantation house they came to. When they got to us, Mama begged them to spare ours. She promised them she'd already freed all her slaves. She cried and pleaded. But . . ." he shook his head, "they burned our house to the ground."

Celia whispered, "I'm so sorry."

"Griff tried to stop them."

Celia's heart was in her throat. She ached to put her arms around him, but she was afraid he would stop talking, stop opening up to her. Every word was a precious treasure.

"Griff picked up a big rock to throw it at them. I was standing on the porch, scared to death, but Griff . . . he didn't see the Yankee soldier who came up behind him. The man pushed Griff down, and my brother hit his head on the rock he was holding. He was unconscious for a week, and when he woke up, it was obvious there was permanent damage."

"I'm so sorry."

"I was only a child. There was nothing I could do, but it hurt to know that I hadn't even tried to defend my home, my mother, or my brother. And now . . . I don't want to be someone who stands by and does nothing, not ever again."

Celia ached to comfort him, in awe that he would entrust this painful memory to her.

"I suppose the war was God's judgment against us. We deserved what happened. No man should keep another enslaved. That's the way I see it now. But how long will it take for this to be a joyful place again? How long does it take before a conquered land is allowed to prosper again? A hundred years? Two hundred?"

He stared up at the sky and she followed his gaze. A few stars had appeared.

"And when Sheriff Suggs tried to hang James, it wasn't the first time he'd executed a man without a trial. He's always done it quietly, making himself judge and jury, and nobody's stopped him." He shook his head. "After the last lynching, I decided to take matters into my own hands. And fortunately, I found out about what he was planning to do, before he tried to hang James, and I was able to save his life."

His eyes met hers with that fierceness she'd seen in him only once before. "As a little boy, there was nothing I could do," he said. "But now . . . That is why I wear the hood and cloak. And that is why I will do it again."

He rose to his feet and pulled her up with him. He lifted her hand up to his lips and kissed the backs of her fingers before pressing her hand against his chest.

An exciting tingle started in her fingertips and spread through her. Seeing the same tenderness and longing that was inside her reflected from his eyes . . . It was almost unbearable.

"Celia, let's get out of here." His voice was gruff and he squeezed her hand, bending his head so close she could feel his breath against her cheek. "I'm tired of this place, everything about it. Let's run away and get married. Marry me, Celia."

Marry? *You're going to get killed and break my heart*, a voice screamed inside her. But he was so beautiful, so noble. Could he actually want to marry her?

Her eyes focused on his lips, so close and inviting. How she wanted to kiss him and hold him and comfort him. *Lord help me, I can't resist.*

She placed her palm against his cheek. Gently drawing his face toward her and rising onto her toes, she pressed her lips to his.

The hunger in his kiss turned her inside out. He still held one of her hands imprisoned against his chest, where she could feel the thundering of his heart. He pulled her closer with his other arm.

She stroked his cheek as they kissed. The ache inside her increased and the only remedy seemed to be to keep kissing him and never stop. Slipping her hand around his neck, she buried her fingers in his still-wet hair.

He's going to leave me just like Daddy. He's going to die.

Panic gripped her. She was kissing him, precisely what she'd promised herself she wouldn't do.

The dream-image of him lying dead on the ground forced itself to the forefront of her mind. No. She couldn't bear it, couldn't bear to love him and lose him that way.

Celia pulled away and clutched at her chest. "I can't do this. I can't—" She gasped, unable to continue. She tried to pull out of his arms but he wouldn't let go.

"No," he growled. "You're not going to do this to me again."

Celia heard the pain in his voice and stopped struggling.

"I know you care for me," he said. "What is it you're so afraid of? What?"

She couldn't tell him.

He gripped her upper arms. "Tell me."

"I-I . . . I couldn't stand it if you died. And you don't seem to care." She spoke the last statement in an angry whisper. "Don't you see? Daddy died and I'm so angry." She drew in a sharp breath at her words, then choked back a sob.

"Nothing's going to happen to me, Celia. You have to trust God."

"God didn't keep my father from dying, did he? How can I trust Him?"

"You're doing all right, Celia." His eyes seemed to plead with her. "God is taking care of you and your family."

"No, I'm not all right!" Celia tried to take a deep breath to calm herself, but her chest couldn't seem to hold the air and all the hurt, too. She shook her head. "I'm not all right. I miss my father. I didn't want him to die."

He pulled her against his chest, wrapping his arms around her shoulders and holding her tight. She sobbed against his shirt. How could Daddy let himself get killed, and how could God let him die? God could have saved him. God was all-powerful. But He let him die and now she would never see her father again. He could never provide for her, never comfort or advise. He was gone.

Truett stroked her hair, murmuring, "I know, I know. It's all right."

Of course he understood. He'd lost two brothers, and Griff too —at least, the Griff he had known before the accident—and it had obviously broken his heart.

She wrapped her arms around the solidness of him. The tears seemed to have loosened the pain in her chest so that she could breathe again. She took a deep breath, still pressing her cheek against his chest. Finally, when she believed she could speak without breaking down, she said, "I'm afraid for you, Truett. I'm afraid you're going to die and leave me broken . . . like my mother." The words made her start crying again. She didn't like hearing the truth in all its stark ugliness.

"For God hath not given us the spirit of fear," Truett quoted softly, "but of power, and of love, and of a sound mind."

"I know I shouldn't be afraid." She lifted her head to look at him. "But, Truett, I—"

His lips pressed tenderly against her forehead and she forgot what she was going to say. He kissed her temple, and then his lips moved down to her cheek.

His mouth, so tender and warm, continued down to her chin, then moved to her lips, caressing gently.

"Celia? Truett? Are you out here?"

Celia instantly let go of him and stepped backward, hitting the tree trunk with the back of her leg.

Had Will seen her and Truett kissing? Her face burned and she covered her lips with her hand, afraid he would see the evidence of Truett's kiss there, where the sensation of it lingered.

Truett grabbed her by the elbow to steady her.

"We're over here!" Truett called. He whispered, bending down to her, "Celia, I—"

"I have to go in. I don't want Will to see us." She turned to run but he caught her arm and wouldn't let go.

"Wait."

She waited. When he didn't speak she turned to look at him.

"Can I come tomorrow night—after supper—just to talk?"

"Yes. But only if you promise to kiss me goodnight." She broke free of his grip and almost laughed at her own brazen words.

By the time she reached Will she had slowed to a walk. She motioned over her shoulder. "He's over there, by the tree."

As she reached the back door, Truett called out, "I promise!"

Celia laughed as she stumbled inside.

But later, after everyone else was in bed, Celia sat on the front porch with her face in her hands. "What have I done?"

Kissing Truett had felt so good, but she never should have done it! She couldn't marry him. She couldn't believe he had asked.

The question had been posed in the heat of the moment. Perhaps he might not have meant it. And she hadn't given him an answer, either.

The thought of marrying Truett terrified her, sending panic straight to her toes. At the same time, it also filled her with longing and delicious anticipation.

Celia bent over and moaned into her hands. "Oh, Lord, this is terrible." She shook her head. "*I'm* terrible."

Celia had never been one to ask her mother for advice. But right now she wished she had someone—anyone—she could talk to. Were her fears irrational? She didn't think so. There was a wanted poster with Truett's face—er, mask—on it, and a sheriff with a complete disdain for the law out to get him.

I have to save him.

That was it. She had to take matters into her own hands and figure out a way to save Truett.

So if that was settled, why did her stomach feel so *unsettled*? Because she wasn't sure she could save him, and she still didn't know what was going to happen. If she was married, could she still take care of her family and open her own shop? How could she ask Truett to move with her to Nashville and leave his family and his medical practice behind in Bethel Springs?

He seemed willing to leave, but what would it cost him? His family needed him—his mother and Griff. How could they get along without him? And this town needed him. They would all hate her if she took him away.

To marry was to doom herself to long days trapped in a kitchen for the rest of her life. At least, that was what she had always thought. If she married now, so young, it would go against everything she had vowed never to do.

But then again, she'd already done things she thought she'd never do, starting with fainting at the sight of blood, then inviting a man to her house, then kissing him—not once, but several times!

Lizzie and Will had teased her about the way she had stayed out so long in the dark corner of the yard, alone with Truett Beverly. And tomorrow she'd have to deal with more of Lizzie's raised eyebrows and secretive smiles, insinuating comments and hopeful inquiries about Truett.

But she had loved being with him, listening to him pour out his painful memories to her, feeling his pent-up emotion in the way he kissed her. Oh my. It was wonderful! But terrifying at the same time.

Celia held her stomach and leaned forward in her chair. "Oh, Lord, I don't think I've ever felt more miserable in my life."

❧

Truett had never felt happier in his life.

In spite of his sore muscles and the fact that he hadn't slept much, he whistled a lively tune as he unlocked his office door the next morning.

The night before, after his "meeting" with Celia, he and Will had waited outside the henhouse for the possum to come back. Sure enough, they hadn't had to wait long before he showed himself. Truett handed the gun to Will and let him shoot it. Then he'd gone home to plan his proposal to Celia—which was what kept him up most of the night.

Strictly speaking, he'd already asked her to marry him, but he hadn't done it right. The words had slipped out before he'd thought. Not that he didn't mean them. His way of asking just wasn't conducive to her taking him seriously and giving him an immediate answer. This time he would kiss her *after* asking, instead of before . . . and during.

He took off his vest and was hanging it on its hook in the back room when the door opened and someone entered.

Truett turned to greet his first patient of the day.

Sheriff Suggs and Almira stood just inside the door, both staring at him with very different looks on their faces.

Almira's face was red and puffy, her eyes wet. Her mouth hung open and she pierced Truett with a pleading, desperate look.

Sheriff Suggs's face was hard and angry, his eyes black. A black shadow darkened his face, defying the early morning sunlight.

"Sheriff." Truett nodded a cautious greeting. "Miss Almira."

The sheriff was holding Almira by her arm, and he dragged her forward.

His insides knotted. "What can I do for you?"

"Doc, Almira finds herself in a bit of trouble. I want you to make the trouble go away."

"What exactly is the trouble?" But he was afraid he knew.

Sheriff Suggs mouth twisted in an ugly half-grin. "She's in the family way. And as you know, she ain't married. And as you also know, she was raped."

Almira let out a strangled cry, like a wild animal caught in a steel trap.

The sheriff yanked on her arm, making her cry out again. "But she don't like to talk about it, as you can probably understand."

Almira began to sob, her hair hanging down over her face.

The urge to plant his fist in Suggs's face almost overpowered him for a moment. But he said a quick prayer and managed to calm his racing pulse.

"I'm sorry," Truett said quietly, "but I don't see how I can help."

"Oh, I think you understand perfectly well how you can help us, Doc. You're a medical man with a medical education. You know how to get rid of this unwanted . . . problem."

Truett's face burned. "Sheriff Suggs, am I to believe that you wish me to forcibly abort Miss Almira's baby?"

The sheriff squinted, looking him in the eye. "See there? You understand me right perfect."

CHAPTER 21

Truett forced his voice to sound calm. "I won't do it. Even if it wasn't against the law, I wouldn't do it."

Almira lifted her tear-streaked face with hope in her eyes.

A muscle in Sheriff Suggs's jaw twitched as he ground his teeth together. He let go of Almira and she ran out the door. But the sheriff's eyes never left Truett's. Suggs stepped menacingly toward Truett until they stood toe to toe and nose to nose. He grabbed Truett by the throat and shoved him against the wall.

Truett knew he should try to make a show of fear, to seem weak, to plead with the sheriff to be reasonable. But it was all he could do to keep himself from breaking the man's face.

"You're trying my patience, Doc."

Truett ignored the sheriff's tobacco juice spittle that sprayed his face. He forced his clenched fists to stay by his sides.

"You know how to do it," the sheriff ground out, "so tell me how it's done. I'll do it myself."

"You'll kill her."

"So be it. It's better than bringing this yellow baby into the world."

"You're an evil-hearted swine, twisted by hate."

"I'm a man, not a weak fool like you."

"No matter what you do to me, it's nothing compared to what God would do. And I'm more afraid of God than of you."

An ugly scowl came over the man's face. He reared back and plowed his fist into Truett's eye.

Truett slumped against the wall, seeing stars, but he managed to stay on his feet. He blinked a few times, then stared back at Suggs. "That all you got?"

"Your high and mightiness just might get you in more hot water than you can handle." Suggs' voice shook with anger as he poked his finger at Truett's nose. "Just remember, I warned you." He spun on his heel and left, slamming the door behind him.

Truett bent over. "Ow. Oh. Ow." He gingerly touched the area around his eye, checking for broken bones. Everything seemed intact.

His face throbbed, but what really hurt was thinking about what Celia would say when she saw his black eye.

In the meantime, what should he do about Almira? He needed to go after her and protect her from Suggs. Who knew what he would do when he caught up with her.

A light tapping came at the back door. That door led to nothing except a stand of bushes behind his office. He went and jerked the door open. There stood Almira.

He gently pulled her inside and locked the door.

"I need a place to hide." Her voice shook. "Do you think Celia Wilcox would let me stay with her?"

"I believe she would. Let's go ask her."

Almira lay down in the back of his buggy and he threw a blanket over her. He glanced around as he drove out of town, but, thank God, he didn't see Suggs.

When he was almost to the Wilcox lane, he stopped the horses. He turned and Almira sat up and looked around. "Why are we stopping here?" Then she looked at Truett and gasped. "What happened to your face?"

He winced. "I don't want Celia to see me. I have a feeling she would get upset."

Almira smiled sadly. "I'm sorry for causing you trouble."

"It's nothing. You have your own worries. I'll be all right." He helped her down. She hurried toward the Wilcox place, turned into their lane and disappeared.

Now he had a letter to write. He just wasn't sure how he was going to tell James about what Suggs was trying to do to Almira and the baby, or how he was going to keep any one of them from getting killed.

How could he ask Celia to marry him now? He had no right to ask her when he was in so much danger. But he should also write a letter that was long overdue, to put an end to Suggs's reign of corruption. He owed it to Celia, if she was ever to become his wife.

～

CELIA REALIZED SHE'D BEEN ROCKING THE DAYLIGHTS OUT OF THE squeaky rocking chair for who knew how long. She forced herself to stop and tucked one foot underneath her.

She'd hurried to clear the table and clean up the dishes after supper. Then she'd made a pallet on the floor of Celia and Lizzie's room for Almira, who'd insisted on sleeping on the floor because she didn't want to take anyone's bed.

That had been two hours ago. Everyone was in bed except Lizzie, who was staying up to finish embroidering a doll dress for Tempie.

Lizzie, ever the sweet, unselfish one. *Lord, why couldn't you have made me more like Lizzie—and less like me?*

Where was Truett? He'd said he would come. She'd been so addled by his kiss, which had been mostly her fault, but now she wasn't so sure she should have said he could come.

She'd started rocking herself again. She stopped. Rocking would only fuel the exhaustion from her nerves, stretched to breaking all day. She was thankful to be able to shelter poor Almira, but even that was an additional strain. If Mama only knew—the mother of her past, before Father died—she would have a conniption fit at the suggestion that an unmarried woman who had gotten with child was being sheltered under her roof.

As it was, Mama hardly noticed there was an extra person at the table.

As a church-going girl who conformed to most of society's restrictions, it *was* a bit disconcerting, Celia had to admit, to know that Almira was with child out of wedlock. Celia was pretty sure how a woman got herself with child, but she didn't like to let her mind go there. Still, even though her own reputation was in danger just by associating with a "fallen woman," Celia wouldn't think of turning the poor girl away with nowhere to go. God, she was sure, would never approve of *that*.

Celia had intended to concentrate on her career as a dress-maker and to start her own business. Marriage, if it came at all, would come later.

Today, hearing Almira speak of her love for her unborn child, Celia began to rethink a few things. Perhaps it would be sweet to have a baby, a little child that belonged to only her and Truett.

Wait! How did her mind jump to having Truett's baby? Clearly, exhaustion was driving her insane.

Celia's eyes were heavy and gritty. She leaned her head against the back of the chair, lulled by the whine and chirp of the crickets and cicadas.

The sound of a horse's hooves clopping up the lane toward the house rose above the drone of the insects. She was pretty sure she recognized Truett and his horse, though she could only see their outline in the dark.

Why was he so late? If he wanted to talk to her, he should have gotten here at a decent hour. She stayed in her chair, trying to feign indifference.

He wore a wide-brimmed hat pulled low over his eyes, making it impossible to see his face. As he stepped onto the first porch step, his low voice drawled, "Waiting for me?"

The deep timbre of his voice sent a thrill through her.

She forgot about pretending not to care. "It is quite late."

He sighed as he approached, then sank down in the wooden chair beside her. "I'm a lot later than I intended. If you're tired and want me to leave, I understand."

Celia said nothing, only stared at him. Something was bothering her besides his lateness. He kept his head down so that his hat cast too much of a shadow for her to see his eyes. Light from the lantern was flooding the porch from the window over her shoulder, but he didn't turn in her direction, so she couldn't see his expression.

A sudden thought made her stomach clench. What if he was acting aloof because he regretted what he'd said to her last night, the part about wanting her to marry him? He might try to take it back.

But Celia didn't want him to think she held him to it. In fact, she too wished he hadn't said it. His little proposal had sent her into a pit of panic and confusion she hadn't climbed out of yet.

But perhaps she shouldn't let him get off that easily. "You said you wanted to talk. So talk."

"Is Almira here?"

"Yes. How did you know? She's asleep in my room."

"I drove her here. Thanks for letting her stay."

"She's welcome as long as she needs a place."

"It could mean trouble for you if her father finds out she's here."

"I'm not afraid of him." It was true, she wasn't—not afraid for herself, anyway.

"Did Almira tell you what happened this morning?" The hesitation in his voice raised prickles of alarm on the back of her neck.

"What do you mean? She only said that her father found out she was with child, that she was afraid he would do something terrible to her, so she ran away."

Truett nodded several times.

"What's going on, Truett? Why aren't you looking at me?"

"I am looking at you."

Celia darted her hand toward him and snatched off his hat before he could react. The light from the windows behind them streamed over the side of his face.

Celia emitted an involuntary squeak. Truett's eye was black and blue. The eyelid was swollen half-shut, and his cheekbone was purple.

"What happened?" Her voice sounded strangled as she choked on the lump in her throat. She reached toward his face but didn't touch him. Even a light touch would probably cause him pain.

"It's nothing. Just a bruise."

He shrank into the shadows so she couldn't see it anymore. She grabbed him by the arm and pulled him toward her, into the light. "I want to see it."

"No." He pulled back.

"Let me see it!" She jumped up and grabbed him by both arms. She tugged, trying to pull him out of his chair. She couldn't even budge him, but he sighed, hung his head, and stood up.

Taking hold of his chin, she turned his head toward the light.

"Someone hit you." She leaned closer. "Have you been fighting?"

"Uh, not exactly."

"What happened?"

"I don't want to tell you."

Celia realized she was standing closer to him than propriety allowed. Not to mention that they were alone together, late at night. If anyone caught them, her reputation would be ruined.

"Please tell me. Why can't you tell me?" She couldn't disguise the anxiety and anger in her voice. Why was he keeping a secret from her?

He stared down at his feet. "Telling you serves no good purpose. It doesn't matter what happened."

"It matters to me. Tell me."

"I can't tell you."

She grabbed his upper arms. He didn't budge.

"Tell me." She ground out the words between clenched teeth.

He leaned his head back and let his eyes roll back in his head. Then he sighed. Again. He finally looked her in the eye and took hold of her, so that they were both holding each other's arms.

"I'll tell you but you have to promise not to cry or fly into hysterics."

It was on the tip of her tongue to retort that she never "flew into hysterics." But she bit back those words and said, "I promise."

He sighed again.

"Would you stop doing that?" All that sighing was fraying her already-shredded nerves.

His throat convulsed as he swallowed. "Everything is all right. Don't worry. But Sheriff Suggs came—"

Celia sucked in a breath so loud it sounded like she was inhaling a cricket. "Sheriff Suggs?"

Truett frowned and lowered his eyebrows at her. "Now, Celia, you promised." He squeezed her arms tighter.

It was Celia's turn to swallow hard. "All right. Go on."

"He brought Almira to me and wanted me to end her baby's life. I told him I wouldn't do it. He got angry and hit me. That's it."

"Oh, Truett." She was breathless and a little dizzy. "That horrid man! He's evil. But you poor, poor thing." She stared at the result of the violence inflicted on his face. She pictured Suggs' fist slamming into his eye.

"I think I better sit down."

Truett helped her back into her chair. "Breathe. It's all right. Just breathe."

Celia kept her head down and tried to comply. *Breathing. In and out.* She began to feel less light-headed. Truett said everything was all right, so maybe it was. Her head stopped spinning and she began to breathe more normally.

She looked up. "You didn't hit him back, did you?" *Please, God, let him not have hit him back!*

"No, I didn't hit him back."

"Oh, thank you, Truett." But the sheriff would hate Truett now. How long would it take him to figure out that Truett was the hooded horseman?

CHAPTER 22

Truett squatted in front of her and held her hands. His heart turned to mush in his chest as he gazed at her. Tears glistened in her eyes as she focused on his bruise again.

"Now, Celia, you promised not to cry."

"Who's crying?" She smoothed her expression. "I'm not crying." She reached up and brushed his hair back from his forehead.

"It's a really ugly bruise, isn't it?" Truett said.

Her eyes were filled with anguish. He might as well take advantage of the situation.

"I think if you kiss it, it will make it feel better."

She stared at his battered eye. Instead of scolding him for saying such a thing, she slowly took his face in her hands and leaned forward. Her breath grazed his cheek in a way that made him ache to hold her and kiss her. But he held his breath to see what she would do next.

She brushed her soft lips against his bruised cheekbone. The spot tingled somewhere between pain and pleasure. Then she pulled his head down an inch lower and brushed her lips over his eyelid.

His heart pounded as her warm lips caressed the corner of his eye.

He opened his eyes just enough to see the halo of light around her head. He could barely make out her features, but her eyes were closed. He leaned forward and kissed her, as if continuing the kiss he had started the night before.

His heart soared. This was going better than he'd imagined. No, wait. He still had to ask her to marry him. What happened to his promise to himself not to kiss her until *after* he proposed?

With great reluctance, he forced himself to end the kiss and back away from her. He cleared his throat, rose, and retrieved his hat from the porch where she had tossed it. He sat down beside her again. When he looked up at her, she was pressing her hands against her cheeks.

"I'm sorry," she said. "I shouldn't have done that."

He was pretty sure she was talking about kissing him, not tossing his hat.

"I didn't mind." Truett felt the goofy grin spreading across his face. "It was very nice." He stared down at his hat. *Now how was this supposed to go again? Oh, yeah.*

He turned to Celia, then sank to his knees in front of her. He placed one hand over his heart while he grabbed her hand.

"Celia, I love you. You are the most beautiful, intelligent, delightful woman I've ever met. God said, 'It is not good for a man to be alone,' and since I've met you, I most emphatically agree with Him. You would make me the happiest man in the world if you would say yes to my proposal of marriage. Celia Wilcox, will you marry me?"

Celia couldn't speak for a moment, but then her spine stiffened. "You talk of your happiness. What about mine?"

Truett blinked three times in quick succession. "P-pardon?"

"You just got hurt by a crazy, mean sheriff. The same sheriff who wants to kill you. Now he knows for sure that you're an enemy. How long before he realizes you're the hooded horseman? And what happens to you then? What happens to me?"

He pursed his lips and sat back on his heels.

"I have dreams and goals and plans. No man wants a wife with such ambitions!" She stood, paced three steps away and back. "I never should have kissed you. I still can't believe I did it—this was the third time! It isn't like me." She realized her voice was rising and she forced it back down to a hoarse whisper. "I've always been self-controlled. But when I'm around you, I lose my mind!" She thrust her finger at him. "And don't you dare smile, Truett Beverly. I never should have danced with you. That's how it all started. You made me forget how much I want to get away from here and get back to Nashville."

"But Celia." He leaned forward and took hold of her hands again, holding them tight so she couldn't pull away. "I wouldn't keep you from your goals and ambitions. We'll go to Nashville, if that's what you want."

He knew it wasn't that easy. Their families needed them here. Thoughts were churning so fast through her mind she could barely lay hold to one. "And what about those wanted posters? What happens when it all catches up to you and the sheriff hangs you?" She was getting hysterical again. "How can you even ask me—"

"Celia, please. We can figure out a way. And if we go away from here, Suggs will not be able to capture me."

"But your family, your mother, and Griff. I couldn't ask you to leave them."

He let go of her hands and rubbed a hand across his face. He knew she was right. Her stomach twisted. She didn't want to be right.

"Somehow things would work out." His voice sounded sad, but he didn't look up at her. He looked so vulnerable, with his bruised face and his hair falling down over his forehead. She longed to brush it back and kiss him again and make him forget what she had just said. Her gaze unintentionally settled on his perfect lips.

No, no more kissing.

He'd just asked her to marry him. *Marry.* The very word filled her with terror.

Truett's voice was quiet and contrite. "I guess you're right after all. A man whose life is in as much doubt as mine has no right to think of marriage. Forgive me." Then he stood and strode off the porch. His boots barely skimmed the steps on his way to his horse. He mounted and started down the lane, away from her.

Celia sank weakly into her rocking chair. "Oh, Truett, I'm sorry," she whispered, too softly for him to hear.

Maybe it was for the best. But she felt sick inside, miserable and confused as he rode away. Would she ever feel normal again, content and at peace, sure of her future, as she had before Father died?

Oh, God, please save Truett from Sheriff Suggs. And help me not to kiss him again until then.

Not that Truett would ever kiss her now anyway.

~

Why didn't I kiss her?

Truett arrived at his office the next morning as the sun began to peek through the trees. He sat his desk, still mad at himself for leaving Celia the way he had the night before, and prepared to write a letter to his father.

He shouldn't have let himself get upset, but her reaction had nettled him. Before he proposed to her, the thought had been nagging him that he didn't actually have the right to ask her to marry him. With Sheriff Suggs breathing down his neck, his life was practically forfeit. And it was true that his family needed him to stay in Bethel Springs. But he had pushed those thoughts away because he wanted her so much, wanted Celia in his arms and in his life. So when she threw his own fear up in his face instead of happily saying yes to his marriage proposal, he'd let himself get so frustrated that he just left.

He'd imagined her accepting him willingly, coming into his arms and kissing him, but it had all turned out so differently. What had he done wrong? If he'd simply pulled her into his arms and kissed her, instead of letting her anger get to him, the night might not have ended disastrously.

Truthfully, though, she was right. She deserved actual assurance that he wasn't going to be killed, and the only way he could give her that was to deal with Sheriff Suggs according to the law, as he should have to start with. He hadn't.

But he would now.

First, the letter to his father. Next, he would write to Madison County Probate Judge William Richardson, a friend of his father's in Huntsville.

In the meantime, Truett would give Celia space. She was a high-strung girl who undoubtedly hated letting anyone see her get upset—and he seemed to make her upset every time he was around. He would leave her alone, even though it would be painful to do so, until he was able to deal with Suggs once and for all.

~

SUNDAY DAWNED CLEAR AND HOT, PROMISING TO BE AS MISERABLE as Celia felt inside. Several days had passed since the ill-fated proposal, and Celia hadn't seen Truett once. She couldn't decide if she was relieved or devastated.

Afraid of encountering her father, Almira didn't accompany them to church. Celia felt her friend's absence, even as she tried to stay calm about seeing Truett again.

Lord, why am I so nervous? She could hardly wait to see him, and yet she had no idea what to say to him when she did. She wished she could stay away from him, but at the same time, she longed to look into his eyes and see that he forgave her and didn't hate her.

Celia didn't intend to tell Truett, but she and Almira had written a letter to a judge in Huntsville. The horrible bruise on Truett's face, and the thought of what Suggs wanted to do to Almira and her baby, had fueled her determination to do something to break the evil man's hold over the whole community. She'd gotten the judge's name from Truett's mother when she'd come for a visit the day after Truett's proposal, putting a hypothetical question to Mrs. Beverly about any powerful leaders she knew in Madison County. Not knowing if it would even get a response, she'd written the judge, outlining the sheriff's crimes, and begged him to at least begin some sort of investigation into the corrupt sheriff.

After arriving at church, Celia barely caught a glimpse of Truett before she sat down with her brothers and sisters. She tried not to stare at the back of his head, but her gaze was drawn to him over and over. She wished she could see his bruise, if it looked better than it had the last time she had seen him, but he never turned his head.

Nothing of note happened during the preacher's usual sermon, except that he coughed several times and looked rather pale. He must have come down with a summer cold.

When the service was over, she watched as Truett put away his hymnal, tucked his Bible under his arm, and made his way quickly down the aisle. She hoped to catch his eye and give him a smile, but he never looked her way.

She couldn't blame him for not wanting to see her or talk to her after she threw his marriage proposal back in his face. And that hadn't been the first time she'd rejected him. He'd probably never trust her again, which must be for the best. She'd prayed so much lately about whether God wanted her to stay away from him and pursue her goals, or if He wanted her to let herself make Truett Beverly "the happiest man in the world." The idea still didn't sit well with her, which must prove—if she needed proof—that she wasn't ready for marriage.

But neither was she able to move her family back to Nashville and pursue her business dreams. She hadn't received any reasonable offers to buy their farm. As she exited the church, Celia wanted nothing so much as to hide herself away somewhere to have a good cry—another thing she never used to do.

How had life become so demoralizing?

~

THE NEXT DAY, CELIA AND ALMIRA SAT ON THE PORCH PEELING THE ripe tomatoes over two big pots. They would cook them and then seal them in jars for the coming winter. It was a monotonous task and Celia was glad to have a companion for conversation.

"Almira," she said, speaking slowly. It was too hot to do anything quickly, even talking. "I'm surprised your father hasn't come looking for you. Doesn't he know we're friends?"

"No." Almira shook her head. "I didn't talk to my father much." She stared at the tomato she was peeling. "He changed after Mama died. It was as if he didn't feel he had to be kind, or even civil anymore. He holds a grudge against all black people—and against Truett and his family, too."

"Truett's family? Why?"

"His father was the overseer for Truett's grandfather's plantation, but according to my father, Truett's grandfather fired him for no reason and hired a Negro to take his place. Truett says his grandfather caught my grandfather beating the slaves and fired him." Almira sighed. "Truett's story is probably the true one."

Almira frowned and let the peeled tomato drop into the pot before picking up another. "My father was never very loving, and after Mama died, he ignored me. I took to following James around. He was so interested in every living thing. He knew which plants were good to eat and how to grow taller cotton plants, which kinds of bugs were beneficial for crops, and which were bad. He got everybody to eat collard greens and watercress and even wrote an article about it that was printed in the Farmer's Almanac. He knew a lot of the poor folks around here don't get much meat, and he said these greens would keep them strong."

"Oh! I read something about that in the Nashville newspaper. I had forgotten his name and hadn't realized that was James. He is something a science genius and only came back to Bethel Springs because he wanted to help his community. I remember the thing about the native plants he convinced everyone to eat." Quite impressive.

"Yes, collards grow wild around here, and so does watercress, around the ponds and marshy places. A good source of iron, or something like that. James is so smart . . . so giving. But Daddy, when he found out how I felt about James, he just hated him with a red-hot rage."

Almira blinked several times, her eyes swimming in tears. "But let's don't talk about my father."

Celia wasn't afraid of Sheriff Suggs, not for herself, but she fervently hoped he didn't appear at their door, asking if Almira was there. She would never give Almira up to him, but she had little power to stop him from doing whatever he wished.

I will take care of Almira and her baby—and you.

The words seemed to appear in Celia's mind. She raised her eyebrows. *All right, God. I will trust You.*

"Celia," Almira said, thoughtfully staring at the tomato under her knife. "What do you think about Truett?"

Celia moaned. "Oh, please, don't."

"What? I was only going to say that he seems sweet on you."

Should she tell Almira what happened last week? She still didn't want to even think about Truett's proposal or their exchange after.

"Not you, too." Celia used the back of her hand to push back the lock of hair that slipped over one eye. "When Lizzie's not hounding me about him, she's giving me these looks to let me know she's thinking about hounding me about him."

"Well, I promise not to *hound* you, but I was curious after the way the two of you were looking at each other at the Fourth of July dance." Almira arched her eyebrows.

A thin stream of tomato juice tickled as it ran down Celia's arm. She grabbed a cloth on the table and rubbed her arm. Sighing, she decided she might as well tell Almira the truth.

"Truett and I are . . ." How could she say this? "I think we both . . . We care about each other. But it can't come to anything." She didn't want to lie, but she didn't want to tell what had happened between them, either. "I've been trying not to fall in love with him." There. That ought to be enough truth for the both of them.

"Why? Being in love is a wonderful feeling."

"Are you joking? Being in love is a terrible feeling!"

"How do you know?" Almira arched her eyebrows again.

"Oh. Well, I don't know, I guess, but I can imagine. It feels scary, as if you're about to dive head first off a cliff into a boulder. It feels stupid! I don't want to do it, Almira. I can't. We both know that women are worth so much more than mere servants and bed partners, and that's all men want us for."

Celia's cheeks burned and she wished she'd kept her opinion to herself, especially since Almira was with child and not married.

But Almira didn't seem to take offense. She smiled and stopped peeling the tomato to stare at the opposite wall. "But isn't it all worth it to have him say he loves you?"

Celia shrugged. No one had ever said they loved her—until last week when Truett said it. It had felt pretty wonderful for a few seconds. But things between them weren't likely to end wonderfully.

She used her knife to stab a ripe tomato from the pan. She should think about how awful being a widow would feel, how she'd vowed never to marry and lose her chance to own her own business.

"I don't want to work in the kitchen all day. I want to work in a dress shop of my own, to create new fashions, to earn money in my own way and at my own trade. The thought of being like my mother ties my stomach in knots."

"Maybe you could have both."

"Both?"

"Sure! All of it—a husband, children, and owning your own dress shop."

"I don't think it works that way."

"Why?"

"Children are wonderful, but someone has to take care of them. I know. It takes all three of us—Lizzie, Will, and me—to take care of Harley and Tempie."

"I think you will see things a little differently when you fall in love. And Truett is a good man, I can tell you that. James, Truett, and I grew up together. We used to sneak off with James to the black church. That's when I learned about the unprejudiced God of love and mercy." She smiled dreamily, lost in her memories. She said softly, "Besides, you couldn't do better than Truett Beverly."

Celia moaned again. If the girl wanted a list of wonderful characteristics, she could name them herself. Noble, selfless, compassionate, brave . . . she could go on and on. "I know he's a good man. That's what I can't stand about him. He's too perfect." She was talking crazy again. She stabbed another tomato. *And a wonderful kisser.*

"I think you are in love with him. You're just too scared to admit it."

CHAPTER 23

Celia wanted to deny that she loved Truett. She wanted to insist that she was independent and ambitious and didn't need a man.

"What if I do love him? Wouldn't it be wrong to make him love me if I had no intention of becoming a meek little wife who stayed at home and had a baby every couple of years?"

Her words conjured up the fact of Almira's pregnancy again. Was that exactly what Almira wished for? To be a wife and have babies? And while guilt assaulted Celia for possibly hurting Almira's feelings, the guilt over kissing Truett when she had no intention of marrying him sent another, stronger stab through her stomach.

But oh, how she liked kissing him. In fact, she wanted to kiss him again, every day for the rest of her life. What did that say about her?

That she was very, very confused. And no better than Almira. How could she judge Almira when she was so carnal herself?

"You wouldn't marry him if he asked you?"

Should she tell Almira that he had already asked her to marry him? But she'd just gotten angry and pushed him away. Truett was probably too angry with her now to still want to marry her. He probably wished he could take it back.

"I don't know if I'd marry him or not. I'm just really scared." Celia stopped peeling. "And confused."

"Have you prayed about it?" Almira half-frowned. "I know. I'm pregnant and unmarried and have no right to give advice, but then again . . . maybe my mistakes qualify me."

Almira's features slackened with sadness. "I think love is the most powerful force in the universe. And although I shouldn't have sinned, I still believe that God is love, and love will one day bring James and me back together." Almira reached over and squeezed Celia's juice-covered hand. "If love is stronger than hate, then love is stronger than your fears, Celia. You just need to let go. Love is so much better than fear."

Part of Celia wanted to think Almira had simply read too many novels. But she also wondered if she was right.

When had she become such a fearful person? She'd always prided herself on being courageous, not afraid of going against other people's strictures to make her own life. But she wasn't sure if love was worth sacrificing a life of independence and . . . well . . . power. She wanted power over her future, power over her own mind, and the power that came with position and earning her own money.

But to get it, she'd always known she'd have to give up love and marriage. That had never bothered her before. Why did it bother her now?

Because she'd seen the tenderness in Truett's eyes, felt the love in his embrace. She didn't want to lose him and the wonderful way he made her feel.

But she was being unfair to him. If only she had the money to take care of her family and get back to Nashville, everything would work out according to her plan and she'd forget about him.

"There is no fear in love, but perfect love casts out fear," Almira quoted as she went back to peeling

Celia stiffened. "If perfect love casts out fear, then my love must not be perfect. Because I'm afraid Truett's love wouldn't make me content."

"How about your fear? Is your fear making you content?" Almira smiled. "You just admitted you love him, you know. You should talk to him about it."

"Oh, no, I should not." She'd already rejected him and hurt him —and herself. "I'll not be throwing myself at a man when I don't know what my intentions are—or his, anymore."

"That was my mistake," Almira said softly.

"What?"

"Not talking things over—about our future. If I had, perhaps we'd be together now instead of several states away from each other. We should have talked instead of . . . kissing and getting into trouble."

"Is that how it starts? With kissing?" Celia swallowed, feeling her cheeks begin to heat. "I mean, you don't have to tell me. I'm sorry."

Almira's white cheeks blushed rosily. "That's how it started with us."

Whoa. No more kissing. Not that she needed to worry about that now, after the way she treated Truett.

~

THE NEXT DAY, CELIA AND ALMIRA WERE IN THE KITCHEN preparing dinner when someone galloped up the lane toward the house. Will, Lizzie, and the twins were out in the back yard plucking a turkey Will had shot.

Celia went down the hall to look out the window. Her heart nearly stalled.

Sheriff Suggs!

She ran back down the hall. "Almira! Go hide! It's the sheriff."

226

Almira went as white as a boll of cotton. She dropped the knife she was using to slice okra and fled to the bedroom.

Celia took a deep breath and forced herself to walk calmly to the front door.

Sheriff Suggs was just setting a boot onto the first step of the porch. Tempie was sitting on the porch playing with her dolls. She stared up at the sheriff. He ignored her as he walked with deliberate steps across the noisy planks toward the front door.

Celia pulled the door open wider. "Good afternoon, Sheriff." Celia pasted on a welcoming smile while each beat of her heart trembled. She forced her voice not to sound as breathless as she felt. "What can I do for you?"

"How do, Miss Celia." He took off his hat and switched his wad of tobacco from one side of his mouth to the other.

Celia's stomach did a queasy flip.

Tempie started screaming. Celia hurried out and discovered she was screaming at a bug that was walking slowly toward her. She picked Tempie up and carried the child inside as fast as she could, calling an apology to the sheriff which she was sure he never heard over Tempie's screams.

Once she put Tempie on the floor, handed her a book and pointed at her tea set, the child stopped crying. She didn't even wipe off the tears still clinging to her cheeks as she reached for the book and calmly opened it to the middle, showing the picture to her doll.

Celia went back to where the Sheriff waited, every nerve jumping, straining to get away.

"Won't you come in and sit a while?" She gave him a weak smile and stepped back, inviting him into the front room.

He shook his head. "I just have a bit of business to discuss."

They continued standing on the porch. The sheriff's expression seemed too nonchalant for a man on the hunt for his daughter. If he'd suspected Almira was there, he would have barged right in. Celia's heart began to slow back to normal.

"Of course. What is it, Sheriff Suggs?" She gave him what she hoped was an innocent, curious smile as she gazed up at him, noticing dried brown spittle at the corners of his mouth.

"Bethel Springs is needing a school teacher and several folks suggested you, Miss Celia, as the most educated woman around. We'd like you to take the job come September first."

"Oh." Should she pretend she didn't know Almira was missing? What should she say?

"You might be wondering about Almira. She won't be back to teach this year." His jaw hardened and a muscle convulsed in his cheek.

"Yes, Ruby told me something about Almira leaving. Do you know where she went?" She stared at him with wide, innocent eyes.

Sheriff Suggs turned his head and spat off the side of the porch. At least, Celia sincerely hoped the tobacco juice made it off the porch.

"Almira ran off. She won't be back." His small dark eyes bore into Celia in a way that made her heart start hammering again.

"I'm sorry to hear that. The truth is, Sheriff, I've been hoping to find a buyer for our farm here so we can move back to Nash-ville. If I get a good offer, we'll be leaving."

"Well, if you don't get an offer, the job's yours. Good day, Miss Celia." He clapped his hat back on his head and turned to leave.

Relief washed over Celia like a waft of cool air. She pulled a nice long draught of it into her lungs.

"Thank you, Sheriff. I'll let you know as soon as I can."

He mounted his horse and tipped his hat without even looking at her. Then he rode away down the lane. She stood watching him, making sure he was truly gone before she went back in the house.

Celia went into the bedroom but didn't see Almira anywhere. "You can come out now."

Almira scooted out from under Celia and Lizzie's bed. "Is he gone?"

"He's gone." She helped Almira up. "He doesn't even suspect you're here." Celia couldn't help the grin of triumph on her face.

Almira's hand shook when she lifted it to brush back her hair. She chuckled nervously. "Thank God for that."

∾

WHEN SUNDAY ROLLED AROUND AGAIN, CELIA FELT SORRY FOR Almira, stuck hiding in the house while they went to church. When Celia asked if she was tired of being shut up all the time for the second week, Almira only smiled and said, "No. I like it here." But there was sadness in her eyes. Almira must be missing James even more than Celia missed Truett.

She hadn't spoken to Truett in almost two weeks. He hadn't even been to the house to see Will. Was he really that angry with her? It was a shame her conflicts with Truett were taking away Will's friend, the man he looked up to and learned from. She sighed, wondering for the thousandth time how she had managed to make things so complicated and messed up.

"I'm so sorry, Will."

Will, seated beside her on the wagon, turned to her with a puzzled look. "What are you sorry for?"

Celia frowned. They were almost to church.

"I'm sorry Truett hasn't been coming around. I'm sure it's my fault. He's just angry with me, but he's crazy about you. You're like a brother to him. I hope you know that."

Will gave her his crooked half smile and shook his head to sling the swatch of blond hair out of his eyes. He needed a haircut. She'd have to cut it when they got back home.

"Don't worry about it, Celia. And I'm sure he's not mad at you —at least, not for long. He's a forgiving kind of man."

Will turned the horses into the short lane that led to the church.

A forgiving man. Sure, but she wasn't asking for forgiveness. She was too confused to even give him an answer to his proposal. She could ask forgiveness for being confused, but that might not be helpful. No, it was better to give him time and let him start coming around again when he was ready.

And pray that God would either make her stop caring about him, or make her stop caring about owning her own business.

Unfortunately, neither seemed likely.

Will ran around to help Celia down. Lizzie and the twins scrambled off the back of the wagon and made their way toward the white clapboard building.

They got inside a little late and had to sit near the front of the church, in the third row. Celia prayed the twins would sit quietly through the sermon and become neither an annoyance nor entertainment for the people behind them, depending on whether the congregants were trying to listen to the sermon, or just endure it.

She allowed her gaze to rove around. Then she saw him. Truett's gaze met hers as he walked down the aisle. He offered a slight smile and walked past, taking a seat in the front row.

After standing and singing three hymns, everyone sat and waited for Preacher Massey to step up to the podium. But instead of the preacher, Truett Beverly stood and made his way to stand before them, holding a Bible in his hand. A slight rustle passed through the crowd.

Celia couldn't help but notice how handsome he looked standing there with his white stand-up collar shirt, his black vest and black coat. His hair was combed neatly into place, and his blue eyes seemed to sparkle in the sunlight that filtered through the windows. She could still see his bruise, although it had faded and was now only a faint yellowish-purple around his eye.

"Good morning." Truett greeted everyone with a serious look as he held his black Bible between both hands. "I'm sorry to say that Preacher Massey is not well. I visited him last night, and his cough has gotten much worse. He cannot be with us today, but he asked me to fill in for him this morning. I hope y'all don't mind."

He smiled, and Celia noticed people across the aisle smiling and nodding encouragement to him. They were probably all thrilled they didn't have to hear Preacher Massey's same old sermon again.

Truett bowed his head to pray. "Dear Lord, we thank you for this beautiful sunny morning and for bringing us together today. Please heal Preacher Massey of his sickness and restore his health. Help us all to open our hearts to your Word, and I pray that you would give me words to speak. In Jesus's name, amen.

"Open your Bibles to Psalm 82, verse two." Truett waited a moment, then started to read. "'How long will ye judge unjustly, and accept the persons of the wicked? Defend the poor and fatherless: do justice to the afflicted and needy. Deliver the poor and needy: rid them out of the hand of the wicked.'"

Truett looked up, his gaze seeming to pierce one congregant, then another. He had that fierce look in his eyes that meant trouble. *Oh, Truett, whatever you're thinking of saying, please don't say it!* Celia clenched her fists by her sides, praying fervently that Sheriff Suggs had decided not to come to church today.

Truett's voice was quiet but authoritative. "Ask yourselves, are we doing what this verse says? Are we defending the poor? Is justice served in our community?"

Celia's heart pounded. Who could he possibly be challenging but Sheriff Suggs? Suggs was the authority in their community, the only "justice" they had. She tried to catch Truett's eye, hoping to plead with him silently to not do this. Of course, everything he was saying was good and right, but it meant death to him. Couldn't he understand that? He would only draw the sheriff's anger—and suspicion.

"Turn to Psalm 94:6." He waited as pages turned. "'LORD, how long shall the wicked, how long shall the wicked triumph? How long shall they utter and speak hard things? and all the workers of iniquity boast themselves? They break in pieces thy people, O LORD, and afflict thine heritage. They slay the widow and the stranger and murder the fatherless.'

"Ask yourselves, has this happened in our midst?"

Celia felt all the blood drain from her face. The "wicked" he spoke of was undoubtedly Sheriff Suggs, and everyone must recognize it, including the sheriff, if he was there. Her heart beat fast and her palms began to sweat. *Oh, Lord, please let him not be here.*

CHAPTER 24

"Turn to Proverbs 31:9. 'Open thy mouth, judge righteously, and plead the cause of the poor and needy.' When was the last time you pleaded the cause of the poor and needy?"

There was no sound, not even the swish of a paper fan. Even Harley and Tempie sat still. Harley's mouth hung open as he stared at Truett, as if he too understood the implication of his words, although that was impossible.

"Turn to Amos 5:12. 'For I know your manifold transgressions and your mighty sins: they afflict the just, they take a bribe, and they turn aside the poor in the gate from their right.' Verse 22. 'Though ye offer me burnt offerings and your meat offerings, I will not accept them: neither will I regard the peace offerings of your fat beasts. Take thou away from me the noise of thy songs; for I will not hear the melody of thy viols. But let judgment run down as waters, and righteousness as a mighty stream.'"

Truett closed his Bible and looked up, staring the people down, but with a peaceful, clear look in his eyes. "God will not tolerate injustice. He will punish not only those who perpetrate it, but also those who stand by and do nothing to stop it."

He relaxed his stance a bit, leaning back on his heels. "This place has seen its share of oppression. The Yankees stole our food, burned our homes, and harassed us for four years during the war. At that time and the years right after, it was sometimes necessary to take the law into our own hands. But the war is over. We have courts of law, judges and lawmakers to see that justice is served and no one is punished without a chance to defend himself." He squinted, his expression growing more intense as he continued. "But when those laws and procedures are ignored, your fellow man is being oppressed, and you're standing by and letting it happen. And God. Is not. Pleased."

Oh, God, oh God. . . Suggs is going to kill him, I just know it. Celia could hardly breathe. The high collar of her dress seemed to be choking her. Her undergarments seemed to grow tighter, pressing into her ribs. Lizzie was staring at her. But Celia couldn't take her eyes off Truett. He was the most handsome, noble, stupid man she'd ever set eyes on. And he obviously didn't care a whit about her warnings and pleas for him to be careful. How could Suggs not know now that he was the hooded horseman? Unless he wasn't at church today.

Truett said some other words about God's mercy and forgiveness, but Celia couldn't take in what he was saying. She was too busy worrying what the sheriff was going to do to him.

Truett sat down and the song leader strode toward the front. All the people were rising to their feet. Celia stood with them, but regretted her hasty rising, as her vision spun like a top and she had to grip the pew in front of her to steady herself. She almost dropped her songbook, but soon recovered enough to open it to the correct page. She didn't have enough breath in her lungs to actually sing, so she simply mouthed the words.

Truett waited up front during the closing song for anyone who wanted to come forward for prayer. But no one came. The song ended and people began filing out of the pews and down the aisle to the door.

Celia sank onto the bench, feeling as if she would give Truett a big piece of her mind if she could get him alone. How could he have made it so obvious that he was condemning Sheriff Suggs' actions?

Of course, everything he said was completely justified, but still, wasn't it foolish for him to attack the sheriff so publicly? Her father had a saying: "God helps the feeble-minded." Well, she hoped it was true and God would help Truett! Because he had surely lost his feeble mind.

As the congregation disbursed, Truett remained at the podium, his head bent over his Bible, as if he was praying. Finding that they were alone except for a few stragglers in the back of the church, Celia stood, wondering if Truett would say anything to her or just go on praying.

Boots clomped down the aisle, coming toward Truett. Celia turned to look.

Sheriff Suggs. His jaw was clenched and his eyes were locked on Truett as he stormed toward him.

Celia's vision became hazy. All the breath left her lungs. *Oh, God, please, not again.* As she started to sit down, darkness closed in around her, and gradually, everything went black.

~

TRUETT LOOKED UP. SUGGS WAS COMING TOWARD HIM WITH HATRED in his eyes, and Celia was fainting.

He knew that pale look and closing eyelids. She was going down. But he also knew he would never get to her in time. She collapsed to the floor.

He ignored Suggs and hurried over to Celia. The sheriff got to her first. Suggs pushed the pew in front of her out of the way.

Sheriff Suggs stood back to let Truett get to her. Truett gathered her in his arms and placed her on the wooden pew. He knelt beside her and lifted her limp hand from where it hung down off the side of the bench.

"What ails her?" Suggs grunted from behind him.

"She fainted." He leaned closer to her face. "Celia? Are you all right?" He touched her forehead, then her cheek, wishing he had some cool water to wipe her face with to help bring her around.

Celia made a sound at the back of her throat. Her eyelids fluttered.

"Celia? It's Dr. Beverly. Can you hear me?"

Her eyes opened and her gaze immediately settled on Sheriff Suggs. Her eyes went wide and she screamed.

Sheriff Suggs muttered an expletive under his breath and stepped farther back.

Truett patted and squeezed Celia's hand, trying to help her get hold of herself. "It's all right. It's just the sheriff." As if *that* would make her feel better.

Her eyes fluttered shut again.

Truett turned to Sheriff Suggs. "Maybe you'd better leave. She seems to be a little upset by, uh, the sight of you."

Suggs pointed his finger at Truett. "I'm not finished with you." Then he turned and stomped back down the aisle and out the door.

Truett and Celia were alone now in the church building. She blinked, beginning to come around again.

"It's all right. I'm here. Everything's all right." He tenderly rubbed her cheek with his fingertips.

She turned her head and stared at him. Her voice was weak as she whispered, "Oh, Truett, is he gone?"

"Yes, he's gone." He squeezed her hand.

"Did I faint again?" She groaned. "Did anyone see me?"

"Just Suggs. And me."

"Is he going to kill you?" Her lower lip trembled.

Truett's heart squeezed in his chest. She loved him.

"No, he's not going to kill me."

"How do you know?"

"Can we talk about this later?" He looked around just to make sure no one had come inside to check on them.

Celia tried to sit up. Truett helped her, then sat on the bench beside her, his arm around her, letting her lean against his side. She laid her head on his shoulder.

This was quite pleasant. He sat staring forward. Finally, Truett shook his head, unable to suppress a grin. "You sure are a high-strung little lady."

"I never was before I met you. You make me crazy."

"Crazy in a good way?"

"Definitely *not* in a good way." Her voice sounded petulant. "Oh, Truett, how could you have said those things?"

"I had to, Celia. The opportunity presented itself and I felt God nudging me to do it." He didn't try to look into her face, and she didn't try to lift her head off his shoulder.

"And now Suggs will kill you," she whispered.

"No, he won't. At least, not in front of anyone. He only kills people he can get away with killing. I have a family who would never let him get away with killing me."

"He'll kill you if he sees you dressed in a black hood and cape, and you know it. He'll shoot you dead."

"Sh. God will take care of me. And besides, I've taken some action that should help us get rid of our corrupt sheriff for good."

"You have?"

"Yes, I have. I wrote Judge William Richardson, the county probate judge in Huntsville."

"You did? So did I."

"You did?"

"Almira and I wrote the letter to tell the judge what he's been doing."

"You'll sure make a mighty fine wife with such a good head on your shoulders."

"I thought you said I was high-strung. High-strung isn't good. And don't say that word."

"What word? I like high-strung. At least, I like you, high-strung or not." He squeezed her shoulder.

She snuggled a little closer. "The 'w' word. You do?"

Truett leaned his head down until his cheek was touching her dark hair. The smell of flowers filled him with images of her. Her hair was pulled straight back from her face into a severe bun. How he wished he could pull out the pins and see it fall around her shoulders. He was sure it would be soft and silky. He took a deep breath and let it out.

"I want to kiss you." His voice sounded as tight as he felt. He would have kissed her, too, but she kept her face turned away from him.

She let out a little huffy breath. "I'm mad at you. Besides, we can't kiss in church. It's shameful to even think about such a thing." But he heard the breathlessness of her voice. She wanted to kiss him just as much as he wanted to kiss her.

"You will kiss me in church," he drawled slowly. "You will kiss me . . . in this church, or another church of your choice . . . right after you say 'I do.'"

"Of all the arrogant things . . ." She sounded mad, but she didn't take her head off his shoulder. "What makes you so sure?"

"Because you love me, Celia."

Her body stiffened.

"You love me, and you care what happens to me."

She stood up, wobbling as she tried to take a step. Truett grabbed her arm to steady her.

"I'm all right. I need to go."

Still she wouldn't look at him. "Celia . . ."

She began walking down the aisle, then turned to glance at him. "Come for supper one night this week. Will misses you."

"When?"

"Tomorrow."

~

WHY HAD SHE ASKED TRUETT TO SUPPER?

Celia ran around shoving biscuits in the oven and stirring the gravy on the stove.

Lizzie entered the kitchen. "I've got the twins cleaned up. Celia, you go and get dressed. Almira and I'll finish supper."

Celia frowned at her sister. Why did she have to look so happy?

"Go on!" Lizzie stripped off Celia's apron and made a shooing motion with her hands.

Celia didn't dare answer her or she might blurt out something unnecessary, something like, *Stop looking at me like that! I'm not marrying Truett Beverly. Who's looking out for* my *happiness? I'd like to know.*

She didn't say any of those things, though it was on the tip of her tongue every time Lizzie or Will or Almira caught her eye and gave her that annoying smirk of theirs that said *Celia and Truett are courting!*

Celia hurried outside and washed her face from the pan on the back steps. She splashed the cool water on her arms. The day was hot and sticky and she felt as if she already needed another bath, though she'd just taken one a few hours ago. There was no time for anything except a change of clothes.

She didn't care how she looked, but she chose the dress she'd worn to the dance, the feminine one with the pink flowered print, and jerked it over her head. She took her hair down and brushed it out quickly before pinning it back up in a bun. Perhaps she should try to style it in a more attractive way.

Who was she trying to impress? Celia glared at herself in the mirror. "No one. Especially not you, Truett Beverly." But the words made her smile. She was lying and she knew it.

Truett's masculine voice drifted in from the sitting room. Her hands shook as she smoothed her skirt. Her dress was still unbuttoned down the back! She stuck her head in the doorway and called in a panicked whisper, "Almira!"

Almira rushed in with a big smile on her face. Why was everyone so happy? Annoying, that's what it was.

Almira hurriedly buttoned her up the back. "Come on. He's here." She took Celia's hand and pulled her toward the door.

Celia pulled her hand away. "I know, I know. Be calm." But she was the one who wasn't calm. She took a deep breath and made Almira lead the way into the sitting room.

Celia hung back and watched Truett greet Almira. He smiled and chucked her under the chin, like a brother would greet a sister. "How ya doin', Mira?"

When Truett noticed Celia standing behind Almira, his eyes took in her dress in a quick sweep and his smile grew wider. Celia bit the inside of her lip at his reaction. She should have worn her ugliest calico work dress. What was she thinking?

Truett stepped toward her. Before she knew what he was about to do, he lifted her hand and bent over it, planting a lingering kiss on her knuckles.

Celia's cheeks began to sting. She couldn't meet the eyes of anyone in the room, the excited grins on their faces. She was forced to look at Truett instead. She tried to frown at him, but her face muscles wouldn't cooperate. Why did he have to be so good-looking? Even with the fading bruise she found herself breathless at the sight of him. His kind blue eyes, reflecting his steadfast heart and chivalrous soul. His gentle mouth, his noble jaw . . . *God, I'm hopeless. But isn't it Your fault for making him so wonderful?*

"I'm going to finish dinner." Celia turned on her heel and fled to the kitchen.

A few minutes later, as they gathered at the table for the meal, Lizzie and Will stumbled all over themselves to make sure they and the rest of the family took all the chairs except the one right next to Truett, forcing Celia to sit beside him. That would have been all right, except that the table was barely big enough to accommodate them all, so Celia's arm ended up brushing against Truett's at least a half dozen times while they ate. But somehow, she didn't really mind.

Truett seemed so at home at their table. She looked around at the way everyone was interacting with him. Even Mama smiled at him and seemed more attentive than usual.

She'd really only wanted him to come and see Will and the rest of the family. They all missed him when he didn't come around, and Celia knew she was the reason he didn't come. That was her only motive for asking him to supper. But somehow, the evening had turned into a "Celia and Truett are courting" party. She could see it on everyone's face, even Truett's.

But the longer she sat beside him, the lighter her heart became. She liked his deep voice and laugh right next to her. She liked the way he glanced at her every so often out of the corner of his eye, and the way he didn't move his arm out of the way when she accidentally brushed against him. She wished she didn't like it, but she did.

Truett complimented all the dishes. Lizzie and Almira were quick to point out the ones Celia made. *Oh, for pity's sake.* She didn't know whether to roll her eyes or laugh.

When the meal was over, they moved to the sitting room. Truett waited to see where Celia would sit. In fact, everyone seemed to be waiting to see where she would sit!

She folded her arms and glared at them. "What are you people waiting for? Sit down."

Lizzie whispered, "Celia! Don't be so rude."

She huffed and finally chose her seat—not on the sofa beside Truett, as they obviously wanted her to, but in a rocking chair. The rest settled around the room with a sigh of disappointment.

They all drank tea until Lizzie and Almira hurried the twins away, saying they needed to get them ready for bed. A minute later, Will yawned and stretched, saying he had to get to bed as well, even though he never went to bed this early. Celia wrinkled her nose at him as he left the room, but he only grinned.

Truett stared at his cup.

"My family likes you." She purposely gave the words a dry tone.

"I like them, too." He smiled across the room at her. They sat in silence a while. Celia could hear the tick of the clock on the mantle and the high-pitched whir of the crickets through the open window. She stared at her hands, folded in her lap, while Truett continued to stare at his cup.

"Well, I guess I'd better go."

They both stood up. He placed his cup on the tray table against the wall and stepped toward the door. Celia followed him. After all, someone had to see him out.

He opened the door and let her go before him. They stepped onto the porch. Celia waited for her eyes to adjust to the dim light as Truett shut the door behind him and stood facing her, his back against the door, as if he was blocking her way of escape.

"I had a good time tonight." His voice was low and seemed to rumble in his chest. "Thank you for inviting me to supper."

Celia didn't say anything. Her eyes focused on the top button of his shirt. She tried to tear her gaze away from the smooth skin of his neck. He was standing awfully close to her. She thought about stepping away from him. She should step away. She should say a hasty good-night and dart back into the house, but her breath seemed stuck in her throat.

He reached out and gently caressed her elbows, drawing her toward him. She knew if she looked up he would kiss her. She kept her eyes focused on his chest.

She let him draw her closer until her forehead rested against his shoulder. She knew she shouldn't let him kiss her, not when she was so uncertain about what she wanted. For that matter, she shouldn't let him hold her like this. Before Truett, she'd never let a man touch her at all. One or two times, a fellow had kissed her hand, and she'd danced with a few partners through the years, but everything with Truett was new.

Where had her anger and bluster gone? They had deserted her, leaving her with a warmth that made her wish this moment never had to end.

CHAPTER 25

Truett held Celia close for a long time, neither of them speaking. What was going through her mind?

She'd been so scared at the sight of Sheriff Suggs walking toward him, she'd fainted. He wanted to reassure Celia that everything was going to be all right, that she shouldn't worry so much about the sheriff killing him, but he didn't want to bring it up if she wasn't thinking about it. Mercy sakes, but she could get upset.

Her head fit perfectly under his chin. Soon he would kiss her good-night, but it felt so good to hold her, he was pretty sure he could stand there all night if she wanted him to.

"I suppose you should go." Celia's voice was muffled against his shirt. She made no move to let go of him or pull away, so he didn't move either.

"I suppose I should."

"I want you to promise me to be careful and avoid Sheriff Suggs."

"I promise."

"Don't get into any more trouble."

"I won't. Not intentionally, anyway."

She pulled away and looked up at him. "No. No more trouble."

"All right."

She reached up and laid her hand against the side of his face. "Your bruise isn't even healed yet."

He tightened his arms around her. His breath seemed to have gotten stuck in his throat. He wanted to kiss her but she looked down again.

"I liked dancing with you," he told her. "We should have dancing at our wedding."

"You're forgetting something."

"What?"

"I haven't said yes to your proposal of marriage."

"But you will."

~

CELIA WANTED TO GET ANGRY AND TELL HIM HE HAD NO RIGHT TO assume so much. But how would that sound, since she was allowing the man to hold her in his arms? If she didn't intend to marry him, she was behaving like a hoyden.

Truett pressed his lips to her forehead. Then he pulled back.

She looked up. Truett stared past her, searching the lane. Then she heard it too. The patter of running feet.

"Miss Celia! Miss Celia!"

Truett let go of her and hurried down the steps toward the girl child's voice. Celia was right behind him.

She caught a glimpse of Annie's tear-streaked face and her heart jumped into her throat.

"Miss Celia, please come quick! Sheriff Suggs, he—" She stopped at the porch steps, bent over, and gasped for breath. "Please come . . . help my Daddy . . . I'm so scared."

"Get in the buggy," Truett ordered. His carriage stood only a few feet away, the horse already hitched and ready to go. He picked Annie up and placed her on the seat.

Celia began climbing up beside Annie, but Truett grabbed her arm. "You stay here."

"No! I'm coming with you." She hoisted herself up without his help. "Let's go."

Truett leapt up beside her, frowning fiercely. He slapped the reins and urged the horse into a canter.

Celia turned to Annie. "What happened?"

"Sheriff Suggs rode up with three other men and started telling my Daddy and uncle that they didn't have no business setting up a store when Bethel Springs already has a store. He told my Daddy he would burn it down. He had a torch. I'm so scared he's gonna hurt my Daddy." Annie sobbed while staring straight ahead.

Celia could only see Truett's profile as he slapped the reins on the horses' backs to urge them to go faster. His jaw looked carved from granite. She could only imagine how intense was the look in his eyes.

The orange glow of a tiny fire became visible ahead. When they were still a hundred feet away, Celia made out the figure of a man holding a torch, the tiny fire she had seen. Three other men were there. The man with the torch, which she recognized as Sheriff Suggs, held one man's hands behind his back. Another man lay on the ground, and another had his boot resting in the middle of his back.

"That's my Daddy!" Annie said. "He's gonna hurt my daddy."

Two women stood nearby yelling and sobbing. Sheriff Suggs's torchlight flickered bright against the night. He handed his prisoner over to the other man and stalked toward the door of the store.

"Hey!" Truett yelled as the horse galloped even faster.

The sheriff halted and turned his head in their direction. He planted his feet apart and faced them.

Celia's heart beat so hard it hurt, but she wasn't sure if it was more fear or anger. How dare the man commit such an atrocity toward innocent people? He was a menace, evil and cruel.

Celia and Truett jumped down at the same time. Rage made her voice screechy. "What do you think you're doing?"

Truett stepped toward Curtis, who was the man holding Annie's father and the other man on the ground. Then she noticed three or four other men standing around with their horses in the shadows.

Truett's hands clenched as he held them by his sides. Annie's soft wailing came from the buggy behind them, the only sound.

"If it isn't Miss Celia Wilcox and Dr. Truett Beverly." Sheriff Suggs spoke slowly, drawing out his words. His features were highlighted by the garish orange light of his torch. His teeth showed and his upper lip curled into an animal-like sneer.

Celia knew Truett wouldn't let the sheriff hurt her, and the men around him, warped as they obviously were, probably wouldn't either. But what would they do to Truett? And to Annie's father and his store?

"The lady asked you a question," Truett said.

The sheriff glared at Truett for a long moment, then he spit a long stream of tobacco at his feet.

"This is none of your business, and if you don't get out of here and keep your mouth shut, you and the lady will be sorry." He glared at them some more. "Now git."

Truett didn't move. Neither did Celia.

"All right, then." Sheriff Suggs grinned. "You can watch while I set fire to this Negro store."

As Suggs turned and walked toward the front door, Truett leaped toward him. Curtis moved away from his prisoners and grabbed Truett by the neck just before he reached Suggs and dragged him back. Suggs disappeared inside.

What should I do? Celia took a step forward, her eyes glued to Truett.

Truett elbowed Curtis, breaking free of his grip, then slammed his fist into Curtis's nose, and he fell to his knees on the ground.

Truett turned toward the store as the sheriff ran out of the front door. Flames leapt in the windows. He threw the torch down and mounted his horse.

Truett ran to the clothesline, which was not far from where they were standing. He yanked down two rag rugs and raced to the well. Celia hurried to help him. They soaked both rugs with a bucket of water.

Over her shoulder, she saw the men leave Annie's father and mount their horses. They fired their guns in the air and filled the night with their hoots and laughter as they rode away.

Truett took one of the rugs and Celia the other and ran toward the burning building.

Inside the store Truett beating at the flames and Celia followed his example. There were so many fires going at once, at least six separate blazes all around the room.

Celia beat at some flour sacks and was quickly able to extinguish that fire. Then she moved to a wooden crate, which took a bit longer. She beat it until it was out. The room was filling with smoke and Celia began to cough. Her eyes and lungs burned and she could barely breathe. She began beating a bolt of cloth that was blazing high. Her chest ached and she wasn't sure she could even lift her rug again.

Truett appeared beside her. He hit the blaze once and left the rug on top of it. Then he grabbed her around the waist and half dragged her toward the door.

They sank to their knees outside in the front yard. Celia coughed so hard she thought her throat would turn inside out. Truett was lying still on the ground beside her. She grabbed his shoulder.

"Truett, are you all right?"

He opened his eyes and smiled up at her. "We did it. We put out the fire."

She laughed, sounding a little hysterical. Then she started coughing again. Truett sat up and pounded her on the back.

Annie and her family surrounded them. The women were weeping and thanking them. The men smiled and shook their hands.

"You saved us. You surely did." He sank to his knees beside them. "My name's Isaac Hartley and this is my brother Sam." He pointed to the man beside him.

"Truett Beverly and Celia Wilcox. I'm afraid you still have a terrible loss on your hands." Truett winced.

"Never you mind that. You saved me and my brother, and the store is still standing. I'm mighty beholden to you." He shook their hands again. "Thank you. Thank you kindly."

Celia wanted to sing with joy at knowing she and Truett had put out the fire, especially when Annie ran over and threw her arms around her neck. When she pulled away, Annie's cheeks were glistening with tears.

"Thank you, Miss Wilcox. God sent you."

"I'm so thankful God helped us." The way Annie was looking at her made Celia ask, "What is it, Annie?"

"Miss Celia, I don't understand. Why is Sheriff Suggs so mean but you and Dr. Beverly are so good? You're white, and the sheriff is white. He wants to kill us but you help us? It don't make sense. My uncle says it's because we live in the South. He says people up North are different, but my granny says that's just a fairy tale. It makes me afraid. I don't know who hates me and who don't."

Celia sighed and squeezed Annie's arm. "I know. But the truth is, whether you live in the South or the North, some people's hearts are full of hate and some people's are not, and it will always be that way, I suspect."

Annie sighed. "I suspect so too. Some people are mean and some are not. It's the same with colored folk." She nodded with a wise look on her young, dark face.

Good and evil would always be warring for men's hearts, but as long as there were good men like Truett, there was hope.

Annie soon joined her kinfolk as they stared at the damaged store. Celia's heart grew heavy again as she ruminated on the fact that Sheriff Suggs would find out his attempt to burn them out was unsuccessful. He would be furious, and he wouldn't give up harassing them.

On the way home, Celia's unease increased with every fall of the horse's hoofs. What would happen now? Sheriff Suggs was fully aware of Truett's bravery and willingness to stand up to him. Would he put the pieces together and realize Truett was the hooded horseman?

He would have to be stupid not to.

Celia twisted her hands together in her lap. It was a miracle that she and Truett had been able to put out the fire and that the sheriff hadn't hurt anyone. But would God give her another miracle, one big enough to save Truett from Sheriff Suggs?

Truett glanced over at her a few times, but Celia pretended not to notice.

They turned down the lane to her house, the trees forming a canopy of limbs and leaves over their heads. Celia began to wonder what she would say to him when he stopped to let her out. She couldn't say, "Thanks for the drive. I had a lovely time." Perhaps just "Good-night" would suffice. Her thoughts and emotions were so mixed up inside her she didn't know what to say.

He stopped the buggy and Celia prepared to jump down, a sudden panic making it impossible to speak.

Truett took her hand and held it tight. "Celia, wait."

She turned to him. His eyes were red and watery, and soot streaked his face. She must have black smoke marks on her face too, and her hair must be a wild, tangled mess. She wiped at her cheeks with the back of her hand.

The look of love and vulnerability on his face made her heart trip and stumble into her throat. She shook her head and stared down at his hand holding hers, a big ball of tears pressing against her chest. "I can't do this. I have to go."

"Why?"

She simply shook her head, but he still wasn't letting go of her hand. "I'm terrified. Sheriff Suggs is going to do something terrible to you." Then an idea struck her. "You must leave this place and get away from Sheriff Suggs—"

"You mean run away?"

"You told me once before that you wanted to run away from here. You could go and stay wherever James is staying. It's just until something is done about this sheriff. Surely we can get help from the authorities in Huntsville."

"I can't just leave, like a coward."

"And I can't just sit back and watch you get killed." She pulled her hand out of his grasp and jumped off the buggy seat to the ground. She ran all the way to the porch and up the steps and inside, shutting the door behind her.

The horse and buggy rattled away down the lane.

The ball of pressure pushed against her chest. "I'm sorry, Truett," she whispered, leaning against the door. "I'm so sorry."

The creaking of the kitchen floor drew her attention. She turned. Her mother was walking toward her.

Celia straightened and took a deep breath to calm herself. "Mama? Are you all right?"

"Getting a glass of water."

"Can't you sleep?"

Mama gazed her questioningly. She stood in her nightgown and bare feet. Celia couldn't remember ever seeing her mother in bare feet.

"Where are your house shoes, Mama?" Celia started toward her, tears springing to her eyes. She clasped Mother's hand. The lump in Celia's throat forced her voice out in a whisper. "Let me get you a glass of water."

She led her mother into the kitchen and used the pump at the sink, then held the glass out to her. She took it and drank several sips, then handed the glass back to Celia.

Celia led her mother back to her room, pulled the covers back, and waited for her to crawl under the sheet. Then Celia covered her to her chin.

"I'm sorry, Mama, for not being very compassionate to you."

Mama stared up at her, and Celia caught the tear in her hand that almost dripped on Mother's sheets. No doubt it would soil them, as sooty as her cheeks must be.

Celia went back to the kitchen and gave her exposed skin a good scrubbing before taking off her dirty dress and going to her own bed. Thankfully, Lizzie didn't wake, or else she might just tell her exactly what she was thinking—that Truett, the man they'd all fallen in love with, who was so good and brave, would soon be killed. Her heart would be broken, their money would run out, and she'd never be able to support her family by making dresses in Bethel Springs. Only God knew how they were to survive.

CHAPTER 26

The next afternoon, Celia stood over a pan in the kitchen, washing turnip greens for supper, when she caught a glimpse out the window of Will running across the back yard toward the house. His face was pale, but he was beaming and out of breath, as if he'd run a long way.

Celia hurried out the door, her hands still dripping water. "What is it? What's happened?"

Will raised his hand in the air, caught his breath, and said, "I did it."

"Did what?"

"I found the Glory Patch right on our land. We're rich, Celia."

It took a while for Will to convince Celia they truly were rich, but once he did, she was so lightheaded she had to lean against the door frame. When she'd recovered both her breath and her wits, Celia and Will each grabbed a bucket and a shovel and trudged off to a sheltered glade on their side of the stream. The other side belonged to someone else, either Truett's family or a man who lived in Killingsworth Cove. But as they descended the hill, Celia's eyes were fixed on a thick patch of green leaves carpeting the entire flat area on their side of the creek.

"Is all this ginseng?"

"Most of it." Will set his bucket down and bent over the leafy plants. "You see those little berries, just starting to show? That's how I knew this was ginseng."

Celia caught her breath. "You're sure, Will? You're sure this is ginseng?"

Will shoved his shovel into the dirt at the outside of the patch. Soon he dug up a big white root, similar in shape to a sweet potato. He held it up.

"Yep. I'm sure." Will spoke in a hushed tone. "It may be too small to be a true Glory Patch, but it's enough to hire someone to help take care of Harley and Tempie so Lizzie and I can go back to school, and to send you back to Nashville, Celia. If you still want to go."

Of course she still wanted to go. But she had to make sure her family was taken care of first. "We shouldn't dig it all up, should we? I mean, shouldn't we leave some for next year?"

Will frowned, then pursed his lips into a grim line. "Once folks hear how much ginseng we brought in to Pettibone's store, they'll come looking for our Glory Patch. There won't be anything left the next morning, much less next year."

"Oh." Celia pictured men combing their land at night, searching every inch for their patch of ginseng. She gripped her shovel and started digging.

∼

TRUETT EXAMINED GRIFF AS HE SAT ON THE TABLE IN HIS OFFICE. He'd gotten a nasty blow to the head when he tripped on a tree root and hit the edge of the back step.

"Does it need stitches?" his mother asked.

"No, he's fine. The bleeding's stopped. This bandage is all he needs."

"I'm fine, Ma!" Griff said with a seven-year-old's petulance and a thirty-year-old's deep voice.

Griff stayed with Truett, sitting at the window watching the few people that went by, while his mother went to buy a few things at the general store. Soon, one of the Posey children came in with a broken arm. Griff watched silently from his perch by the window as Truett set the bone and splinted it, wrapping it tight. He'd just sent the boy home when Greenbrier Lee burst through his office door, still wearing his black-stained leather apron.

"Well, the dung heap's stirred up now," he said, shaking his head.

"What are you talking about?" Truett asked as he put away his splinting materials.

"You know those black folks down t' other end of Cove Road who opened a store a while back?"

Truett's stomach sank.

"Sheriff Suggs don't like them having that store. I bet Pettibone's been giving him a reason to get shed of that Negro store. I hear he tried to burn it down, but somehow they managed to put out the fire. Now Suggs is planning on lynching those folks as soon as he can get enough men to ride down there with him."

Truett pointed his finger at the blacksmith. "You agree with what I was saying Sunday at church."

Greenbrier nodded.

"We need to round up our own group of men and put a stop to this hanging. It's wrong and you know it."

"Well, now, you're right, Tru, you're right." The blacksmith rubbed his chin, avoiding his gaze. "But I got a wife and five young'uns. A man's got to think of his family first, don't he?"

"Suggs can't fight the whole community. If we all pull together he'll be forced to stop this killing of innocent people."

Greenbrier continued rubbing his jaw, staring at the floor.

"You know I'd like to help, but it seems too chancey. Once you get on his bad side, Suggs would just as soon kill you as look at you."

"I never took you for a coward."

"It ain't that and you know it." The blacksmith pointed a thick finger at Truett. "I got my family to think of. You can take chances. You ain't got no wife, no young'uns to raise up."

His words struck Truett with more force than he cared to admit. No, he did not have a wife or children. And if he risked his life again, he might lose Celia forever—if he didn't get killed.

But how could he live with himself if he let those innocent people be killed for the sake of one man's greed and another's pure evil?

Aubrey Pettibone was behind this, but Suggs would enjoy helping the local merchant get rid of his competition.

Truett's blood pulsed hard through his temples. Even if it meant sacrificing his prospects of marrying Celia, or cost him his life, Truett could not sit by and let Suggs kill Annie's father and uncle, maybe even their wives and children. No, he couldn't—wouldn't—leave those good people to the devices of Sheriff Suggs. And he had a feeling Celia wouldn't either. For all her warnings and begging him to be careful, he believed she'd go to their aid herself, if she found out about it.

The blacksmith mumbled something else about being sorry he couldn't help and then shuffled out the door. Perhaps there was no real threat. Truett wasn't stupid. The whole thing could be a trap. Suggs could be trying to lure the hooded horseman into the open so he could capture him—or kill him. After all, it wouldn't be dark for several more hours, and Suggs generally did his lynching at night.

But Truett couldn't let Suggs kill those men. He would be there, and he would stop him.

CHAPTER 27

"I'll help you, Truett."

Truett glanced over at Griff. He'd been so quiet during the exchange with Greenbrier, Truett had forgotten he was there. The offer was sincere, but he couldn't put his brother at risk. He would have to get away from Griff, but how?

"Everything's all right. Why don't you go across the street and see what Mama's doing? She may have bought a peppermint stick for you."

Griff crossed his arms and glared at Truett.

"I have to leave. You're just going to have to stay with Mama."

"No. I go with you."

Truett gritted his teeth and strode out the door, Griff following right behind him. He went across the red clay street to the general store and found his mother examining a bolt of cloth. He touched her arm and leaned his head close to hers. Aubrey Pettibone stood behind the counter, watching him with beady hawk eyes.

"I need you to take Griff home." Truett kept his voice low. He stared hard at his mother, hoping she could see the seriousness in his eyes and would not question him.

"Mama, no!" Griff's voice rose to almost a shout, resounding through the whole store. "I want to go with Truett!"

"Come on outside, Griffy." Mother tried to soothe him with a gentle tone.

"No!" That agitated look came over Griff's features, the one that said he was losing control. His face turned red and he puffed out his cheeks.

"We'll go looking for a Glory Patch in the morning. How does that sound?" Truett smiled, feigning a calm that he was far from feeling. "We'll go fishing, too, if you want."

A smile broke over Griff's features. "Let's go now!"

Still Aubrey Pettibone stared at them, obviously listening to every word.

"Let's go outside." Truett looked his mother in the eye and used his head to motion toward the door. Then he escorted them both out into the street.

"Truett's taking me fishing!" Griff leapt out of the store and started jumping up and down.

"Tomorrow, Griff. All right? We'll go later."

Griff's mouth hung open.

"Right now I have something else I have to do."

"I want to go too."

To keep Griff's agitation from getting out of hand, he knew he had to stay calm. He took a deep breath to get control of his voice.

"Griff, you know you're my buddy, right?"

"Yeah, Tru."

"You also know I'm a doctor. And doctors help people. Right now I got to go help somebody, all right?"

"I come with you. I can help, too."

"Griff, you can help Mama. Let's make Truett an apple cake." Mama smiled, moving in front of Griff so he would look at her. "Come on, honey. Won't that be fun? We'll make that burnt sugar icing you like and you can lick the spoon. Then tonight, when

Truett gets back, you can show him the cake you helped bake, and you can go digging for fishing worms." She began moving toward the horse and buggy hitched nearby. "We better hurry home so we can get the cake finished before Truett gets back."

The confused, petulant look on Griff's face gradually changed to a smile. "Truett, we're gonna make you a surprise."

"Whew-ee. I love surprises. I'll be there before you know it."

Truett hurried toward the livery stable to get Colonel. But every time he looked back, Griff was looking over his shoulder at Truett. He might still try to follow. Truett picked up his pace.

Truett saddled up Colonel and rode at a modest clip out of town, not wanting to attract attention. But once he was away from the notice of people, he urged his horse into an all-out gallop, heading straight for the cave at the line between his family's property and the Wilcoxes'.

Too late, Truett realized he had caught up with Mama and Griff just as they were turning into the drive leading to the house. Truett slowed Colonel to a walk but Griff turned and saw him just before he disappeared behind the trees that lined the road.

Truett galloped past, praying Griff wouldn't try to follow him. Mama couldn't stop him if he was determined to leave.

Truett was soon at the mouth of the cave. He dismounted and ducked inside. He stripped off his shirt, which was already damp with sweat, and slipped the cloak over his undershirt. He fastened it at the top and pulled the hood over his head. Finally, he grabbed his rifle from its hiding place.

As he emerged from the cave, a sound like a twig breaking made him freeze in his tracks. He searched the area through the eye holes in his hood. He waited, looking for movement and listening for any sound. A bird fluttered down into the tree in front of him, but nothing else.

Truett cautiously moved toward his horse, holstered his gun, and mounted. He guided Colonel toward the glade of ferns, still looking over his shoulder occasionally to make sure no one was following him. He pushed his horse to go as fast as he dared through the forest toward the clearing of wildflowers and the huge oak tree where Suggs liked to do his lynching.

He drew near the clearing and peered through the leaves. Late afternoon sunlight streamed in, revealing two men standing beneath the hanging tree, nooses around their necks. Suggs and his son, Curtis, sat atop their horses, guarding the men.

Truett searched the area for any other men who might be standing guard nearby but saw no one. Perhaps his sermon had made an impact after all. Aubrey Pettibone was a coward and a hypocrite not to be here himself.

Suggs took his time with first one rope, then the other, and slung it over the thick branch of the tree above the men's heads.

As Truett crept closer he could make out the faces of the men. Just as he had known, it was Annie's father and uncle. Their hands were tied behind their backs. The sight filled Truett's head with heat that beat against his temples.

He took a deep breath. He had to control the urge to shoot Suggs and be done with his ugly evil. But he remembered David, finding King Saul and refusing to kill him, cutting off a piece of his robe instead.

Truett slipped from the saddle and made his way quietly around the clearing, toward where Annie's father and uncle stood. As he came close, he pulled his knife from his belt.

Truett was directly behind Annie's father. He waited until the sheriff and Curtis started talking, looking away from their prisoners. Truett whispered, "Step back. Slowly. Take two steps back until you're almost touching the tree."

Annie's father stepped back, using tiny steps, until Truett was able to hide in the large tree trunk's shadow. He slipped his knife between Isaac's hands and sawed furiously at the rope that tied them.

"Now don't move. Pretend your hands are still tied. I'll give you the signal. You take the rope off your neck and run." Finally, the rope gave way to his knife's blade and snapped in two.

The other man had heard at least part of Truett's whispered instructions. He slowly moved back as Annie's father moved forward, back to where he had been standing.

Suggs looked up. "Hey! You! Where you think you're going?" He pointed at Annie's uncle.

Curtis narrowed his eyes at them, then shook his head. "He can't get away. He'll just choke himself if he tries." The two laughed. "Save us some trouble."

Truett moved forward, hoping the other man's slightly broader frame would keep him hidden. He sawed at the rope binding the man's hands as perspiration beaded his forehead and ran down his temples underneath the hood.

His hands were sweating, too. His grip slipped on the handle of the knife, but he managed to hold on. Finally the rope broke free. Sam's arms jerked down with the sudden release of the rope, but he quickly righted himself, holding his hands behind his back.

Truett slowly stepped back until he was once again in the cover of the trees. He found Colonel and led him back around to the other side of the clearing, staying hidden among the trees and stepping carefully.

When the sheriff and Curtis were between Truett and the Hartley men, Truett mounted Colonel, took his rifle from its leather case, and nudged Colonel forward. He pointed his gun toward the sky and discharged it with a resounding boom.

Sam and Isaac tossed their nooses over their heads and raced into the trees behind them. Suggs and Curtis both drew pistols from their belts and twisted their bodies this way and that, searching for the source of the gunfire.

Truett wheeled Colonel around and kicked him into a gallop.

A gun shot split the air just before a stabbing pain pierced his side. He pitched forward onto Colonel's neck, but the horse kept running.

Truett held on to Colonel's mane, trying not to fall off. He had to stay conscious . . . had to guide Colonel to the cave. The pain intensified. He blinked, trying to focus on his course ahead. *Keep me conscious, Lord.*

Oh, God, don't let me die. Celia would never forgive me.

CHAPTER 28

C elia turned from the window. "Ruby's coming up the lane."

"I'll be in the bedroom." As Almira hurried away, she tossed a smile over her shoulder, and Celia felt reassured that she didn't mind having to hide herself away when they had visitors.

Celia stepped out on the porch to greet her friend, glancing at the sky. In the east, dark clouds gathered, and the oppressive stickiness in the air warned of a storm on its way. Ruby must have important news to be out in this weather.

"Hey there." Ruby ran up the porch steps and hugged Celia. "I'm still so excited about Will finding that Glory Patch, I don't know what to do."

"I know. It hardly seems real, but the money's real enough."

"I reckon you'll be going on back to Nashville, won't you?"

Celia sighed but tried to look cheerful. "I suppose. It's what I've always wanted, what I've prayed for." But an unsettled feeling rested heavy inside Celia, the same feeling she had every time she thought about leaving her family—and Truett—and going back to Nashville.

Yes, she wanted to get back to working and saving her earnings toward opening her own shop, but . . . was this what was best for her? Had she ever cared what God wanted? Was she too focused on what she wanted to even wonder?

The Bible said God's will was good and perfect. For the first time, she wondered if she had missed the perfect will of God because she was too busy embracing the imperfect—but very strong—will of Celia.

Celia would have to think about that later. Right now she needed to ask Ruby a favor, for Almira's sake.

"Ruby, since I'm leaving," she swallowed the lump that came into her throat before continuing, "and Almira's gone, would you be willing to teach the Bethel Springs children come September?"

"Me?" Ruby's eyebrows disappeared beneath the hair curling on her forehead. "You think I could do it?"

"Almira told me you were her best student. You can do it—with God's help," she added.

"Well, if the young'uns and their folks'll have me, I think I'd like that." Ruby's eyes widened, as though she was surprised at her own words.

Celia hugged her friend. "I know you'll be a good teacher."

Ruby clutched Celia's arms and pushed away to look into her eyes. "I almost forgot what I came to tell you! Sheriff Suggs is causing trouble again."

"What do you mean?" Celia held her breath.

"Well . . ." Ruby's skirt swayed around her ankles as she stepped toward a chair and sat down, drawing out the suspense. Celia sat on the edge of the chair next to her, her eyes glued to Ruby's lips.

"I heard tell that Sheriff Suggs is gonna lynch a couple of Negroes. You know, the ones that opened that store?" Ruby shook her head. "I can't help but wonder if he did it just to spite Dr. Beverly, after that sermon he preached on Su— Why, Celia, whatever's the matter with you? You're whiter than a sheet."

Celia stared at Ruby without seeing her. "How did you hear this?"

"Everybody's talking about it. Some folks think the sheriff is just trying to smoke out the hooded horseman."

If everybody was talking about it, then Truett would have heard. And Truett would never sit still and let those men be hanged.

A shot rang out, drifting to them from a long way off, but still distinct enough that the source of the sound was unmistakable.

Two more shots.

Celia jumped to her feet. Ruby stood too, grabbing Celia's elbow. "You aren't fixin' to faint, are you, Celia?"

"I have to go!" Celia broke free from Ruby's grasp and ran off the porch.

"Where?" Ruby called after her, but Celia neither answered nor slowed down as she raced into the trees.

Oh, God, please let him be all right. Please don't let anyone be hurt, except maybe Suggs.

No, she shouldn't pray like that.

God, please let no one be hurt, especially—

Images from the nightmare filled her mind—Truett lying on the ground, hurt, probably dead. *Please, God . . . Please keep him safe.*

Her heart pounded in her throat as she ran. After several minutes she couldn't run anymore. She was gasping for breath and had to slow to a walk. She didn't know if she would find him, but something told her that he would go to the cave to hide.

Lord, how can I bear it if Truett dies?

My grace is sufficient for you.

Celia almost stopped in her tracks as God spoke to her spirit. His grace was sufficient. She would be all right. God would help her.

She kept heading in the direction of the gunshots, toward the cave.

Celia focused on what she would do when she found him, safe

and alive. Would she start another angry tirade, accusing him of putting his life in danger and disregarding her warnings? *Oh, Truett, forgive me for being so hard on you.* If he was alive, if she were able to find him, she would tell him she loved him. Tell him he was noble and brave and good. Tell him she'd marry him. *Oh, how I want to be his wife, God. What a fool I've been. I've loved him all along. Nothing is as important as that.*

Sweat tickled her neck in the hot August afternoon. A low rumble of thunder rolled in the distance. She wanted to run faster but the humid air was suffocating.

At first Celia couldn't find the cave's entrance. Where was it? She yanked back another tree branch and—there it was. But before she could go inside, she was greeted by the click of a gun's hammer being pulled back.

She froze. "Truett?"

"Celia. Thank God."

It took a moment for her eyes to adjust to the semi-darkness, but it was easy to see Truett was much too pale and sweating more than even this heat should allow. And why was his arm wrapped around his middle? She sank to her knees beside him.

"You're hurt! Tell me where!"

His face was scrunched into a grimace, but he shook his head. "It's all right. Nothing to worry about. But if you could get something for me . . ."

"Yes! What?"

"Look in my saddlebag and get out the roll of bandages."

His horse standing farther inside the cave. She hurried to him, pawed through his saddlebag, and finally found the narrow roll of white cloth inside.

Her heart still pounded, though her breathing was slowing back to normal. She knelt beside him, searching his body with her eyes. "Where is it?"

"Now, Celia, I don't want you to see it. You just give me the bandage and look away."

"No! I can do this, Truett. You need help. Let me help you."

Truett raised his eyebrows at her.

"Please."

He sighed. "All right. But I want you to know it's not serious. The bullet went all the way through, and that's a good thing."

All the way through. Celia swallowed and tried to breathe. *I will not faint. I will not faint . . .*

"It missed all the organs. God was looking out for me."

Celia still wasn't sure where his wound was located, but she reached for the clasp on his cloak and got it unfastened. She swept off the black cape. A bright red stain made a large blotch on his undershirt at his lower left side.

Her stomach lurched. *I will not get upset. I will not faint.* She should pray. *Oh, dear God, you won't let him die, will you? I trust you, God. Truett is yours. Keep him alive.*

Truett needed her. She would be strong and capable—for him. Her voice squeaked out of her tight throat, "Not serious, you say?"

"Now, Celia, if you start to feel faint—"

"No, I'm fine. What do I do?"

"We have to wrap it around, tight, to stop the bleeding. Here, I'll hold it while you wrap."

She placed the end of the roll of fabric against his bloody side. She concentrated on breathing in and out, and forced herself not to think about the warm, sticky blood on her fingers or the pain in his face. He placed his blood-covered hand over the end of the bandage and held it in place while she wrapped the bandage roll around his middle and his back. She had to lean over him, almost in his lap to get the bandage all the way around.

"Make sure it's tight."

Celia pulled it taut.

"Tighter."

She pulled harder. Truett moved his hand so she could keep it as tight as possible. She kept winding carefully until she came around the wound again. He sucked in a breath through his teeth.

"I'm hurting you."

"No, no, it needs to be tight."

She continued winding the bandage across his stomach and around his back. A tear dripped off each cheek. *Please let him not notice.* She bit her lower lip to stop it from trembling.

She continued wrapping the bandage. He bit his lip, too. As she leaned toward him to get the bandage around his back, more tears dripped from her eyes onto his chest.

"Why are you crying?" His voice was strained.

She ducked her head and kept on with her task.

His fingers slipped under her chin and lifted her face, forcing her to stop. He gave her an intense, searching look.

"I love you, Truett." Her voice broke. She knew her chin was quivering but she didn't care. "I love you and I'm sorry if I caused you pain. I'm sorry for being such a fool."

"You're not a fool, Celia. I'd never think that about you." He put his arm around her and pulled her against his chest. She didn't even mind his sweat and laid her head against his shoulder. Her arms were already around his waist as she held the bandage behind his back.

"I should have accepted your marriage proposal. I'm so sorry for letting my fear stop me."

"Are you saying you will marry me?"

"Yes, that's what I'm saying."

"You're not afraid I'll die on you?"

"I am still afraid." Her voice hitched but she continued. "Almira said love was better than fear, and I know she's right." She lifted her face to his and kissed him.

She sat up and continued with the bandaging. Her tears had dried and she was now much more aware of his state of undress and her closeness to him. Her heart fluttered as she tried to avert her eyes from his chest.

When she came to the end of the bandage, she pinned it down. "I hope it's tight enough."

"Perfect. I'm so proud of you, Celia. You make a very lovely and capable nurse."

"I bet you say that to all the girls who are in love with you."

"No, just you." He gave a half grin before grimacing.

Celia settled in beside him and leaned her back against the wall of the cave. "What now?"

Another clap of thunder, this time much closer, shook the ground beneath them. Fat drops of rain began to strike the leaves at the cave entrance, just a few feet from them.

"I figure we ought to wait for the storm to pass."

Celia sat still beside him. She wanted to hold his hand, not caring that it was covered with blood, but she didn't dare. She'd either start crying or want to kiss him again. Instead of holding his hand, she needed to think of a way to get him somewhere safe.

"After the storm I'm taking you to my house. Suggs might go to your house looking for you. If he sees you've been shot, he'll know you're the hooded horseman."

She waited for him to argue with her, or to have a better idea.

"I suppose you're right."

His voice sounded weak. She sat forward and looked at him. Was he lying to her? Was his wound more serious than he had said? Was he dying? No, she couldn't think like that. She had to stay calm. She couldn't help him if she became hysterical.

"Truett, is there anything else I can do for you? Do you need water? I can go to the stream and get you some. It's not far."

"No. Having you beside me is all I need."

"Truett, tell me the truth. Are you going to . . . die?" Her voice went up three octaves on the last word, then cracked.

Truett smiled, and then winced. "The worst thing is that I lost a lot of blood. But I think I'll live. 'Then may I dare to boast how I do love thee.'"

"This is no time for poetry. I wish you'd be serious."

"I am serious. You just need to trust me. And trust God."

Trust was not her strong suit. But neither was nursing, and she'd just done pretty well at that.

She gazed at him a long time. He was so dear to her.

She got up and took the blanket off the back of Truett's saddle. "Do you want to lie down?"

"No, I think I'm better sitting up."

She made a rectangle out of the blanket and tucked it behind his back and head.

"Thank you, darling. Now sit down and relax. The storm's just starting."

Darling. He called me darling. Her heart swelled again, forcing out a sigh.

She snuggled up to him, letting him lean on her. She prayed silently, asking God to heal the man she was unequivocally, irrevocably in love with, as the rain and wind began their deafening onslaught.

～

Truett closed his eyes and tried to sleep, but the pain in his side kept him too tense. Lightning flashed and the rain poured down, driven sideways at times by the fierce winds as he watched it through the cave entrance. Soon, the thunder and lightning grew less frequent and the wind and rain less violent. The storm seemed to be passing over them.

Celia's head rested against his bare upper arm. Her hair had come loose from the pins and a few strands lay across her cheek. Every so often she would lift her head and look closely at his face and ask, "How are you feeling? Do you need to lie down?" The concern in her voice put a smile in his heart and almost made him forget the pain.

She had said she would marry him. He stared at her profile, memorizing her features.

He reached out and gently smoothed the hair back from her

face. But he didn't take his hand away. Her skin was as smooth as silk, and he rubbed her cheek with the back of his fingers.

Her eyelids fluttered and she lifted her head. "How are you feeling? Are you sure you don't need to lie down? Has it stopped raining?"

"Not bad, yes, and yes."

"We'd better go, then."

She put her arms around him and let him use her shoulder as a crutch to help him up. He stayed propped against the wall until she could bring Colonel to him, just inside the mouth of the cave.

He stuck his foot in the stirrup, his hands on the pommel, and tried to propel himself into the saddle, but the pain stabbed all through him and he weakly fell back to his feet. With his next attempt Celia helped, pushing him up, and he finally managed to throw his leg over and pull himself into the saddle.

He closed his eyes, unable to breathe. The pain was so intense he almost lost consciousness. He rested his forehead on his horse's neck.

Celia took the reins and led them through the woods.

It was almost completely dark when Will met them in the back yard. Will and Celia helped him off Colonel and half carried him inside. The pain was more intense than ever after the jostling he'd taken in the saddle. Sweat broke out on his forehead again, even though the rain had cooled things off.

"You can have my bed, Truett." Will grinned at him, but there was fear in his eyes.

Truett grabbed Will's arm. "Will, I need you. . ." He had to pause to catch his breath, as the pain was making it hard to breathe. ". . . to tell me . . . if you see . . . the sheriff."

"Sure will, Tru. Don't worry, now."

NOT SURE HOW LONG HE'D BEEN LYING IN BED, TRUETT OPENED HIS eyes to Celia standing over him with glass of dark red liquid. Her voice seemed to come to him through a fog. ". . . Father's medicinal wine."

She slid her arm behind his back and raised him up, holding the glass to his lips. He drank a few sips and closed his eyes. She murmured something soothing and he drank some more, and then she eased him back onto the pillows. He immediately drifted into a strange dream about being chased by a bear with a big human nose and long, sharp claws.

The next morning Truett awakened long enough to eat a little bread. He gulped two glasses of water and then drank some warm tea. Celia was so happy to be able to tell him what she'd heard from Ruby—that Annie's father and uncle had escaped from the sheriff and were hiding where Suggs was unlikely to find them. Then Truett went back to sleep.

~

CELIA STOOD IN THE DOORWAY, WATCHING HIM SLEEP. HE WAS SO very dear.

She pressed a hand over her mouth. He actually loved her.

Since Will had discovered the patch of ginseng, Celia could go back to Nashville. The prospect filled her with excitement, but also with sadness and dread at the thought of being so far away from Truett. Would he still want to marry her if she went away? How long would they wait? Would she ever have her own shop? Questions whirled in her brain, but still, that old desperate feeling didn't come back. Somehow, things would work themselves out.

Celia sighed. He was so noble and courageous. He deserved love and admiration.

She was such a selfish person, not like Lizzie and Will, who never asked for anything for themselves. They served the family and loved and cared and never tried to protect themselves with distrust and a hard heart—like she had. *Oh, God, I don't deserve him. I don't even deserve my family.*

My grace is sufficient for you.

Celia whispered softly, "God, I don't deserve You, either. But your grace is sufficient for me."

Lizzie hurried toward her. "Why are you crying? Is Truett all right?"

Celia wiped her face with her hands. "Everything's all right. I've just been stupid, that's all."

Lizzie hugged her, and Celia hugged her sister back.

"Someone's here." Almira's words drifted to them from the front parlor.

Celia and Lizzie exchanged a wary look and hurried toward Almira, who stood staring out the window, one hand clutching her neck.

"What are you doing, Almira?" Celia couldn't imagine why she was still standing there.

"Shouldn't you go hide?" Lizzie asked, touching her arm.

Almira didn't move. Her eyes misted over. "It's him."

Celia peered out the window. The brown-skinned man pulled off his hat as he mounted the porch. His shoulders drooped slightly, as though tired. Celia had never seen the man before, but his dark skin—and Almira's reaction to seeing him—told her exactly who he was.

"James." Almira flung the door open and leapt into his arms.

He hugged her, then backed away, holding her at arm's length and staring down at her stomach. "I'm sorry, Almira."

She shook her head. Her voice trembled as she said, "I'm not sorry." She paused. "I'm not sorry I'm having your baby. I'm just sorry we're not married."

"Truly?" Hope was evident in the way his voice rose at the end. Almira nodded.

James sank to one knee, clutching Almira's hand. "I love you, Almira. Will you marry me?"

"Yes."

James stood and she fell into his arms again.

Will was already backing away, his cheeks red. Lizzie and Celia turned to go as well.

Heavy boots clomped up the steps outside. Sheriff Suggs was stomping across the porch.

James and Almira started running through the parlor toward the back of the house but had barely reached halfway across the room when the door burst open. Sheriff Suggs stood with a rifle pointed at James.

"I'm gonna kill you, boy!"

CHAPTER 29

Screaming added to the confusion as James pushed Almira behind him and Will jumped in front of James.

Celia was closest to the sheriff. She grabbed the gun barrel and shoved as hard as she could, slamming it into the side of the Suggs' head.

James and Almira ran. Suggs turned on Celia and grabbed her around the neck with one enormous hand.

Lizzie screamed.

Will ran forward, grabbing the sheriff's gun and yelling, "Don't touch my sister!" He kicked the sheriff in the shin.

The sheriff howled and let go of Celia to wrest his gun away from Will. Celia gasped for breath.

Suggs grabbed Will by the shoulder, holding him at arm's length. "Who else is here?"

Celia's heart stopped beating. What if he found Truett?

Strength surged through her and started her heart again. She grabbed Suggs' arm from behind but he shrugged her off.

"Stop! I forbid you to come into my house! Get out. Now!"

Suggs ignored her and stomped down the hall, peering into

the bedroom she shared with Lizzie. He pointed the gun inside, glanced around, then moved on to the next room.

Celia and Will both jumped in front of him when he got to the doorway. The sheriff easily peered over their heads.

"Who we got here?" An evil grin spread across his face and he took his time moving his chew of tobacco from his left cheek to his right.

Celia glanced over her shoulder and saw Truett standing behind her. He'd somehow managed to pull on his pants and shirt. Truett and Suggs stared each other down.

"What are you doing here? Say!" Suggs' thunderous voice reverberated in Celia's ear.

"He's my fiancé. He has every right to be here." Celia thrust out her chin and glared at the sheriff. "But you do not. Leave this place immediately."

"I'm the sheriff and I'll go wherever I want." He roughly pushed Will and Celia aside, forcing his way into the room.

Suggs pointed his gun at Truett and moved closer. "It's awfully late to still be in bed. I'm afraid you have sullied this young lady's reputation."

Celia ran and stood in front Truett, shielding him with her body. She'd die before she'd let that evil man hurt Truett.

"Get out of here."

"I'm not finished, Missy." Suggs growled and used the barrel of his rifle to tap Celia on the shoulder.

Truett placed his hands on her upper arms and gently moved her aside. "It's all right, Celia." He faced the sheriff. "What do you want, Suggs?"

The sheriff poked Truett in the ribs with the rifle barrel. "I want the hooded horseman. And I believe you're him. Take your shirt off."

"Excuse me, Sheriff, but that wouldn't be appropriate in front of—"

"Take it off!" Suggs didn't wait. He stepped forward, shifting his gun under his arm, and grabbed Truett's shirt front in both hands. He ripped the shirt open, sending buttons flying in all directions.

The sheriff's eyes fastened on the bandage around Truett's middle. Blood had seeped through, creating a dark red splotch.

"There's a reward for your capture, Mr. Hooded Horseman." Sheriff Suggs smiled, showing brown, tobacco-stained teeth.

"No!" Celia raged, her voice strong while her hands shook. "You can't take him! You have no proof."

"I *will* take him. He's under arrest."

Sheriff Suggs reached a hand toward Truett, but Celia stepped between them again.

"Don't you dare touch him." Celia clenched her hands into fists. Rage filled her so that she could barely see.

Truett caressed her shoulder and spoke softly in her ear. "It's all right, Celia. I'll go with him. It'll be all right."

~

TRUETT COULDN'T LET CELIA AND WILL CONTINUE TRYING TO defend him. Besides, he had no choice. They were all powerless to fight Suggs.

He stepped around Celia. "All right, Suggs. I won't resist arrest, but I've done nothing wrong. My father and his friend, Judge William Richardson—I believe you know him, the probate judge? —are coming into town. Could be here any time today."

Of course, Truett was bluffing. He hadn't heard from either his father or Judge Richardson.

"Will," Celia spoke up, her shoulders back and her chin high, "go hitch up the wagon. I will not have Truett walking or riding a horse with his injury." She crossed her arms and glared at the sheriff. "Though it is slight . . . a slight injury. Not serious at all."

Truett almost laughed at her clumsy attempt to make the sheriff think he wasn't hurt bad. Not only was she high strung, she could spit fire, too. And it was more fun to watch when it was directed at someone besides him.

Celia made the sheriff wait until she had fixed blankets and pillows for Truett to rest on in the back of the wagon. When she told the sheriff she had one more pillow to get, he yelled at her and jumped up onto the seat. Truett squeezed her wrist and whispered, "I'm not hurt that bad. A slight injury, remember?"

She sat down beside Truett and his nest of blankets. "Sheriff, you may go now."

Suggs grumbled under his breath, spit a long stream of tobacco juice at the dirt, then set the horses in motion.

At least James and Almira had gotten away.

Once they arrived at the jail, Celia refused to go home. She gave Truett all the blankets and quilts, pushing them between the bars, since the sheriff wouldn't let her carry them into his cell herself. Then she settled herself on the floor and leaned against the wall next to his cell. She said she just wanted to make sure the sheriff didn't do anything to him on the sly. Truett thought about telling her that if the sheriff wanted to kill him, there wouldn't be anything she could do about it. But he decided against it.

The sheriff locked the cell and walked out, leaving them alone.

"Is your side hurting you?" Celia asked.

Truett was propped up, half-lying, half-sitting on the cot, the scent of mildew and sweat rising from the thin straw mattress. "No, not much."

"Can I run over to your office and get you something? Some medicine?"

"Later I'll need to change my bandage. You can go get some things for me then."

She brightened. "Of course."

After they'd been there for an hour or so, Sheriff Suggs came back in. He thrust out his chest and wore a satisfied smirk.

"It looks like there's going to be a hanging after all."

Celia sat up straighter. Truett waited for the sheriff to say more.

"I'll be hanging the Hartleys before sunset."

Celia gasped and covered her mouth with her hand.

"It seems they thought they could hide out in an old shack in the woods, but I found 'em. Got 'em tied up outside."

Celia sprang to her feet and looked out the window. "Oh, you're horrible! Those men don't deserve to die just because they opened a store. And it's against the law for you to hang them without a trial. What kind of beast are you?"

"You look a-here, missy. I've had enough of your mouth." He shook his finger in Celia's face.

Truett wished he could break that finger. He stood to his feet and walked to the other side of his cell.

"She's right, Suggs. You won't get away with it this time. The authorities—"

"Shut up!"

Truett shrugged, feigning indifference. "All right. But the hooded horseman will probably stop you again."

"You're the hooded horseman!" Suggs roared, stalking toward him.

Suggs grabbed the bars and Truett stepped back, not wanting to encounter his foul breath.

"You're the hooded horseman, and you'll hang for it. Nothing can save you. You assaulted a sheriff and his deputy. You shot at a lawman, and you'll hang. Not even your daddy or his judge friend can save you."

Truett regretted the sheriff had said those words in front of Celia. She turned white as cotton. He hoped she didn't faint on this stone floor. He couldn't catch her and she might hit her head.

"Celia, go sit down."

She didn't obey, but the color came back in her cheeks as she glared at the sheriff. "You're an evil man. If you hurt those men or Truett . . ." She appeared to be trying to think of something, clenching and unclenching her hands by her sides. Finally, she blurted, "God's going to punish you!"

"So I'm going to hell?" Suggs laughed an ugly belly laugh. He continued laughing as he sauntered out the door.

Celia approached him, her eyes locked on his. He went to her, his heart twisting as she reached through the bars and put her hands around him. He drew her as close as he could. She rested her forehead against his chest, her cheek pressed against a bar.

"I'm so sorry about this," he whispered in her ear. "I behaved foolishly. I should have written Judge Richardson a long time ago."

"It's not your fault. You were just trying to do the right thing. Who knows if the judge will even respond to our letters?"

A hitch in her voice told him she was crying. He pulled out his handkerchief and wiped her eyes.

"Hey, now, don't cry. Of course the judge will respond. The sheriff is probably bluffing. The townspeople will finally stand up to him and keep him—" . . . *from hanging Sam and Isaac.* He stopped himself from finishing the sentence. He didn't want to remind her. Besides, it was almost too painful to say out loud. After all, if Truett hadn't interfered, the men would have lost their store in the fire, yes, but they'd at least be alive tonight, instead of possibly.

. .

"Let's pray, Celia. Pray for a miracle."

Celia nodded and closed her eyes. Truett whispered a plea for God to save Sam and Isaac from getting hanged by Suggs. "God, we need a miracle."

Celia was still crying. He dabbed at her cheeks until she took the handkerchief away from him and wiped her nose.

She looked up and took his shirt in her fists, gazing intently into his eyes. "I love you, Truett. No matter what happens, I love you, and I think you're the most wonderful man in the world. God has shown me how wrong I was, how twisted and confused my thinking had become. Nothing is more important to me than loving you. And I just want you to know that."

Truett's slid his hand behind her neck and he kissed her lips. He longed to pull her closer, but the bars prevented it.

He pressed his forehead to hers. "You're so beautiful when you tell me you love me."

She gave him a shaky smile. "Is that the only time I'm beautiful?"

"No. You're also beautiful when you smile, and when you're mad at me, and when you're yelling at Suggs, and even when you cry. You're beautiful all the time . . . especially when you've just been kissed."

She caught her breath and stared at his lips.

The sound of a door squeaking on its hinges forced them apart. Truett winced when his mother walked in. Would she break down at seeing him injured and in jail? But when his father followed right behind her, his heart soared as hope filled his lungs.

∼

"Mr. Beverly!" Celia gasped, relieved at the sight of Truett's father. The man was a strong presence and carried himself with a cool aloofness that commanded respect. But somehow Mrs. Beverly's panicked clucking and hovering also calmed her. Celia leaned against the wall while Truett reassured his mother that everything would be all right. His father, on the other hand, stood stoically glaring into space, limiting his words to short, half sentences about not tolerating these outrages.

Celia continued sending up silent prayers for the miracle they needed, the miracle that would save Annie's family, her father and uncle, and Truett too. God was making a way to rescue them, she was sure of it. She only hoped He would hurry, since Sam and Isaac's time was very short otherwise.

After the passing of perhaps another hour, Grady Skidmore, who'd helped them fell their leaning tree, burst through the door.

Truett moved to the edge of his cell. "What is it?"

Celia's stomach sank. Had Annie Hartley's father and uncle been hanged already?

"I've got news. And it's not good, I'm afraid."

"Let's hear it." Mr. Beverly demanded.

"The Hartleys didn't get lynched. Someone came and rescued them."

"Who?" Truett asked.

"The hooded horseman."

"What?" Celia glanced at Truett. *How could that be?*

"The bad news is that the hooded horseman was . . . well . . . Suggs shot him."

Celia held her breath as she waited for him to continue.

"Who?" Truett gripped the bars, his knuckles turning white. "Who was it, man?"

"It was Griff."

CHAPTER 30

Truett's heart jolted. Mother cried out, a little shriek, then sank into Father, who held her up and helped her to a chair.

"He was still breathing, last I knew," Grady added quickly. "He was shot in the shoulder."

Truett's knees went weak. But then he grabbed the bars and shook them. "Let me out of here! I have to tend my brother."

"Where is he?" Father swiped a hand across his chin.

"Suggs's men are bringing him back to town on a wagon."

"Suggs will pay for this." Father's voice boomed inside the small jail house.

"Yes, he will."

Everyone turned to see who had spoken. The man was well-dressed in a dark frock suit and black tie, and he made his way from the door to Truett's father.

"John." He clasped Father's hand and placed a hand on his shoulder. "I'm here to help."

Celia pressed herself against the bars of Truett's cell. "Oh, Truett."

He raised his eyes to hers. His legs felt heavy and wooden as he held her hand through the bars.

Suggs walked in the door. "What's going on here?"

"That is what I would like to know." It was the stranger who turned and faced the sheriff. His eyes blazed. "Are you Sheriff Suggs?"

"Yes. Who are you?"

"I'm Judge William Richardson, and you are under arrest."

Sheriff Suggs's jaw hardened and a muscle twitched in his cheek.

"I'm taking you back to Huntsville," he continued, "to face a grand jury investigation into your alleged illegal activities, including the lynching of several men. And if the boy doesn't survive you shooting him, I'll have you convicted of the murder of Griffith Beverly."

Suggs seemed to have cleared his face of all expression. He stared straight ahead, his lips pursed.

Judge Richardson glared at Sheriff Suggs and pointed at Truett, "I demand you release this man, as he obviously is not the hooded horseman."

Suggs reached into his pocket and pulled something out. Judge Richardson took it from him. Then he tossed it across the room at Celia. She caught the key and inserted it into the lock. The door swung open. Truett rushed outside to find Griff.

~

CELIA STOOD FROZEN AS TRUETT RAN OUT OF THE JAIL.

"You." Judge Richardson turned to Grady. "Come with me. I want you to take me to Isaac and Sam Hartley so they can identify the rest of the sheriff's men." Judge Richardson looked out the window. "Though I believe my deputies have them all rounded up right outside."

Truett was free, but would he be able to save Griff? His last brother.

She stood in the doorway and watched as Judge Richardson, with six or seven deputies, took Sheriff Suggs away, his hands cuffed behind his back. The sheriff's face was red as a beet, and he spewed curses at everyone in sight. When the sheriff slowed his step, one of the Huntsville lawmen shoved his shoulder.

Celia and Truett's parents hurried out with one mind, no doubt—to find out if Griff was still alive and if there was anything they could do to help Truett tend him.

Poor Griff. He must have stolen Truett's black cape and hood, which they'd left in the cave, and gone after Suggs. Mrs. Beverly's face was white, almost ashen, and she gripped her husband's arm.

Her chest hollowed out at the thought that Griff might die. And her stomach wrenched at the pain Truett and his family would feel if he did.

~

TRUETT LEANED OVER GRIFF'S SHOULDER AS HE WORKED TO GET THE small round bullet out of the bloody flesh that just wanted to close in over it. Finally, he pulled it out and held it up, examining it to make sure it was intact. Convinced no fragments were left behind, Truett dropped the metal slug in the slop bowl and reached for the needle he needed to sew up his brother's wound.

Sweat beaded on his forehead and upper lip and the pain in his side from his own bullet wound became more difficult to ignore. His blood loss made his legs weak and trembly, and his hands were beginning to shake. But he had to get this wound sewn up.

Someone touched his arm. When he glanced up, Celia offered him a glass of water. While he drank, she dabbed the sweat from his forehead with a handkerchief—which was a good thing. He didn't want his sweat dripping into Griff's wound.

"You shouldn't be here," he rasped after gulping the entire glass of water.

"Someone has to look out for you." She took the glass as he went back to stitching. Thankfully, Griff was still asleep from the laudanum he'd given him.

"Not feeling faint, are you? Just stay back and don't look at what I'm doing."

"I'm fine."

"Is Mother all right?"

"She's well. She's lying down in the back room, and your father went to speak with Judge Richardson."

Soon he'd finished the last stitch and tied it off. He wiped most of the blood away, and Celia helped him bandage it.

"You make a good . . ." He paused, blinking as the room tilted. ". . . nurse."

"Sit down." Celia took his arm and led him the two steps to the bench along the wall. He sank down and stretched out, face first across the bench.

When he opened his eyes, Celia was bathing his face with cool water and a cloth.

Two men picked him up and carried him, and he was too weak to protest.

The next time Truett opened his eyes, he was lying on one of two cots in the back room of his office. His mother and father were standing nearby.

"Where's Griff?" He tried to sit up, but everything started going black again, so he lay back down.

"I'm here, Truett." Griff's voice sounded calm, if not very strong. He was lying on the other cot.

"Are you all right, Griff?"

"Uh-huh, all right. Mama said you were sick."

"I'll be well soon."

"I brought you some water." Celia's face came into view.

Father helped him sit up and he drank down the glass of water.

"Is Griff drinking enough?"

"Yes," Father said. "He's been up twice."

"Walking?"

"Yes, but he's still a bit weak."

Truett was grateful for his father and mother's presence, but he couldn't take his eyes off Celia's face. Could it be true that she loved him? Her expression certainly was different from her usual look. Kind of soft and sweet, kind of like when they had just kissed.

He reached out his hand to her and she took it, squeezing it.

"Your bandage needs changing." Celia swallowed, as she was obviously thinking of the blood that had soaked through his bandage.

Although he'd rather have Celia help him, he was afraid of her fainting. Besides, of course, that it wasn't proper.

"We shall help him with that, my dear." Mother squeezed Celia's arm and gave her a quick hug. "You go on home and get some rest."

Celia opened her mouth as if to speak, but then she bit her lip instead. She nodded and gazed into his eyes as she walked toward the door and out of sight.

～

A FEW DAYS LATER IT WAS SUNDAY. CELIA GOT HERSELF READY FOR church, then helped get the twins ready as she urged Will and Lizzie to hurry—but gently, her heart feeling oddly peaceful.

The sky was gray and overcast, and Celia glanced around for Truett's mother so she could ask how Truett and Griff were doing. Will had gone every day to check on them at their home, where they were convalescing, so she knew they were both improving, but it was a surprise to see Truett and Griff sitting side by side, with their mother and father next to Griff, when she entered the church.

Her heart tripped over itself. Did she dare? She strode right down the center aisle to their pew and held her hand out to Truett's mother.

Mrs. Beverly took her hand, breaking into the widest smile, and stood and embraced her. "You sweet thing. Thank you for sending that soup to us. It was delicious. I think it had healing properties, because just look at Truett and Griff!" She pulled back and extended her arm to the two young men.

"They look as if they are nearly recovered."

She felt nervous as she smiled first at Griff, then at Truett, but when he winked at her, her smile widened and she nearly laughed.

Celia longed to sit beside him and hold his hand through the church service. But that would not be proper, as there had been no official announcement about their plans to marry. Instead, she sat in another pew with her family.

After three songs and a prayer, Preacher Massey, apparently recovered from his summer ague, stood to deliver the message. "'Greater love hath no man than this, that a man lay down his life for his friends.' One of us here today can boast this kind of love. Griffith Beverly. His noble, selfless acts will become a legend in these parts . . . a true story the people of Bethel Springs will tell their children, grandchildren, and great-grandchildren, of how he risked his life to deliver innocent men from the noose of a lawless sheriff.

"Griff is known by all, but did any of us realize what a big heart he has? Did any of us know what a difference he would make in Bethel Springs and Madison County?" Preacher Massey solemnly bowed his head. "Let us pray."

After the sermon, Celia stood with the congregation to sing the final song. As she did, she noticed several people looking over their shoulders. She turned too. Isaac and Sam stood at the very back row, along with Annie and several others from Annie's family. Celia gave a tiny wave, and Annie smiled and waved back.

When the last song was sung and the last prayer said, Celia hurried into the aisle, but Annie and her family were gone.

When Celia and her siblings arrived back home, they found Mama in the kitchen, cooking.

"It's for the Beverlys. They have two sick boys, and I wanted to bring them some dinner."

Celia, Will, and Lizzie stood frozen.

"Aren't you going to help me?"

"Of course." Celia and Lizzie helped Mama while Will went to fetch the wagon. They loaded up all the dishes and drove over to the Beverlys. When they arrived, Mrs. Beverly insisted they all stay and eat with them, as there was so much food.

After dinner, Celia watched as Mama, looking almost like her old self, with her hair freshly combed and pinned into a bun on the back of her head, spoke quietly to Mrs. Beverly. She was much thinner and her black dress hung loose on her hips, but Mama was talking again. Somehow, the shock of recent events—the sheriff catching James in their house and taking Truett to jail, followed by the news of the two Beverly "boys" being shot and the sheriff himself being arrested—had reached through her grief, jolting her out of her stupor.

Celia, Lizzie, and Will exchanged several looks but didn't mention her startling change, afraid Mother would retreat into herself again if they said the wrong thing.

Celia sat in a chair in the corner as Truett and his father discussed politics nearby. Griff was sitting quite still on the sofa, staring at Tempie and Harley as they sat on the floor, playing with wooden soldiers.

How different this day would have been if Suggs's bullet had struck just a few inches lower. The mirror beside Celia would have been covered in black crepe, and the clock on the mantle would be stopped at the time Griff had been shot. Or if the bullet that struck Truett had been several inches higher, they would be having a funeral today instead of a relaxing Sunday afternoon eating and talking with friends.

The painful thought stole her breath. Her hand shook as she pulled out her fan and used it to fan her face, taking slow, deliberate breaths.

Mr. Beverly was talking now with Will and Lizzie about their nearby pond. Soon, they were standing and heading out to see if they could find any ducks or geese. Even Mama was going with them, walking beside Mrs. Beverly.

Truett stood too, but instead of going with them, he strode toward her, his eyes riveted on hers. He reached for her hand. Celia stood and he led her into a tiny alcove under the stairs. What was he about?

~

Truett could no longer stand being in the same room with Celia, but not able to talk with her alone. He needed to hold her, just for a moment, to relieve the ache in his chest.

He led her to the only place he could think of where they might get a moment of privacy—under the stairs in the hall between the kitchen and the parlor. He backed himself against the wall, into the corner, and she came willingly into his arms, burying her face in his neck. He held her tight, pressing his cheek against her hair, and took a deep breath.

"I'm so glad Griff is going to be well." Celia whispered.

"I know. Me too. When we were children, before his head injury, he used to take me fishing." It was a random thing to say, but he'd been remembering that all morning. "Since the gunshot wound, he's been so much calmer. But he could have been killed." We both could have.

He stood still, holding her. She was so soft and warm. "It's my fault," he whispered.

"Oh no, Truett. Of course it's not."

"He followed me to the cave. I thought I heard someone. Now I know it was Griff. That's how he knew where to find the cape and hood. He heard people talking about the sheriff going to hang those two men and went to stop it. He was fascinated by the hooded horseman, and I knew that."

"It wasn't your fault at all. But everything is going to be all right. That's the important thing. You're both going to be all right."

He concentrated on her words and ignored the painful taunts that had been plaguing him the last three days. God was merciful. He hadn't allowed Griff to be killed, sparing him and his family from crushing pain.

Truett pulled back and brushed her cheek with his knuckles. *Celia.* She was everything he wanted. To think that a few weeks ago he'd felt tormented by thoughts of her. Now . . . he wasn't sure he could bear to be without her.

"Father will be gone back to Tennessee tomorrow. Can I call on you then?"

"Of course."

Someone was coming. Celia tried to pull away, but Truett pulled her closer and plastered himself against the wall, deep in the shadows. Whoever it was walked on by without noticing them.

Truett took another deep breath of her. She smelled of lilac soap and Celia. A wonderful combination.

"I love you," Celia whispered.

Truett kissed her hair. "I love you, too."

"Truett?" His mother called.

Celia stepped back, out of his embrace. Truett let her go. She squeezed his hand and hurried away.

~

THE NEXT MORNING, CELIA WAS FINISHING THE BREAKFAST DISHES

when she thought she heard a horse snorting out front. *Let it be Truett!* She dried her hands on a towel and went onto the front porch.

Truett sat on the wooden bench. "Where is everybody?"

Celia was all fluttery inside at seeing him again. She couldn't help smiling.

"They're all out back. Mama's hanging out the washing and Lizzie and Will are playing with Harley and Tempie."

"Good." He reached out his hand to her and pulled her onto his lap.

"Truett Beverly!" She giggled in spite of herself. "What would our mothers say?"

"Do you want to know?"

"No, I think not." Celia smiled, grateful to be alone with him. She straightened. "But what about your wound? Am I hurting you?"

He shook his head. "It doesn't hurt, not when you're near."

He was teasing, but he didn't look like he was in pain. She snuggled down against his shoulder.

He sighed deeply. Celia imagined all the things he was feeling, all that he was releasing in that sigh. She didn't think words were sufficient, so she lifted her hand to his face and stroked his jaw, enjoying the feel of the prickly stubble against her fingers.

"I got a letter today from James and Almira," Truett drawled softly.

"Already?"

"Yep. They stopped off in Kentucky. James knew a preacher there who would marry them. When he sent the letter, they were on their way to Ohio."

"Is that where they'll live?"

"James knows a community there where they'll be accepted. It'll be a little easier for them in Ohio than it would be here."

"That's wonderful." Celia rested her head on his shoulder

again. How happy Almira must be now. It must be so wonderful to marry the person you loved.

"Let's get married tomorrow."

Truett's words sent a tingle down her spine. "You know we can't. Your family will want to gather for the wedding, all your Tennessee relatives, they'll all have to be notified, and—"

"I know." His fingers brushed her cheek.

It was hard to talk, with the way he was staring at her lips. But they needed to talk. "I found a woman who will help out with the twins when Will and Lizzie go back to school in a week."

He sighed again. "I guess that means you'll be going back to Nashville."

Was he angry that she was going away? She didn't think so, or he wouldn't be letting her sit on his knee. But she shouldn't be sitting on his knee. Celia's cheeks stung and she tried to get to her feet.

"What?" Truett asked.

"What if someone sees us? Let me up."

He let her stand. "Are you only worried about someone seeing us?"

"No." She was also worried about her own reaction to him. But how could she tell him that? "I just think it's . . . well . . . it isn't proper."

He smiled slowly, and she was sure he was reading her mind. Heat crept up her neck and into her cheeks. She crossed her arms.

"All right. Will you sit with me?" He stood up until she sat down on the bench, then he sat back down beside her.

He took her hand in his and looked her in the eye. "Will you marry me, Celia? I know your mother is doing better now, and because of the ginseng, you have the money to go back to Nash—"

"Yes."

"You probably can't leave Bethel Springs fast enou— Did you say yes?"

"Yes." Celia smiled into his deep blue eyes. "How many times do I need to accept your proposal of marriage before you will marry me, Truett Beverly?"

He laughed, then kissed her hand. "So, about where we will live . . ."

"I just assumed we would live here, in Bethel Springs."

"Is that where you want to live?"

"No. I mean . . . I don't know. Where do you want to live?"

"You don't want to live here, Celia, I know that."

"You're right. I don't. But I don't want to live without you, either."

He was drawing lazy circles on the back of her hand with his thumb, sending tingles all through her. She desperately wanted to kiss him.

He closed his eyes, as if he was fighting the same temptation she was. Finally, he cleared his throat and went on. "Since you need to continue to pursue your dream of opening your own dress shop, we'll live in Nashville."

Celia stared at him. "You would do that? You would leave Bethel Springs and go to Nashville?"

"Of course. I thought you knew that, Celia."

"How could I know that?"

"As soon as things settle down here, and I've had time to scout out a new doctor for Bethel Springs, I'll come to Nashville and set up an office there."

"You would do that? And would you let your wife work as a seamstress? And later, own her own business?"

"Why shouldn't I? I don't want to control you, Celia. I want to love you."

Celia realized her mouth was hanging open. She closed it. "So —you could—work as a doctor in Nashville?"

"Why not? I have friends there. I even completed some of my study there. I'd always hoped to go back and study under a certain surgeon, Dr. Hollenberry."

She leaned into his side, not sure what to say. "But once I have children," she said, thinking out loud, "I couldn't possibly run a shop."

"Perhaps not. Perhaps you could. We'll see when the time comes."

"Dr. Truett Beverly, you are too good to be true."

"Then marry me, as soon as possible. I don't like waiting." He leaned over, pulling her toward him, and kissed her forehead. His lips moved downward over her temple and cheek.

"We probably shouldn't be kissing anymore," she said breathlessly as he kissed his way slowly across her chin. "Not until after we're married."

"I know. We shouldn't." He kissed her lips briefly, then stood up, bringing her with him.

"Mother will be disappointed not to invite everyone she knows and plan a big shindig. And it'll be hard to keep my lips off yours. I'll have to pray a lot to get through these next few weeks."

"Amen." The word just slipped out. They both laughed, and the laugh ended in another kiss.

"I guess I better go ask Will and your ma for permission to marry you."

"I guess you better." Celia tucked her hand in the crook of his arm as they started down the steps to the back yard. Her heart was so full she could hardly breathe as she gazed up at him.

❧

SIX WEEKS HAD PASSED. CELIA BLINKED BACK TEARS AS SHE WALKED down the aisle of the church. All the people she loved had come to her wedding. There was little Tempie, looking deceptively sweet in her pink dress and ribbons. Harley stood stoically beside her, looking older than his five years. Will grinned at her and winked —the adorable thing. Lizzie was already sniffling, her face beaming even as tears swam in her eyes. Their new step-father, Horace Pouncey, stood beside Mother. He'd come to Bethel

Springs a week after Griff got shot to look into buying their farm —and got more than he bargained for. He and Mother fell in love and got married.

Mama smiled, then reached up with her handkerchief to wipe a tear off her cheek.

Celia had to look away to keep her own tears at bay.

There was Mr. and Mrs. Beverly on the other side of the aisle, nodding approvingly at her. Mrs. Beverly's face seemed pinker and a bit plumper. She and Griff were living with Mr. Beverly in Columbia, Tennessee now, as Griff had become more easy-going and calm after the accident, not minding the move.

Mrs. Beverly looked content tucked into her husband's side.

For so long, Celia struggled to understand why she had to come to Bethel Springs last summer, why she had to agonize over her own and her siblings' future, worried she'd never get back to pursuing her dreams and would end up like her mother, stuck forever in Bethel Springs. But now . . . now she understood, and she was so thankful.

Straight ahead stood the most wonderful man she had ever met. She came to stand beside him and had to tear her eyes away from his and try to listen to the preacher's words. But in a few short minutes the preacher would announce her as the wife of Dr. Truett Beverly, telling him he could kiss his bride, and she could hardly wait.

Author's Note

Growing up in rural South Alabama, there was a sense that, in some areas of life, things hadn't changed much in a hundred years. And so it wasn't hard to imagine life in the 1800s.

Two of my favorite books—and movies—were *To Kill a Mockingbird* and *Gone With the Wind*, and growing up with the last name "Lee," my life was total immersion in all things Southern, all the time. But as an adult looking back, there was so much about race issues and injustice that went right over my head, as my parents taught me never to mistreat anyone, especially those who were mistreated by others. Still, I couldn't write a story set in Alabama in 1880 and pretend racial injustice and cruelty didn't exist.

I got the idea for this story more than ten years ago when I was touring the antebellum house in Spring Hill, Tennessee, called Rippavilla Plantation. The tour guide spoke about a sheriff in a nearby town who lynched people whenever he felt like it. In my recent research, however, I found no evidence of any such person. But there was plenty of evidence that many "ordinary" white people formed lynch mobs and, in all, murdered more than 4,400 black men, women, and even children over a period of a hundred years after the Civil War had ended. In nearly every instance, it was the common people who unjustly and unlawfully took it upon themselves to take another person's life who had been accused. And the authorities, in most instances, simply looked the other way.

I also discovered in my research that there was someone in Madison County, Alabama, my home county for the past twenty years, who stood up against lynch mobs more than once, sacrificing his own safety to try to save a life, and getting injured by the would-be lynch mob on at least one occasion. He was William Richardson, the Madison County Probate Judge, and I took the liberty of placing a fictionalized version of him in my story.

To learn more about this horrendous practice of lynching and racial terrorism, I recommend the book *The Sins of Madison County* by Fred B. Simpson; the Lynching in America website, https://lynchinginamerica.eji.org/; and the Legacy Museum and the National Memorial for Peace and Justice in Montgomery, Alabama, https://museumandmemorial.eji.org/. Just as we must never forget the Holocaust, we must never forget the injustice and terrorism committed right here on American soil. We must stand up against hate and discrimination anywhere we find it.

I hope I have presented, in my historical romance story, a bit of truth and reality. The South has many wonderful, desirable qualities, and I am thankful for how far Alabama has come in their race relations and justice, but I do not want to pretend that evil did not and does not exist. "He who forgets history is doomed to repeat it." No one should feel terrorized or treated unjustly because of the color of their skin, or for any other reason. Ever.

ACKNOWLEDGMENTS

As I originally wrote this story more than ten years ago, many people have had a hand in making suggestions. I am grateful for all of them, including Kim Moore, Debbie Lynne Costello, Kathleen Maher, and probably many others I've lost track of. I especially want to thank my agent Natasha Kern for her suggestions, as well as my excellent content editor, Serena Chase, and my wonderful line editor, Grace Dickerson. Thanks also to beta readers Terry Bell, Toni Shiloh, Piper Huguley, and Faith Dickerson.

ABOUT THE AUTHOR

Melanie Dickerson is the New York Times bestselling author of the Christy Award winning novel, *The Silent Songbird*, and the author of fairy tale retellings set in Medieval Europe and a trilogy set in Regency England. Before she was an author she was a teacher and has taught in Ukraine, Germany, Georgia, and Tennessee. She has two amazing daughters and lives in north Alabama, where she writes full time. See all her books on her Amazon page https://www.amazon.com/default/e/B003BAAJG6/ or on her website http://www.melaniedickerson.com/ and follow her on Instagram, melaniedickerson123 or on facebook https://www.facebook.com/MelanieDickersonBooks/

OTHER BOOKS BY MELANIE DICKERSON

The Hagenheim/Fairy Tale Romance series:

The Healer's Apprentice

The Merchant's Daughter

The Fairest Beauty

The Captive Maiden

The Princess Spy

The Golden Braid

The Silent Songbird

The Orphan's Wish

The Warrior Maiden

The Thornbeck/Medieval Fairy Tale series

The Huntress of Thornbeck Forest

The Beautiful Pretender

The Noble Servant

The Regency Spies of London Series

A Spy's Devotion

A Viscount's Proposal

A Dangerous Engagement

DISCUSSION QUESTIONS

1. Why did Truett risk his life to save James?

2. Why did Celia come to Bethel Springs? How long was she hoping to stay? Why did she want to go back to Nashville?

3. Why did Celia not flirt with Truett or act impressed with him?

4. What was the wager Truett made with himself about getting Celia to change her opinion of him?

5. Griff frightened Celia when she saw him tying little Tempie's bonnet strings. Why was Celia frightened for her sister?

6. Why did Celia feel guilty when Will accidentally cut himself with the ax? Why was she so embarrassed when she fainted?

7. At the dance, did Celia enjoy dancing with Truett? Why did she suddenly give him the cold shoulder? What was she so afraid of?

8. What were Celia's reasons for not wanting to get married? Do

you think her fears—of not wanting to lose her identity or her ability to own her own business—were justified?

9. Who do you relate to more—Celia and her fears of losing herself and her identity? Or Almira and her belief that love was better and more powerful than any fear?

10. How did Celia feel when she discovered Truett was the Hooded Horseman? Why was she so determined to warn him to be more careful and not expose himself to danger?

11. Fear kept Celia from accepting Truett's proposal of marriage. Have you ever had a fear, whether rational or irrational, that made you do things that didn't make sense to other people?

12. What was it that finally helped Celia overcome her fear of accepting Truett's proposal of marriage?

13. In the beginning, Truett came across as a bit arrogant. What events in the story helped him change and become more humble?